Last Writes

C.A. LARMER

ISBN: 978-0-9942608-2-6

To writers,
everywhere

CONTENTS

PROLOGUE

The drugging had been relatively simple, but it wasn't over yet. He needed to leave a message, to make him pay.

He searched around the room until his eyes settled on a butcher knife resting on a battered chopping board on the kitchen bench, a few bread crumbs scattered around it. Yes, that would do nicely. Slowly, methodically, he made his way over to it, brushing the crumbs away before picking it up and returning to the bed. His hands shaking now, he held up one thin, white wrist and began to slash at it, first this way, then that.

"This will teach you to mess with me," he said. "Now you'll be sorry."

Then he let the blood-splattered knife drop to the floor.

CHAPTER 1

A shrill sound blasted through a thirsty sleep and Roxy Parker sat up with a start, glancing bleary-eyed towards her clock radio. It was just after 8:00 a.m. and the phone was screaming like a demented catbird. She groaned and, feeling the full force of one-too-many champagnes, grappled for the hands-free receiver.

"Hmmm?"

"Roxy?"

"Hmmm."

"Don't tell me you were still asleep?"

Roxy located her black Ray-Ban reading glasses on the bedside table, wedged them into place and checked the clock again.

"Oliver, it's 8:04 on Saturday morning, you're *supposed* to still be asleep." She propped up on one elbow, a little more alert now. "Speaking of which, what the hell are you doing up at this hour?"

Roxy's agent, Oliver Horowitz, was your classic insomniac. That meant late nights pacing his Kings Cross apartment and late mornings catching up on his Zzzs. Olie rarely got to work before 10:00 a.m. and, it being Saturday, should not even be vertical for another three hours.

"What's going on?"

"Just had some bad news. Tragic, actually."

"Oh?"

"One of my writers is dead."

"Oh." She digested this for a few seconds. "Shit. Who? What happened?"

A deep sigh. "Don't really wanna go over it on the phone. Can you come meet me? For a coffee. I need to unload."

Roxy grimaced. She liked death stories as much as the next person. Actually, a lot more, if truth be told. It was her one true indulgence, her "sick little fetish", as her friend Max Farrell would say. But it was 8:04 a.m. on a Saturday morning, for God's sake. She glanced again at the clock. Make that 8:06.

"Come on, Roxy, I'm down at Peepers, five seconds from your place." A pause. "The death could be suspicious. Maybe even murder. Coppers have already grilled me."

Now he had her hooked, as he knew he would. Roxy rubbed the sleep from her eyes and said, "I'll be there in ten."

As she wrestled her way out of the sheets and into the bathroom, Roxy wondered which of Oliver's clients had kicked the bucket. She hoped it wasn't investigative reporter David Lone. She'd only just met the guy.

I bet it bloody is, she thought, scowling at herself in the mirror. It would be just her luck. Roxy had met the luscious Mr Lone the night before, at his film premiere, and there had been an instant spark between them, or at least *she* had felt one. Of course it could have had something to do with the three champagnes she'd knocked back before he'd even caught her eye. Roxy didn't normally drink a lot but last night she couldn't help herself. Not only was the alcohol free—and who can resist free grog?—but it had been weeks since she'd gone out and she was determined to have a good time, even if it killed her.

And it *had* been a good time, Roxy thought, as she surveyed the evidence in the mirror in front of her: smudged mascara, blood-shot eyes, a pillow crease across one cheek.

Bloody hell, she was going to need more than ten minutes to smooth this mess out. She turned the tap on, squirted some cleanser onto her face and got scrubbing, erasing the remnants of the night while the memories flooded back.

Roxy recalled vacuous air kisses, tinkling champagne flutes and Oliver's nauseating smile as they stood wedged in one corner of the glitzy, inner-city bar that had been chosen as the party venue for David Lone's film launch. The place was packed to the rafters and on her side alone, Roxy could make out at least a dozen celebrities, from TV stars and fashion designers to models and gossip columnists. And there in the centre of them all was the author-of-the-hour, David Lone. Like her, David had been a long-time client of literary agency Horowitz Management and, until his last book, a little-known and seemingly mediocre one. He was an investigative reporter by trade and, from what Olie had told her, wasn't exactly turning heads with his work. He had even tried his hand at crime fiction, apparently, with little success. Then, one day he began poking his nose into the so-called "Supermodel Murders"—a string of highly publicised crimes that took place over a two-year period with only one thing in common: each victim had, at one time or another, been a model. In fact, most had worked for lowly chainstore catalogues and only one of the five victims had ever really made The Big Time, so to speak, but the press had leapt on the case with relish, exalting all the victims to Super status. Much sexier that way, of course. And much more sellable.

Especially for David Lone.

His investigations resulted in a series of probing articles that not only blew open the lid on rampant drug abuse, eating disorders and underage sex within the modelling industry, but also helped solve the murders. The articles won several journalism awards, including a Walkley, and a book deal was promptly signed. His tome, *The Supermodel Diaries*, was a runaway success and very soon David and his agent, Oliver, were raking it in. When the film deal came through, they were on cloud nine. With that deal came an enormous advance that would help see David, and to a lesser extent Oliver, through any tough times ahead. Although, having just attended the film premiere, Roxy reckoned the toughest thing on David's schedule right now was how to spend the millions that would clearly be pouring in.

As he finished shaking yet another hand, the author caught Roxy's eye and gave her a wide, confident smile. She felt her stomach flutter, and then unwittingly ran one hand through her glossy, black bob, patting down her fringe and smoothing out the ends.

Easy, girl, she scolded herself. *He's not even your type.*

David was of the metrosexual, well-groomed variety, his slick blond hair obviously streaked and styled, his face shaven within an inch of his life, and his deep blue suit meticulously pressed with a crisp, white shirt underneath. She usually went for men who didn't know their way around an ironing board, let alone a shaving kit, yet there was something about David Lone that made her sit up and take notice. Perhaps, she thought, he wouldn't be quite so attractive if he wasn't quite so successful.

Within minutes, David was dislodging himself from the main crowd and moving towards her. Roxy readjusted the long strand of white beads she had worn over her lacy blue dress, and tried to look casual.

"Stop looking so constipated, Rox, Davo's on his way," Oliver said between clenched teeth, his smile still in place.

She sneered at him.

"Oh much better," he said, "that'll really win him over."

"I'm not here to win him over," she retorted. "Anyway, you're one to talk. You've got some major making up to do."

Oliver's smile dropped. "Me! Why? Without me, he would never have snagged the six-figure film deal. He should be thanking me."

"He might not be so appreciative if he knew you walked out halfway through the flick. I saw you sneak out, Oliver. Get bored, did we?"

Her agent blushed, a slight crimson beneath his flabby cheeks, and it caught Roxy by surprise. Oliver didn't regularly display human emotions like embarrassment. He was too thick-skinned for that.

"Jesus, Roxy, you don't miss a beat. Anyway, it's nothing personal. I've seen the bloody thing so many times, I couldn't stomach it again. I was gaggin' for a fag."

"Don't panic, Olie, I doubt Lone noticed. Besides, you made it back in time to see your name up on the big screen and that's all that really matters, isn't it?"

"Gotta love those endless credits," he said just as David reached their side.

"Hey, here's the man who helped make it all happen," David was saying to Oliver, yet his eyes were firmly on Roxy and the flutter in her stomach turned gale force. "It's Roxanne Parker, right?" Her jaw must have dropped because he laughed and added, "Yes, your agent has mentioned you once or twice. You write magazine articles and ghostwrite other people's autobiographies. Correct?"

"Correct. Good to see Oliver's actually doing his job. Congratulations on the movie, it was impressive."

She wasn't being disingenuous. Roxy really liked the movie. It had taken her quite by surprise. She had read and enjoyed the book on which it was based, but had come to expect most film versions of books to be disappointing at best. This time the story had been beautifully transplanted to the big screen and she wondered whether it was largely because David had been intimately involved.

"Yes, it was pretty awesome, wasn't it? I can't take any credit for that, I hate to admit. Brilliant director, actors were sensational. Although I think Matt Damon would have done a better job of me."

Roxy laughed. "I would have preferred Brad Pitt."

"Really?" he said, intrigued, looking her up and down. "So you're a Brad Pitt kind of girl?"

She blushed. "Aren't we all?"

Oliver glanced from one to the other and snorted. "Brad schmad, I still think they should have let you play the part, Davo."

"I'm a writer, Oliver, not a thespian. You have to know your limitations."

"What limitations?!" Oliver turned to Roxy. "We've just cracked the best seller lists in the US and the UK, and now, with this film, we should be stuck there for a while."

"Double congrats," she said, making sure to include them both in that.

Just then an elderly man stepped out of the crowd, and shuffled towards them, his watery blue eyes dancing above a charming, crooked smile. He had a black beret on his bald head and a baggy suit that only worked to accentuate his emaciated frame.

"Hey, you made it! That's great," Oliver said taking the man's hand gently, then turning to the others. "Have you guys met William Glad, of the Glad Gardening series?"

Roxy swooped in to plant a soft kiss on William's leathery cheek. "Of course I've met Mr Glad. Although I haven't seen you for a while. How are you feeling these days?"

"Ah, as good as can be expected," he said, shaking the subject away. "You look lovely as always, Miss Parker." He turned to David. "As for you, young man, that movie was magnificent and you should be very proud of yourself. I just wanted to stop by and congratulate you before I head off."

David beamed, thrusting his own hand out. "Thank you, Mr Glad, I appreciate you saying so. It means a lot to me. I know your gardening books very well. My father couldn't live without you, although I believe my mother has cursed you from time to time."

William chuckled. "Ah yes, another gardening widow, sorry about that."

"Not at all. You're clearly doing something right. Don't tell me you're a client of Oliver's as well?"

"For now," he said, his smile wavering slightly. "It's been a good innings, eh, Oliver?"

The agent agreed, a flicker of a frown across his forehead. "It's not over yet, William. We can still re-publish that impressive back catalogue of yours, you know?"

He dismissed this with a shrug. "Pointless and egotistical, I've told you that before, Oliver. No, no, let the new guard do their thing." He turned back to David. "I'll leave you young 'uns to it. I need to get home to bed or I'll have Erin on my case, she's loitering by the door looking anxious as always. I just wanted to let you know you've done a swell job."

"Thank you," David replied. "Can I help you out?"

Oliver stepped forward. "No worries, mate, I got it." He took the older man gently by the elbow. "Thanks for making the effort, William," he was saying as he began steering him through the crowd towards the exit and a middle-aged woman who was indeed looking anxious, hands on her hips, frown across her face. The woman looked completely out of place at the venue, wearing a frumpy floral dress, her hair pulled back in a tight ponytail, her face plain and makeup free.

"Erin?" David asked Roxy and she nodded.

"William's daughter. Oliver says she's a bit of a nightmare, very bossy with her dad. But I guess she has a reason to be now."

"Oh?"

"You haven't heard?"

"Heard what?"

Roxy took a quick sip of champagne. "Poor man has cancer, bone marrow, I believe. Hasn't got long to go."

"Oh that is a pity. Well, I guess he's right, though, he's had a good innings. Those gardening guides of his were huge sellers. My dad had about ten of them."

"Still, not much consolation when you're staring death in

the eyeballs."

"I disagree. He can go to his grave knowing he was a success. He left a legacy. That's not something to be sneezed at."

"Yes, but he's only in his sixties. Wouldn't you give all that up for another twenty years?"

David dropped his head to one side. "No, I don't know if I would. Would you?"

"Well, I guess it depends how I planned to spend that next twenty years."

He laughed. "I'm glad Oliver invited you along."

Roxy smiled awkwardly. "I think Olie invited every client he's ever come in contact with! I'm sure I saw Miss Erotica, Tina Passion, loitering around the bar earlier. In any case, I have to confess it took a bit of coaxing—no offence. I'm not much of a night owl, but I'm glad I came. So, how's your next book selling? I believe you wrote one about the terror cells in Sydney?"

His smile deflated just a fraction. "Oh, it's early days. We haven't got official sales figures in yet. Where is that waiter? I think he's neglecting us and it's all paid for by the film company so we might as well make the most of it." He strode off in search of a drink just as Oliver reappeared.

"So the second book's a fizzer then?" Roxy said to Olie.

"'Fraid so. I think he's missed the boat on the whole terrorist thing. People are bored stupid with the subject. Just between you and me, it looks like being a bloody flop. You're only as successful as your last book and a few of the reviewers are already calling Davo a 'one-hit-wonder'."

Roxy winced. That was one of her greatest fears. She wondered then if it was better not to succeed at all than to be considered a fluke. Having never had the glory of a top-selling book, the jury was still out on that one.

"His next book is on drug cheats in sports, he's about halfway through, but I'm not sure that's any more exciting, to be honest. So, a few muscle pigs are using performance-enhancing drugs. Who cares? I keep telling Davo he needs another glamorous murder, something that'll really grab the nation's attention."

"Well, you never know your luck in the big city," she laughed. "This very moment, some gorgeous young thing might be meeting a grisly, Hollywood-style ending."

As they drained their champagne flutes and kept the small talk flowing, little did they know that's exactly what was happening.

Roxy stared at the mirror suddenly, slamming herself back to reality.

Forget gorgeous young things, it has to be William Glad, she thought. *He must have passed away sooner than expected.*

She pulled on denim shorts, a silky white T-shirt and blue cotton scarf, then stopped, squishing her lips to one side. *So why then had Oliver mentioned suspicious circumstances, murder and cops? What could possibly be suspect about an old guy dying of cancer?* She shrugged, added a few dangly necklaces and blue flip-flops, then headed outdoors to find out.

CHAPTER 2

"**The** day was divine—a cloudless sky, a soaring sun, a gentle breeze fluttering from the shores of Elizabeth Bay—yet Roxy barely noticed. Her head was still thumping and her eyes were scrunched into slits, squinting at the cursed sun. She wasn't much of a fan of summer, at the best of times. It was way too bright and sparkly for her liking but it didn't help that today she felt like death warmed up. Replacing her Ray-Ban specs with dark prescription Gucci sunglasses, she zipped her oversized leather handbag up tightly, then made her way down the street from her apartment block to the small café on the corner.

Oliver was slouched at an outdoor table, one of only two in use at this hour, and didn't even notice her approach. He was holding his head up with both hands as though fearful it would drop off, and staring down at his coffee, glumly.

Not a cheerful character by nature, Oliver was also no sulk and usually weathered life like he did most of his clients—with a quick shrug and a no-nonsense attitude. That was one of the many reasons Roxy liked him and had continued using him as her literary agent over the past decade. Today, though, he looked wretched, and she noted that he was still wearing the same shirt he had on last night—an old, black and white bowling shirt with the words *"The Fearsome Four"* sewn in cursive writing across the top pocket. He'd lost the jacket, though, and stubble was already appearing on his heavy jowls, adding to the desolate facade.

"Bloody hell, Olie, you look as bad as I feel," Roxy said, dropping into the empty seat across from him and placing her handbag between her feet. "You okay?"

He looked up at her as though surprised she'd actually shown. "Urgh, I've had quite the night, I can tell you."

"You don't *need* to tell me, sweetie, the clues are abundant."

She indicated the plate of greasy bacon and eggs that was half demolished in front of him, the cheap sunglasses that were shielding his eyes, and the box of Paracetamol that looked like it had recently—frantically—been ripped open.

"Besides," she said, "last time I saw you, you were heading to Party Central with Tina Passion in one hand and a nicked bottle of champers in the other. Finally have our merry way with Miss Erotica, did we?"

"'Course I didn't. Never do, she's hot and cold that one. But it's nothing to do with her."

"No, of course not, sorry."

The waiter appeared and she ordered a latté and a croissant before saying, "So, tell me, what's happened. Who's shuffled off our mortal coil this time?"

She didn't mean to sound flippant but she really wasn't expecting what Oliver was about to say.

"Do you remember Seymour Silva, the author behind the *Alien Deliveries* series?"

His change of tack surprised her and Roxy had to take a few moments to catch up. "Well, I'm not really into sci-fi but I've heard of him, obviously. He's a pretty successful author, right? And isn't he one of yours?"

"Was until a few months ago. His manager cancelled our contract."

"Why? You weren't delivering?"

"Oh it's a long, ugly story. Sales *were* starting to drop off and they hooked up with some slimeball agent called Amy Halloran and that was that. She promised them the world, you know how it goes. Tried to steal Tina off me once if I recall. Luckily that didn't pan out. Doesn't matter now anyway."

"Why?"

"Seymour's dead."

Roxy sat forward with a start. "Really?! So William Glad's okay then?"

"Glad? Still alive and kicking as far as I know. Nope, it's Seymour. I got a visit this morning just as I was getting in, from the police. They had just found his body and wanted to ask me a few questions."

"Why you?"

"Apparently he still had my details down in his mobile phone as his agent. Don't know why they didn't have Amy's deets or why they even needed to speak to his agent, but there you go. I got them up to speed, set them on the right path. Couldn't even think about sleep after that, though. So here I am." He waved towards the clutter on the table in front of him.

Roxy's latté arrived and she tested the glass before pushing it aside. "So did they say what happened? How he died?"

He cocked his head to one side. "What do you reckon? The Filth never give anything away. But it was obviously a suspicious death because they asked me where I was between about 8:00 p.m. and midnight last night which was obviously when he died."

"Well, you were with me, at David Lone's film launch, of course."

"Yes, Roxy, I do remember that much, thank you. I told 'em all that. Have a hundred witnesses to prove it."

"Well, there was that—" She stopped mid-sentence. Roxy was about to mention Oliver's little disappearing act during the film preview, his quick exit for a smoke around

8:30 p.m., but the look of despair on his face stilled her. She decided not to mention it. It had nothing to do with Seymour's death, after all. Still, she couldn't help the tiny chill that was now sweeping over her, and she hugged her arms tightly around herself.

Sensing something, he said, "Don't worry, Rox, they're obviously just looking into all avenues."

"And *you're* one avenue?"

"Can't understand why, I hadn't seen the bloke in months, hell, probably a good year."

"How come? I thought you said he'd only dumped you a few months ago."

"Yeah, but I always dealt with Norm."

"Norm?"

"Norman Hicks, Seymour's manager. Odd bastard. Anyway, I sent the cops off to see him. He'll be cut up, those two were thick as thieves. Quite a team. It is bloody sad. They had real potential in the sci-fi scene. Internationally, I mean. The books were dropping off a bit here, but the world was their oyster. I helped get *Alien Deliveries* translated into a few languages and they could've cracked the almighty US market if they'd played their cards right."

Roxy touched the coffee glass again and then took a tentative sip. "So what's the story with family, etcetera? Did Seymour leave a rich and happily grieving widow behind?"

"Trust you to be considering the culprits."

"I'm just asking."

"Not that I know of. He was only young, mid-twenties I think, and, besides, Norm was his main man."

"Oh? Lovers?"

He shook his head, then speared a piece of dripping bacon and thrust it into his mouth. Chewing on it, he said, "Not the vibe I got. More like good buddies."

"Maybe they had a falling out? Not so buddy buddy suddenly?"

"Hey, steady on, Rox. Nobody's even saying it was murder at this point."

"Actually, you did, on the phone earlier but I won't hold you to that. It's just that he seems a bit young to die of natural causes, wouldn't you say?"

"Yeah, but he might have had an accident or topped himself. The cops certainly weren't giving anything away." He paused, then offered her one of his lopsided grins. "So, gonna put this one in your *Book of Death*, are you?"

Roxy flashed him a quick sneer, thought of a smart retort and then simply said, "Yeah, probably."

There was no point pretending otherwise. Roxy did have an obsession with death, particularly murder, and was compelled for reasons even she could not fathom, to catalogue these grisly crimes in a series of large scrapbooks she called her Crime Catalogues each week. Meticulously, she would cut out every newspaper article she could find and paste them in, just as her old friend Amanda used to do with clippings on Pearl Jam back in their high school days. Unfortunately, unlike Amanda's work, Roxy's scrapbooks were never-ending. There would be no break-up tour, no sudden decision to quit, to hang up their knives and guns, poisons and pillows. Murder was one consistency you could count on. And so, over the decade, her scrapbooks had grown. At last count, Roxy had twenty-three. She glanced across at the Saturday papers beside him.

"Surely it hasn't made the news yet?"

He shook his head. "It'll be all through them tomorrow, though, so sharpen your scissors. This is big news, Rox. The guy had plenty of fans."

"And at least one enemy," she replied softly, sipping her coffee again.

CHAPTER 3

By the time Roxy returned to her apartment, her head was reeling, and not just from the hangover. She had pinched a couple of Oliver's headache tablets but they had yet to take effect, and her mind was going a million miles a minute.

Who would want to kill science-fiction writer Seymour Silva?

It had her intrigued, but Olie was right, she didn't even know if it was a suspicious death and it certainly hadn't made the papers yet. Instead, there were several other sordid tales worth cataloguing: a drive-by shooting in Cabramatta, a guilty verdict on the Shaken Baby story she'd been following closely, and a husband-killer out on appeal. She did a little victory salute. She wasn't into corporal punishment but the poor, battered wife had probably done the world a favour.

Seated at the small desk in her sunroom, the place that served as her home office, Roxy snipped away quietly, methodically, making sure to retain every precious word. Then she reached for the latest scrapbook in a lower drawer and the gluestick beside it, and began to paste the clippings in. As she did so, she wondered again why she did this, why she felt the need to cut and paste in all this misery. Was it simple, morbid curiosity? Or did she believe that by containing the violence neatly in a catalogue, she would somehow control the uncontrollable?

The ringing phone broke her from her reverie, and Roxy picked it up quickly, forgetting to look at the caller ID number as she normally would.

"Roxy speaking," she said breezily.

"Hey, Parker," came a deep drawl on the other end and her heart skipped a beat.

"Oh, um, hi," she managed, now just sounding breathless.

It was Max Farrell, her best friend. That is, until about six months ago when their relationship took a nose dive. Long story short: Max had declared his undying love, Roxy had run screaming into the night, and they had never quite moved past it, despite several attempts to do so. Yet Roxy wanted to move past it desperately, and not just because Max was a gorgeous human being and a hunky one at that (think: stubbled square jaw, breathtaking smile, and tall, athletic build). They had met at a press conference almost three years earlier and connected over a mutual loathing of the whole celebrity scene. Despite being a top-gun photographer, as in demand for his celebrity snaps and funky fashion spreads as he was for his aspirational advertising images, Max kept it all at a sardonic distance, and loved the way Roxy didn't buy into it, either, more content in each other's company than an A-list crowd.

And that's what Roxy missed most. She missed Max's company. He was the only person in the world who could snap her out of a bad mood with a few beers and a bit of light banter. The only one who could drag her out of the house when she was determined to stay in, and who knew when to get involved and when to leave her the hell alone. Unfortunately, after her rejection, he had left her more than alone, he had left her lonely and pining for him. But she wasn't about to tell him that.

"How're you doing?" he asked, perhaps for the second time.

"Me? Fine, yeah, fantastic actually. Really, really fantastic." She clamped her lips shut. Scrunched her face up. She hadn't meant to sound so enthusiastic.

"Oh, right, well, that's good to hear." Yet he sounded a little deflated. Would he have preferred to hear that she was miserable? "Listen, I won't take much of your time. I was just wondering if you're doing anything next Saturday night."

Now Roxy's heart was racing. Was her old friend asking her out? On a date?

As if reading her mind, he quickly added, "It's just that I'm throwing a bit of a thing at my place and thought, you know, you might wanna come along. Maybe bring a mate."

"Oh, right. Sure." Her heart returned to slow-mo speed again.

"Maybe you could bring Gilda what's-her-name. She seems pretty cool. For a cop."

Gilda Maltin was a police officer Roxy had befriended eighteen months earlier while working on a ghostwriting assignment for an elderly Sydney socialite called Beatrice Musgrave. Roxy's job had been a simple one—to interview Beatrice and turn her words into a fabulous book for which Beattie got all the credit and Roxy got all the money, or at least enough to pay her mortgage for six months. Sadly for both of them, the ghostwriting assignment went belly up when the client, herself, was discovered belly up in the rocky bay below her mansion. She'd been murdered. Gilda had been the detective in charge and was not at all perturbed when Roxy began poking her nose into the case, unable to just let it go. In fact, they had worked together to solve the case, and had remained in touch ever since. Both women were strong-willed with an irreverent sense of humour but Roxy doubted it was Gilda's jokes that had Max singling her out. It probably had more to do with her sexy good looks.

She felt suddenly depressed. "Sure, I could do. Or maybe I could bring Oliver. He's having a bad week."

"Really?"

"Yeah, one of his old clients turned up dead this

morning."

"Seriously?"

"Seriously. The police aren't giving much away at this point, but it's pretty tragic." She took another breath. Was that a voice she could hear in the background? "How have you been, Max?"

"Good," he said, hurriedly. "Look, sorry, can't talk long I've, um, got someone here."

As if on cue, a woman's throaty laughter filled the ear piece, plunging Roxy's heart back down into her stomach. Talking to Max was like playing ping pong with her internal organs, and she wasn't sure how much more of this they could take.

"So you can come?" he asked.

"Huh?"

"To the party? Next Saturday night. From nine."

"Oh, yeah, sure, I'll be there."

"Good, see you then."

And with that he was gone and Roxy was left staring forlornly at the phone, her heart now as flat as a ping pong bat.

CHAPTER 4

"Men can be such bastards, darling," Lorraine Jones said matter-of-factly as she scanned the menu with one long, varnished nail. It was now lunch time on Sunday and mother and daughter had met at the Flower Pot Café as scheduled. "He was never right for you anyway. At least you can move on now."

"I don't want to move on, Mum," Roxy snapped back. "He was a mate and now, because I won't sleep with him, I'm suddenly taboo."

"He invited you to his party, didn't he?"

"Yeees," she had to concede.

"So, stop your whining and see it as an opportunity to meet someone else. Surely Max has got some lovely friends with real jobs and clean hair that he can introduce you to?"

Roxy rolled her eyes. "Oh, yeah, I'm sure he'll be throwing them at me. Anyway, that's hardly going to improve things, me going out with one of his mates."

Lorraine placed the menu down and turned her eyes upon her daughter, shaking her head as she did so. "What am I going to do with you?"

"What?"

"You're almost thirty-two and you still haven't learnt. Men and women can't be friends darling, it's—"

"A cliché," Roxy interrupted, "straight out of a bad Meg Ryan movie. Look, let's just drop it, okay? What are you having?"

"The salmon bagel. Hold the capers and red onion. And a mineral water. Sparkling."

"Good, I'll go and order." Roxy jumped up. "Before the queue builds up."

The Flower Pot Café was beginning to fill with patrons, most of whom had just purchased a selection of flowers or potplants from the adjoining nursery. It was a bright and boisterous eatery with a decent-enough menu and quick service if you got in at the right time. Lorraine and Roxy had begun meeting here each fortnight only recently and found the atmosphere mutually compatible, having tried several other venues before with varying degrees of success. Roxy's favourite haunt, Lockie's Café in Surry Hills, proved far too downmarket for the aspiring Mrs Jones, and it didn't bother her daughter who had grown tired of hearing her mother gripe about gays and "grotty inner-city types".

Their next choice, the Ivy in Lane Cove, was certainly plusher but they had swung too far the other way. Roxy felt completely out of her depth there, and lamented the way her mother spent most of their luncheons waving to one "darling friend" or another, duly pointing out their bachelor sons as she went. And so Roxy decided, this, too, would not do. Then one day, quite by accident, mother and daughter ran into each other at the Flower Pot Nursery, which, they realised, was located almost halfway between their two homes. Here was the perfect solution. If only Mum could change her attitude, Roxy thought, plonking back down in her seat.

"The food won't be too long," she said and before Lorraine could return to the conversation about her love life, or lack thereof, added quickly, "Did I tell you I've got a new book to write?"

Lorraine looked pleased. "Really, who is it this time? No eccentric hoteliers, I hope?"

She was referring to another client of Roxy's who had shown up dead, murdered for her precious boutique island resort in the Pacific. This time, Roxy had gone on to write the hotelier's life story, thanks to her generous daughter, but it had been a gruelling experience so soon after the death of Beatrice Musgrave, and she had shied away from ghostwriting biographies for a while, instead choosing to write relatively simple, albeit vacuous, articles for women's magazines and supplements in the Sunday papers. Life was much less traumatic that way. But it was ghostwriting she loved most—turning people's life stories into an entertaining narrative that their family and friends could enjoy—and she was now looking forward to sinking her teeth into another one.

"I don't actually know who it is," she told her mother. "It's early days. Oliver's going to brief me tomorrow."

"Oh, dear, well, I hope this one's deadly dull and not an ounce of blood is shed."

She had a point. With her last two clients murdered, Roxy's life was beginning to resemble an episode of *Murder, She Wrote.* Some would call her cursed, but Roxy knew it wasn't as unpredictable as you'd think. After all, when people write their life stories, hanging the family laundry out for all the world to see, someone is bound to get upset.

"In any case, it should keep you nice and busy," her mother was saying. "I know you like to be busy. It's the perfect distraction for you."

"Mum, don't even go there, okay?"

"Darling, it's a fact. You're a classic commitment-phobe. I read about you in *Cosmo.*"

"*Cosmo,* hey? That all-knowing source of spiritual sustenance. Seems a little downmarket for you. I would've thought you were more the *Vogue* magazine type."

"Well, one has to read *something* while waiting for their hair to set." Lorraine patted her neatly blow-waved, ivory blonde hairdo, managing to mess it up in the process. She wasn't wearing her trademark black, velvet headband but she did have a set of pearls in her ears and a matching pearly coloured dress that, teamed with the hair, left her looking like a blob of whipped cream. Probably not the effect she was after, thought her daughter snidely.

"Honestly, I'm going to have to find a new stylist," Lorraine was saying. "Scottie keeps me waiting far too long, even for him." Her eyes darted across Roxy's razor sharp, black bob. "Of course, it wouldn't hurt *you* to pay him a visit. He can't quite work miracles but he can come close."

"I like my hair as it is, thanks."

She sniffed. "Well, it's hardly very friendly, is it?"

Roxy laughed. "Friendly? Now there's one for the books. What exactly is 'friendly' hair, pray tell? Should I get Scottie to weave it into a door mat? Should he dye a big 'Hello' in my fringe?"

Lorraine smirked back at her daughter. "No need to be sarcastic, Roxanne. I'm just saying, your fringe practically covers your eyes, which is very unappealing. You have such beautiful green eyes. And as for the colour? Let's face it, darling, black is so *dreary*. I don't know why you insist on looking like a … What's the word? Goth, I think it is."

"They call it 'Emo' these days, and I'm nothing like one."

"Well, whatever they call it, it doesn't look nice. You should go lighter. You'd look really sweet and we all know how much men love blondes."

"Ahh, another popular cliché. This is going to surprise the hell out of you, Mum, but appealing to men isn't exactly my top priority."

"You can honestly tell me you don't want to settle down one day and have children? Are you saying I'm never going to get the chance to hold a grandchild in my lap?"

She was pouting now and Roxy felt like screaming. She couldn't even picture a wriggly little kid on Lorraine's bony lap. Besides, she'd been perfectly happy to keep her own child at a convenient distance when she was young, what on earth did she want with grandkids? Roxy glanced around eagerly searching out the waiter.

Where was the damn food?

"Oh, Mum, of course I hope to have kids one day. All I'm saying is that I'm into my career right now. I love my work, and men and kids are just not on my immediate agenda."

"But you're going to Max's party, right?" The pouting had turned into a look of sheer panic.

"Yes, I suppose so."

"Good! Well, if you won't fix your hair, how about buying a sexy little frock? We can go shopping this afternoon if you like."

"I don't think that's necessary. I'm sure everyone'll just be in jeans."

Lorraine frowned. "Honestly, you young people have no idea how to dress yourselves, do you?"

"We're not salad, Mum," Roxy said, relieved to see the food arrive.

Over lunch, Roxy could tell something was on her mother's mind, other than her listless love life, of course, and eventually she said, "Spit it out, Mum. What is it you want to say?"

Lorraine took a deep breath. "I was thinking it might be nice for Charlie to come along next time we catch up. What do you think?""

I think I can feel a migraine coming on, Roxy thought, groaning internally this time. It was bad enough that she was subjected to her stuffy stepdad's antics at the end of every month when she visited their North Shore house for dinner, but now he was inviting himself along on these mother/daughter catch ups? She'd had enough.

"Actually I think it's a terrible idea. Can't he go and play golf or something?"

There was a sulky silence and Roxy could feel her temper rising again. Her mother was an expert at sulking her way towards what she wanted but Roxy was adamant this time.

She tried a different tack.

"Look, Mum, this is supposed to be *our* time, remember? Quality time together."

"Yes, I know that, but, well, Charlie feels a little left out. He wants to get closer to you, darling, he wants to be the father you don't have. Why won't you let him in?"

Because he's not my dad, she wanted to tell her. *Because he's nothing like my dad.* She reflected then on the tiny, framed, black and white picture of her father that was sitting beside her bed. It showed a young man, his hair tussled, a smile wide across his face as he held a small girl in his arms. Her hair was perfect with a ribbon in place but her smile matched his. They looked as though they hadn't a care in the world. One year later that man would be dead and the girl would never be quite so quick to smile again.

"Not going to happen, Mum. So let's drop it. Okay?"

Another silence, a snippy, "fine" and then a sulky, "Well, will you at least come over for dinner, soon? He'd like to catch up with you. Says you need a decent feed."

Roxy scowled at this but let it drop and promptly changed the subject.

Half an hour later, as she made her way home, Roxy wondered whether she would ever learn to tolerate Lorraine Jones. She loved her mother dearly, couldn't help herself, but Lorraine was like an alien species most of the time, like someone from another planet. This brought the smile back to Roxy's lips. It had reminded her: the Sunday papers were still waiting to be collected. Perhaps there were more details of the sci-fi writer's untimely demise.

******

That evening, as Roxy slowly snipped away at the edges of the various newspaper articles on Seymour Silva, somebody else was also keenly devouring the news. He was surprised how little space it was getting. After all that effort, he had expected the front pages of both Sunday papers, but only one seemed to care. The other had hidden the article on page six and this irked him.

A famous writer had died, surely that was big news? If there had been more than one murder, say two or three … that would have made them sit up and take notice.

The thought sent a shiver down his spine, and something else, too.

The gem of a good idea.

CHAPTER 5

Roxy threw open her closet doors and stared pitifully at the contents inside. Nothing. Not a shred of inspiration reached out to entice her in. She glanced at her watch: 9:29 a.m. She had better hurry or she'd be late again. She had dawdled far too long on the Sunday papers last night, reading over every scintillating detail of Seymour Silva's life which had been covered in both papers but most comprehensively by "crime reporter" David Lone in the *Telegraph*. She had forgotten he wrote for the *Tele* and was surprised he had managed to get this article together so quickly after his big film launch. Unlike her, he obviously had no trouble focusing with a hangover.

David's article was spread over the entire page and read like a gripping yarn. (He was good at gripping yarns, that was obvious.) Born into a dirt-poor Dubbo family, Seymour Silva had lived, according to David, a fairly ordinary life until one fateful night at the age of nineteen when he simply vanished. Missing without trace, his family had been frantic until he reappeared ten days later, naked, dehydrated and disoriented, insisting he'd had an extra-terrestrial experience. He claimed he'd been abducted by aliens.

The family sought psychological help, of course, but Seymour refused counselling and eventually disowned them, moving to Sydney where he began his incredible writing career. In the six years since his supposed abduction, Seymour had written five novels and, while always insisting they were not autobiographical, his own eerie past helped propel them to healthy sales for a young, and if truth be told, fairly average, Australian science-fiction writer.

It was all about the back story, of course, Roxy understood that. If he had just been an ordinary bloke from the 'burbs, writing extraordinary tales about ETs, his manuscripts might never have made it out of his hard drive. Thanks to his spooky past, and local success, Seymour's future as a global entity was also looking on the up, or, at least, that's how David portrayed it, and quoted Seymour's new agent Amy Halloran to that effect.

Sadly for all, Seymour's "incredible career" was now cut short, his body discovered early Saturday morning by a cleaning woman in his apartment in an inner-west suburb of Sydney. The police were yet to comment, but according to David, Seymour's death was "highly suspicious" and there was blood splattered across his bedroom. He didn't elaborate further yet it didn't matter to Roxy. She was firmly hooked. This was going to make for some riveting reading in the weeks to come.

Enough of that! Shoving the coat hangers to one side, she whipped each one across separately, hoping something, anything, would leap out at her. But zip. She sneered back at her wardrobe like a sulky child, reminding herself of her mother. Winter was much easier for dressing up, she decided. All you had to do was add a scarf or a jacket and old outfits were instantly renewed. There wasn't much you could do with a summer frock that had been worn one too many times. Not that Oliver would care, or even notice for that matter. She finally settled on a black and white spotted blouse, flowing black skirt and thick red belt, then finished her makeup, scraped a comb through her hair, smoothing down her thick fringe in the process, slipped into some black ballet flats and headed out.

Oliver was in his usual spot, wedged behind the desk in his inner-city office, when she waltzed in, and Roxy didn't wait for an invitation, simply sat down in the scrappy armchair in front of him and smiled.

"You better today?" she asked and he shrugged, scratching his stomach where it bulged out of a lairy, Hawaiian-print shirt.

There was a brown smudge down the front, probably the remnants of breakfast, a greasy kebab, a sloppy burger or something equally as nutritious. Oliver wasn't what you'd call health-conscious and his expanding girth, not to mention grease-splattered clothing, were proof of that.

"Sure, the hangover's gone and the cops haven't called again," he said. "I'm sailing on cloud nine. Let's get straight to it, eh?" He dug about his messy desk for a file, located it and threw it towards her, spilling some of the contents as it went. "So, remember our hot-shot author David Lone?"

She laughed. "Well, I would if it wasn't for the brain cells I managed to destroy at his premiere. That was quite a night. David's been busy on the Seymour Silva case, I see."

"Yep, that is his job when he's not moonlighting as a celebrity. Anyway, he's your man. We've been commissioned to write his life story."

Roxy's jaw dropped and for a second she was uncharacteristically speechless.

"The publisher wants a racy book looking at his background, how he came across the Supermodel murders, the ins and outs of the case, a bit about his love life, that sort of thing. Coffee?"

"Um, yeah, sure." She was still processing it all as Oliver yelled out to his assistant.

"Shazza! You in yet?!"

There was a hoarse cough in the front room and then a loud, "Whatdaya want?"

"Two coffees, if it's not too much to bloody ask. Roxy's here."

A mop of frizzy red hair appeared at the doorway followed by a skinny, middle-aged woman wearing an acid-wash skirt and a frilly, red blouse that dipped far too low across a flat, leathery chest.

"Hi, love, how are ya?"

Roxy waved hello. "Great, thanks, Sharon. How's the Big Guy treating you?"

Sharon glanced across at Oliver and shrugged. "Like crap as usual. It's milk and two, right?"

"Thanks, yes." Sharon disappeared and Roxy turned to her agent. "Explain this to me, Oliver: why on earth does a hugely successful writer need another hugely *unsuccessful* writer to write his life story? It doesn't make any sense."

She held up David's bulging file of press clippings and book reviews and waved it at him.

"Jesus, you're a suspicious beast! You can never just say, 'Thanks for the work, Oliver, I'd love to do it.'"

"I'm allowed to ask!"

He sighed. "Two reasons. The first is he's right in the middle of his drug cheats book. Deadline is looming so he hasn't got the time to do it himself, but we need to get the book out while he's still big news. Second, it's what the publisher prefers. Apparently it's cooler that way, sells better, too. It's gonna be like an unauthorised biography that's, well, secretly authorised." Roxy looked at him sideways and he cleared his throat. "We're gonna market it as a bit of a tell-all. You know, the hidden story behind the famous writer and the famous book. The stuff you don't know, that sort of thing."

"And David Lone has approved all of this?"

"Yeah, loves the idea. Hell, if I recall rightly—and we did discuss it over one too many shots of tequila, I have to confess—it might even have been *his* bloody idea. We just all reckon it'll sell better than an autobiography. It's gonna be a bit steamy, a bit sexy."

Roxy sat back in her chair considering the well-groomed man she had met at the film premiere and couldn't quite equate the two. Sure, he was a little smarmy but he certainly didn't seem like your average playboy Lothario. Oliver took her silence as hesitation.

"Look, there's good money in this for you. Half a year's freelance salary, plus royalties, so it's in all our interests that we make it as juicy as possible."

"But is there anything 'juicy' to say?"

"Christ, yeah!" Oliver's grin lopped to one side. "So you fell for his nice boy image, eh? David Lone is a bit of a party boy, big with the chicks. Well, especially since the book came out, and now with the film, he's on the A-list. I'm sure I saw him at the end of the party smooching that new blonde soap star from *Home and Away*."

"Sounds real A-list," Roxy replied wryly as Sharon reappeared with the coffees.

The receptionist glanced at the file in Roxy's hands. "Oooh, I love Davo," she said with a wink. "Dirty great spunk, that one."

"Thank you, Sharon, that's very insightful. You can close the door on your way out," Oliver said and she flipped him the bird as she did so.

Roxy sipped her coffee for a moment and had to admit the thought of spending more time with the handsome reporter was tempting. He was clearly an intriguing character, and it was good money after all. Still, the idea of writing something so trashy gave her pause for thought. Even Roxy Parker and her lowly bank account had their standards.

Oliver was one step ahead of her. "Look, Rox, I know you're usually more high-brow than this, but it's a good story and it needn't be tacky if you write it right. We just want a gripping yarn about a gripping guy. Why don't you get together with David and nut it out between you? See how it feels?"

"Well, it can't hurt."

"Blood oath! Plus it gives you a break from all that girlie crap you write about for those no-brainer chick rags."

"Ahh, I think you mean all those probing social issues for women's magazines," she corrected him. "And you're right. I could do with a bit of variety about now. Okay, give me his number and I'll give him a call."

Oliver reached into his back pocket, pulled out a wallet and located one of David Lone's business cards. He flung it towards her. "Actually, we've already set something up. Tonight at Piago's, 8:00 p.m. His shout."

Roxy glanced at the card and then raised an eyebrow at her agent. "How very presumptuous of you both. So he's expecting me then?"

"Tells me he's looking forward to it. Hey, there might even be a romance in this for you if you play your cards right."

She almost choked on her coffee, spilling a little down her blouse, and jumped up to swipe a tissue from the box on his desk.

"Jesus, Olie, cut it out," she said, dabbing at the stain. "You sound like my mother."

"I don't think your mother's thinkin' what I'm thinkin'."

Roxy scrunched up the tissue and lobbed it at her agent's head while he continued chuckling away.

CHAPTER 6

Piago's Ristoranté & Bar was as pretentious as it sounded, bursting with ageing executive types in creased Italian suits and obscenely young wannabe widows in designer frocks, and, hovering around them, a flurry of starched waiters who clearly found the whole world distasteful, their noses turned high. Roxy despised places like this but it didn't exactly surprise her that David Lone had chosen it. It certainly befitted a man who was moving up in the world. He laughed when she suggested as much.

"Oh, I can't stand the place. I just find it such a laugh. Look around you, this is all great fodder for our books, yes?"

"I guess so," she replied, not convinced.

"And I have to tell you I do love Monday nights out. They're the real deal."

"How do you mean?"

"You know, less of the riff-raff out and about, just the important people."

"Oh, I see, and that would be you and me, would it?"

He smiled. "You're quick, I like that. That's why I wanted you for the book."

They were seated across from each other at a candle-lit

table right in the centre of the room, and David gave Roxy a piercing look that saw her shifting in her seat, her confidence waning. She hadn't noticed how blue his eyes were until now. They were almost translucent, like shallow rock pools, and they were beguiling.

What is it with this man? He was not her type at all, and yet he certainly knew how to push her buttons. It didn't help that he was less clean-shaven today and had swapped his expensive suit for a more relaxed tight T-shirt and tailored leather jacket. Not quite something Max would wear but close enough. For reasons she wouldn't admit to herself, she had dressed up tonight, and was wearing a silky magenta coloured dress, heeled boots and beads, but she noticed that she was still the most casually dressed woman in the room. And she was proud of herself for that.

"So you asked for me, specifically?"

"Absolutely. I've read your stuff, seen you around. In fact, I met you with Oliver at his office once about two years back."

"Really?"

A slight shadow flickered across David's eyes, muddying the waters. "We talked for a few minutes, you don't remember?"

Roxy shifted again. "Hey, sorry about that, but you can't take it personally. My memory is like a sieve at the best of times. Wouldn't remember my own name if I hadn't tattooed it to the inside of my eyelids."

"That's what they all say." He glared menacingly for a split second before breaking into a wide smile. "I'm just messing with you, Roxanne. Can I call you that?"

"If you like. I do prefer Roxy, though."

"Really? I don't think it does you justice. In any case, I think you and I would make an incredible team, whatever we call each other." He leaned back in his seat. "I think we have chemistry."

"Oh," she said, feeling a blush creep up and she breathed deeply to push it back down. "So! Where is that waiter? I'd kill for a merlot."

He didn't seem to notice her discomfort. "Allow me."

David signalled for a waiter and, after some discussion, settled on a pricey Margaret River cabernet Shiraz. When the bottle arrived he made a bit of a show, swirling the glossy red liquid in his glass and sniffing it before taking a slow, tentative sip. She half expected him to slush it around his mouth then spit it out into a bucket but he simply swallowed the mouthful and indicated for the waiter to pour.

After the waiter had left, David raised his glass and said, "To a great working relationship." Then he toasted her, holding the glass to his lips while his eyes never left hers.

He was getting way ahead of himself now, she thought, taking a good gulp. "First things first, hey. What exactly are you after with this book?"

He shrugged. "Surely we don't have to launch into work just yet?"

"Well, no, but—"

"So you read about Seymour Silva?"

"The dead writer, yes. Mostly thanks to you. The other paper barely mentioned it. I see you're in the thick of it. What's your theory?"

"It has to be murder, no question."

"Really? I thought that hadn't been determined yet. Why do you think it's murder?"

He winked. She didn't really like blokes who winked, especially blokes with gorgeous blue eyes that should remain open and staring firmly at her, as unsettling as it was.

"You'll have to read tomorrow's press to find that out," he told her and then, when she groaned, he laughed.

"Come *on*," she said. "If you want to work with me, you're going to have to show you can trust me."

"Okay, okay, I'll give you the scoop for free. Suffice to say, he wasn't just found dead, there were some circumstances that dispute the whole suicide theory."

"Oooooh ... Such as?"

"For starters, there was no suicide note."

"So?"

"So, he's a writer. Surely a writer would leave a long and dramatic good-bye letter to be published posthumously. Wouldn't you?"

"I wouldn't kill myself, so I guess I don't know."

He ignored this. "Plus he has a very bizarre manager who I'm looking into as we speak."

David's hand instinctively reached for the expensive smartphone he'd placed on the table earlier, and he checked it quickly before placing it back down, as though expecting an urgent call at any moment.

"And how do you know all this?" Roxy asked.

"I have my sources."

"Oliver Horowitz?"

"Hardly. No, I go a lot deeper than that."

"Let me guess, Oliver's been wining and dining his forensic friend Kay Chong again?"

Lone paused for a moment, surprised. "You've met Kay, then?"

"Yes, I have."

"She's certainly very useful, that woman. But she's not the only one."

There was a cheeky gleam in his eyes and Roxy wondered whether Kay had also proven useful to David in the case of the Supermodel murders. She made a mental note to ask him about that, later.

"So, what's the goss?"

"I just told you."

"You told me nothing. Come on, you're holding something back. Spit it out."

"Okay, okay." He took another mouthful of wine and then launched in. "According to ... well, let's just call them 'sources', Seymour was also heavily drugged when he died and his wrist was slashed."

"Sounds exactly like suicide to me."

"Don't be too quick to judge. That's clearly what the culprit intended. The answer is all in the wrist."

"Huh?"

The gleam in David's eyes had intensified. "Seymour's wrist wasn't just slashed." He paused. "It was slashed from the top of the left side down and then from the top of the right side down."

She looked at him blankly. "Okay, and that's intriguing because?"

"Think about it."

Roxy blinked several times then began tracing the line of the cut along her own wrist, from one side down and then the other. "You mean he was sliced with an X-shape?" He nodded, smiling. "Sorry, David, I'm still not following."

"An X-file, of course."

Roxy couldn't help scoffing. "You're serious? You think he was deliberately marked with an X for *The X-files*? The old TV show about aliens and stuff? Why? Because he was a sci-fi writer?"

"Obviously." Just then the waiter arrived to take their orders and David waited until he had done his duty before continuing on, his face increasingly animated. "I believe he was clearly trying to make a point, leave a message, so to speak."

"He?"

"Yes, you're right, it could be very well have been a woman. I wouldn't put it past any of you."

"Hey, watch it!"

He laughed. "It's intriguing, though, isn't it?"

Roxy had to admit it was. "Look, you're preaching to the converted here. I love a good true crime story more than most people, but I think you might just be stretching this one a bit too far, David. For starters, *The X-files* hasn't been on telly for years, so it's a tenuous link at best. Plus, the 'X' could purely be the result of a frantic knife wound. A coincidence. Or if it was intentional, who's to say Seymour didn't do it to himself?"

"I don't know, I think there's something very suspicious about the whole thing. It's just a hunch I've got. I'm going to get to the bottom of it, I can tell you that for sure."

Roxy stared hard at David and then broke into laughter, quickly trying to swallow it back down as she watched a wounded look sweep across his face.

"Am I really that amusing?"

David's sensitivity made him even more attractive to Roxy and she leaned towards him, one hand at her lips. "Sorry, David, I'm not laughing at you, honestly I'm not. I just cannot believe I have met someone as interested in all of this as I am."

"What's not to be interested in? While we were all happily watching my new movie in a cosy cinema, some monster was slashing the life out of another human being. If it really was murder, what made him—or, yes, *her*—do it? Was it premeditated? Spur of the moment? It's fascinating stuff and anyone who tells you differently is a liar."

David was starting to get worked up, his eyes were sparkling again and he was now sitting forward, gesticulating with his hands. "I hate the way we have to pretend that murder is not polite conversation when it's often all anyone can think about, read about. Humans are fascinated with death and particularly murder. It's the reason the *Supermodel Diaries* did so well—sex, lust, murder, that's what sells, it's what people want to read whether they'll admit to it or not."

"Easy, tiger, I'm with you there. It's always grabbed my attention and I'm more than happy to admit it."

He seemed relieved by this and raised his wine glass to hers, giving it a solid clink. "See, what did I say? I knew we'd be perfect for one another."

This time she couldn't suppress the blush that was sweeping across her cheeks.

CHAPTER 7

The following morning Roxy awoke with yet another hangover, unusual for her so early in the week. She moaned as she dragged herself into the shower. This David Lone character was proving to be a bad influence, she thought, then smiled at the memory of a truly enjoyable evening out. They had followed up dinner with drinks at Bar 11, an inner-city lounge bar that was just as pretentious as the restaurant, and she even recalled a little dancing before she'd had the good sense to flee into the night.

David was certainly charming but Roxy knew she had to watch her step. This was business, after all, and what was that saying about never mixing the two?

She lathered herself with soap, and couldn't help smiling. Until now she'd never had to worry about that. Murder mysteries aside, her past ghostwriting clients had all been relatively dull; usually monopolised by the only people who could afford to have a book written for them—the old and the wealthy. But David Lone was different. He was young, good looking and a riveting conversationalist. For the first time, Roxy could actually relate to one of her clients. And he was right. On paper, at least, they were a perfect match. Not only were they both passionate about writing, she also discovered as the evening progressed that David was interested in many of the things she found important, like politics, the environment, travel. And, yes, even murder.

She had to admit that she was particularly drawn to his fascination for death. For the first time in her life, Roxy felt comfortable chatting with a man about true crime. He *got it.*

"Just because you're interested in murder doesn't make you any more evil than anyone else," he'd said and she had nodded her head vigorously, the warm red wine tingling through her veins. "It just makes you more fascinating as far as I'm concerned."

She had felt a sense of jubilation wash over her then, recalling the numerous conversations that Max Farrell had aborted over the years often angry with her at the mere mention of death. How often had she tried to chat about an article of interest or a news story on TV only to find him tense up and wave her away? At last, here was a man who did not shy away from the reality of life which, like it or lump it, includes death, some of it unexpected and macabre.

Roxy stepped out of the shower and dressed casually before heading to the sunroom to put her thoughts down on her trusty laptop. She created a new folder marked "Lone Wolf" (she always named her files cryptically, it was an odd habit she couldn't explain but persisted with nonetheless) and then opened a Word document, this one plainly titled "Q&A". At the top of the page she typed: *If I decide to do it!* Then she added a few quick questions, including, *"Where does David source his information from?"* and *"What first sparked his fascination with death and murder?"*

Roxy then sat back and rubbed her temple, squinting out past the fluorescent green ferns to the gleaming yachts bobbing about in the bay in front of her apartment block. She lived in the inner-eastern suburb of Elizabeth Bay which was a high-density area bursting with an eclectic mix of low-income, arty, bohemian types, well-to-do socialites and DINKS (double income, no kids). Roxy didn't really feel she belonged to any of these sub-cultures, but she loved the area nonetheless, and she loved her tiny little pad, its chipped, whitewashed walls and sunny perspective. The view, alone, was worth the sometimes crippling mortgage. She stared out at it now as she tried to gather her thoughts.

At this stage, Roxy didn't have a lot to work with. They'd barely discussed David's biography last night and, thinking about it now, she realised that every time she turned the conversation towards it, he just as smoothly steered them back off track.

Was he avoiding something? she wondered. *Or was he just having too much fun?*

In any case, it meant they would have to meet again, this time at a more sober location—there were so many things yet to nut out before she would sign on the dotted line. Still, as she searched for David's number through the cards in her purse, Roxy knew very well that there was no turning back now. This was one man it seemed she could not resist. Her mother would be proud.

Several phone calls and a few hours later, Roxy was back in Oliver's office, sitting in the battered old armchair, pen and paper in hand. Beside her, on a squeaky new director's chair, was David Lone, dressed casually now in a chambray shirt and jeans, looking fresh as a daisy with a wide smile on his lips.

Did the man never suffer hangovers? Roxy wondered, begrudgingly.

Oliver's mind was elsewhere. "Come on then, Davo, spit it out. What have you got to be so smug about? Happy with your X-files scoop in the paper today, eh?" He nodded in the direction of the tabloid newspaper that was folded over itself on his desk.

"Not that, no," David said. "Although my scoop has hit the airwaves. That's all they're discussing on talk-back radio today. Have you been listening to the dialogue?"

"Mate, I'd rather slit my own wrist with an X than listen

to talk-back. So if it's not that, why are you looking like the cat who ate the canary?"

Roxy raised one hand high in the air, like an eager school child. "I know! I know! You've uncovered some *more* juicy details about the Seymour Silva case."

David chuckled. "Top of the class for you," he said. "But we're not here to talk about Seymour Silva. It's all about me today." Now both Roxy and Oliver scowled at him and he laughed again. "All I can say is, I could have a very big scoop coming out in tomorrow's paper, bigger even than the X-slash. If my investigations pan out, and I think they will, it's going to ruffle quite a few feathers, I can promise you that."

Oliver looked apprehensive. "Really? What have you found out?"

"Nothing confirmed yet," he said, reaching around to pull his iPhone out of his back pocket. He glanced at it quickly, then placed it on the desk in front of him. "I'll know more soon. Until then ..." David pretended to zip his lips shut and Oliver glared at him for a few moments.

"You do know what you're doing, right?"

"Naturally."

He sighed. "All right, let's get on with it then, what's to discuss?"

"I haven't got any questions. I say we just get started on my book as soon as possible."

"Ah ... hang on a minute," Roxy stammered. "I haven't actually agreed to do it yet, in case anyone hasn't noticed. I need to confirm a few things before I sign up."

"Fair enough," David said. "What can I confirm for you?"

"Well, for starters, let's discuss the tone of this book. I'm not real big on the sleazy tabloid style, if that's what you're after."

David grabbed at his heart as if in shock and Oliver leapt to his defence.

"Er, I think, Roxy, I might have given you the wrong impression yesterday."

"You mean the impression that you wanted me to write a sleazy tell-all?"

He grimaced. "Yes, that one. I've since spoken to the publishers and Dave here, and they don't want 'sleaze' so much as 'best seller'."

"That's right," said David, turning his whole body to face her. "I don't want it to be sleazy. I'm not sleazy, so why would my book be? But I do want it to be a fantastic read. I want to sell copies, I mean, what's the point of doing this otherwise?"

Roxy could think of many reasons to write someone's life story—to create history, set the record straight, entertain and inform—but she chewed her lower lip and let them continue.

"We just want a fantastic read," Oliver repeated. "And we want to strike while the iron's hot. The film's just out, David's books are soaring up the charts, it's time to get his story told."

"And, again, tell me why you don't want to write it yourself, David?" He shrugged as though it were unimportant. That wasn't going to cut it. "I mean it," she said. "I understand why people normally employ me—most can't write to save themselves, or don't know how to get started—but you're different. You're a pro. Why not write it yourself?"

He sighed impatiently. "Because, Roxanne, I want you to write it. I'm a little young to be writing my memoirs, yet my story is kind of intriguing, if I don't say so myself." He winked, grinning. "Plus, I think the audience will perceive it as more revealing if it's written by a so-called 'outsider'. Then of course there's the fact that I just don't have the time. I'm pretty busy right now, in case you hadn't noticed. I'm trying to finish this blasted book on doping and elite athletes, and I'm also on the Seymour Silva case for the *Telegraph*."

"This book about Davo really needs to come out soon," added Oliver. "Gotta strike while he's hot."

"I'm always hot," David said, winking again.

She ignored that and said, "But are we calling it 'Unauthorised'?"

This was a sticking point for Roxy. It smacked of overt sensationalism. Oliver laughed nervously.

"Oh, Roxy, I was just throwing that about the other day. Let's just get started on the book and see how it goes."

David grabbed one of Roxy's hands, taking her by surprise, and she felt a jolt of electricity race through her. His skin was warm and smooth, and he cupped her hand between his own, staring deeply into her eyes. "Roxanne, let me assure you I am after as tasteful a book as you are. But I also want it to reach as wide an audience as possible, so it needs to be entertaining. Not sleazy but scintillating. There is a difference and you can pull it off, I know you can. You did it with your last book, and you can do it with this one. I'm happy to lay myself bare for the book—so to speak. I will answer every question you ask, and you can follow me anywhere you choose. You'll have an all-access pass." He raised his eyebrows a few times, teasingly, and she couldn't help laughing.

"All right, fine, let's do it. What's the deadline?"

"Yesterday," said Oliver.

"Then we better get started." She released her hand from David's grip, anxious to regain some control. "Let's talk word count, chapter ideas, that sort of thing."

"We're one step ahead of you," said Oliver. "The publisher has already sent through a bit of a brief, I'll print it out for you."

Over the next two hours the agent and his writers nutted out a rough profile of the David Lone Story. They agreed on word count—about 60,000—with two colour sections of photos and illustrations, and discussed some rough chapter headings. David also drew up a preliminary list of interviewees and provided Roxy with contact details, and they scheduled their first "official interview" for the following Thursday morning. Oliver then printed out a standard contract for them all to sign.

Just as they were reading through the small print, a curvaceous blonde burst into the room, decked out in a tight pink and silver dress, with skyrocketing black heels and numerous silver necklaces dribbling down her exposed cleavage, some lost within the spongy folds.

It was Tina Passion, of course. Roxy recognised the romance writer from the large cardboard cut-out that Oliver used to keep as pride of place in his office. She was another of Oliver's clients and, if memory served Roxy well, was once a lingerie model before she tried her hand at erotic fiction, the type of love stories that left *Mills & Boon* readers blushing under their crisp cotton sheets. As far as Roxy could tell, Tina Passion sold very well, helped along, no doubt, by the fact that she was a regular on the social circuit, her billowy bosom popping up at every tacky nightclub opening and horse racing event going. She had a kind of Dolly Parton charm, too, that won over the women, although Roxy was about to become an exception.

"Oliver, *gorgeous*!" she said, ignoring the curious writers as she flung herself across the desk and towards the agent, planting a sloppy kiss on his cheek and leaving a bright pink smudge behind.

He pulled away, a giddy grin on his face, and waved one hand towards Roxy and Lone, spluttering, "Tina Passion, meet Roxy Parker and David Lone, two of my top writers."

"And here I was thinking I was the only one," she purred, giving Roxy the once-over before turning her attentions to David.

"Mr Lone. How delightful! I saw you at your film premiere the other evening. Couldn't catch your eye, though." She sounded slightly offended, and David swept in and took one of her hands, planting a slow kiss on the back of it.

"Apologies for that, Ms Passion," he said. "I can not believe I missed someone as stunning as you."

Tina's eyes lit up, Roxy looked ready to throw up and

Oliver just looked flustered.

"Er, you're early, Tina," the agent cut in. "I'm not quite finished here—"

She removed her hand slowly from David's, her eyes still firmly upon him, and said, "No need to rush. I just dropped in to postpone."

"Aw, really?"

She turned back to Oliver who was no longer grinning. "Yes, schnooky, enormous apologies and all that, but I have to get a rain check. Papa's in town, freaked out by all the nonsense in the press about Seymour Silva being bumped off." She shot Lone a wicked smile. "So I'm stuck entertaining him this evening, would you believe?"

"What's your dad worried about?" asked Oliver.

"Oh he's just being *protective*, you know what he's like." She scooped her long locks up with one hand and swept them back behind her while the other hand readjusted the necklaces that were still half hidden down her décolletage. "How about we get together Saturday night instead? I should be able to get rid of him by then."

"Er, sure. He doesn't want to meet with me, does he?" Oliver's eyes looked panic-stricken and she giggled.

"Not after your last get-together, no, no, no! I wouldn't do it to you, darlink!" She giggled again, her nose pinching up where the cosmetic surgery interfered with her usual laughter lines, and the look of relief that now swept crossed Oliver's face had Roxy intrigued. She wondered what that was about, but there was no time to enquire. Tina was already flinging herself back across the desk, smothering Oliver's cheek with more kisses.

"See you at Pico's, Saturday night," she said, straightening up. "Ciao!"

Then she waved her long, spidery nails at David and ignored Roxy completely before clicking back outside, her powdery perfume choking the air behind her. The two writers turned to Oliver with undisguised smiles.

"We're just heading out for a bite to eat. It's business.

That's all."

"Of course it is," Roxy said, indicating his cheek. He swiped at the lipstick mark, only managing to spread it further. "And Pico's to boot!"

"You don't have the monopoly on the place," he retorted, knowing only too well it was once the venue for Max and Roxy's get-togethers.

"Monopoly? I barely have a memory of the place it's been so long. It's all yours." A twinge of regret swept through her as it always did when she thought of Max and their flailing friendship. "Although I wouldn't have thought it was your style."

"Well, it's about two blocks from Tina's townhouse so …"

"Ahh, I get it," Roxy laughed. "Hoping for an invitation back, are we?" When he ignored this, she asked, "What's your history with Tina's dad? Sounded like bad blood."

Before Oliver could answer, Sharon's voice came through the intercom: "Got Erin Hayden on the phone for you, Ol'. Put her through or what?"

"Oh, yeah, sure," he said and then turned to the writers. "Just read through the contracts, this won't take a moment." The call was put through and as Oliver spoke to Erin it was clear he was getting bad news. "Yeah, right ... Oh, dear, I'm sorry to hear that, Erin ... Okay, well that all makes sense ... Yep ... Yep ... Can I call him or ...? Okay, well then give him my best."

Roxy looked up from her paperwork, an eyebrow raised and he shook his head at her, then bid good-bye to Erin and hung up.

"Not good?" she asked.

"Nah, I don't think we'll be seeing much more of poor old William Glad around the place."

"Oh no."

"Yep. Erin tells me his condition has worsened considerably in the past few days. He's at home now, bed-ridden. They're bringing in a full-time nurse on the weekend, to help him through his palliative care."

"Can't his daughter move in, help him out?" asked David, putting his contract aside.

"I'm sure she'd like to but she's got a brood of her own to take care of. She's a single mum, you know. Four or five kids."

Roxy gasped. "Yikes, that's a lot on her plate. Poor Erin. Is there anything we can do?"

He shook his head. "Erin just says he's bedbound and trying to tidy up loose ends. Saying good-bye to friends and family, that kind of thing. Oh, it's such a shame. He was one of the greats, at least in horticultural circles."

David's phone beeped suddenly and he jumped on it, reading the incoming text, his eyes lighting up as he did so.

"Now what?" asked Roxy and he held a hand up, finishing the text before getting to his feet.

"Sorry, gang, but I've got to cut this short. It's just as I'd hoped."

"What is?" asked Roxy. "Is it to do with Seymour Silva's death?"

"Yes it is. I have the scoop to end all scoops!" He beamed, looking like a young boy holding up his first soccer trophy.

"Well?" said Roxy. "Spill!"

"No can say. You're going to have to read it in tomorrow's *Tele*."

She groaned. "You're not always going to be this secretive, are you?"

"Apologies, but I've still got to double check a few things first. I don't want to get ahead of myself."

Oliver looked worried. "Give us just a hint, Davo, something to whet our appetites."

He considered this. "Okay, well, all I can say is I now have conclusive proof that Seymour's death is suspicious. There is at least one person who had ample motive and opportunity." Then to their wide eyes, he added, "That will have to tide you over until tomorrow. I've really got to run.

The editor is going to want my copy pronto."

He dashed out leaving them both staring after him, perplexed.

Roxy looked at Oliver, her emerald green eyes squinting inquisitively. "What the hell was all that about? Do you know who he's talking about? Who is this person with motive and opportunity?"

Oliver shifted his gaze and shuffled the papers in front of him. "Er, well not really. I mean, I'm not sure what he's gonna say. I guess we'll have to wait and see if it makes the *Tele*."

CHAPTER 8

As it turns out, David Lone's "scoop" not only made the next morning's paper, it was all anyone could discuss on talk-back radio, TV chat shows and at office bubblers across the nation. And with good reason. It was riveting stuff.

David's front-page article was headed, *"Space Invaders! Shocking literary fraud"* and in similarly sensational detail, revealed that Seymour's agent, Norman Hicks, was in fact the real writer behind the *Alien Deliveries* sci-fi series and Seymour merely the "front man". The story went on to suggest, very strongly, that this "literary fraud" might, in some way, have a bearing on Seymour's sudden death, yet stopped at pointing the finger directly at Norm. The paper's lawyers would not have allowed that, but the inference was clear and Roxy could read between the lines, which she was doing now, over the phone to Oliver.

"I can't believe it!" she said, pulling the pages a little closer with one hand as she held the hands-free receiver with the other. "According to David, Seymour Silva didn't write the books, his so-called manager did. What a shock!"

Expecting Oliver to gasp along with her, Roxy paused for a few seconds but Oliver remained oddly quiet. That's when it hit her. "Oh my God. You knew, didn't you?!"

"Knew?" he managed.

"Of course you knew, that's why you were so worried yesterday. How long have you known? Were you in on the whole thing?"

"No, I bloody wasn't."

"You must have known something, Oliver, you were his agent."

He paused again before saying, "Not initially I didn't. But, yes, okay, eventually I cottoned on."

"Oh my God!" She dropped the paper and switched the phone to her other hand, tucking her legs up underneath her on the living room sofa where she was sitting. "How did you work it out?"

"Can't believe I didn't work it out sooner, to be honest. Seymour's as thick as a brick. Every time I ever asked him a question, about the books or plot or whatever, he always deferred to Norm. It was pretty bloody obvious in the end."

"But why? Why would Norm let someone else take the credit for his work?"

"Think about it, Roxy. You said it yourself to me several times—the books aren't that great. Wouldn't sell half as many if there wasn't such a sensational story behind the supposed 'writer'. Seymour had the good fortune of being abducted by aliens, for Christ's sake. Who better to front a series of books about aliens than someone who was actually abducted by one?"

She rolled her eyes. "Hate to break it you, Olie, but I suspect that Seymour wasn't *actually* abducted by aliens."

"Irrelevant, his readers believe it and that's all that matters. You couldn't ask for a better marketing pitch. Look, I don't know who approached who first, although I suspect Norm had some rejected manuscripts gathering dust in his top drawer, then he sees the amazing news stories about Seymour's supposed abduction and decides to approach him about ghostwriting his books."

"That's not ghostwriting, Olie," she said defensively.

"Norm was writing fictional stories and using a celebrity to sell them for him. It's verging on fraudulent."

"It can't be illegal if both parties agree to it, surely. Either way, they came to me as a team with the first book and I never cottoned on. I don't honestly reckon they meant to continue the charade for so long, but after that one sold so well, and then the second and third ... Well, they just went with it. I only worked it out myself during promotion for the last book, the fifth one. I told them they needed to come clean, to spill the beans before something like this happened. I knew it'd come out eventually. Always does."

"Is that why you were sacked?"

"Yeah, probably. They didn't quite say that but ... well ..."

"Why didn't you tell anyone? Leak the truth?"

"Hey, my loyalty is to my writers, you know that. I promised Norm I'd keep it quiet and I did. Besides, it's not my job to do David Lone's job. If no one else twigged then so be it. Doesn't matter now."

Roxy shook her head. "I think it does. David's absolutely right, it shines a totally different light on the whole death. Certainly provides motive. Maybe Seymour was demanding more of the cut from the royalties, or threatening to reveal all and Norm wanted to shut him up before the truth came out."

"But how does that help Norm? With Seymour dead he can hardly write any more books, can he?"

She thought about this. "He could say there were a few extra books in the pipeline, lots of deceased authors bring books out posthumously. Hell, they even brought one out by Patrick White recently. He's been dead for over twenty years."

Oliver was not buying it. "Look, Roxy, think about it. How does it benefit Norm to kill off Seymour? There's only so many books you can bring out posthumously before people start suspecting. And from what Norm told me, neither man wanted to come out of the closet. Now Norm's forced to if he ever wants to write another book. Maybe no one wants to read a book from an ordinary, unknown bloke called Norm, who never got 'abducted by aliens'."

"You're doing that annoying curly thing with your fingers, aren't you?" Roxy asked. It was another of her pet hates.

"Here's another thing to consider," he said, ignoring her. "What if the readers don't believe Norm is the real writer? What if they think he's taking the credit now Seymour is dead? Only Seymour can verify the story and he's gone. What if Seymour's fans don't buy it? What if they think Norm is just cashing in? It's risky."

"*You* could verify it."

He snorted. "Me? I'm just a sleazy agent, no one believes anything agents have got to say."

"Yeah, you've got a point. So why, then, would Seymour kill himself?"

"Dunno that either, I'm afraid. But Seymour Silva was hardly the full quid. I mean, the guy was convinced he'd taken a trip to outer space with little green men. Clearly delusional. Maybe he thought the little green men were coming back for more. Look, this is all very lovely, but I can't sit around gasbagging all day. The reason I called was to see if you can come to Seymour's funeral with me tomorrow."

"Really? They're releasing the body? After what David's just revealed? Surely he's right—this does suggest motive."

"Not to the cops it doesn't. I got a group e-mail about twenty minutes ago—the funeral's on tomorrow, 10:00 a.m. sharp."

"Oh, right."

"Will you come along?"

"Well, I didn't exactly know the guy, Olie. I wasn't—"

"Please, Rox. I could do with the moral support."

She sighed. "Of course, okay. What are the details?"

"It's at the Halloson Crematorium, out past the airport, you know it?"

"No, I don't. Got an address?"

"Oh shit, Shazza's screaming at me, got someone on the other line. Look, I'll pick you up if you like. In the morning, about quarter past nine. That'll be easier."

He hung up and Roxy stared down at the newspaper again and then had a sudden thought. *Damn it.* She would have to put off her first interview with David Lone. They were scheduled to meet at Lockie's Café right when the funeral was on. She knew which one she'd prefer but she had promised her agent, so she phoned David to postpone. He was furious, but luckily not with her.

"Funeral?!" he cried down the phone five minutes later. "You mean they're releasing the body?"

"I guess so. The police must be convinced it was suicide."

"That's utter bull—!" A beeping noise interrupted him and he said, "Hang on a second." After a long wait, David returned. "Sorry, that was my editor. She's not happy. The paper's just heard about the funeral, they need me in there ASAP. Arrrghh! Makes me look like a bloody fool. The whole premise of today's article is that Seymour was murdered. It's so obvious that his sleazy manager is the culprit. I mean, I practically handed him to the police on a platter, and now ... What did Oliver say? Why did they change their mind?"

"He didn't say much. I don't think he knows. He just heard the funeral's on and asked me to tag along. They must have cleared Norm of any involvement."

"It doesn't make sense! Have you ever met Norm? He's a total nut job. Nuttier even than Seymour, and that's saying something. More aggressive, too ..." He stopped. "Tell me they're not cremating him."

She scrunched up her face. "It is at the Halloson Crematorium. Sounds like it to me."

This infuriated Lone even more and he began to discharge a string of expletives before he caught himself and apologised.

"You're taking this to heart, David. Surely suicide's better than murder?"

"In whose book?!" He took a deep, calming breath. "Sorry, Roxanne, I'm being very ungentlemanly but I just can not believe the police are so bloody stupid! I mean, this is dumb, even for them. They are blatantly ignoring viable evidence. Seymour was obviously drugged, he had that suspicious 'X' on his wrist, don't forget, then I find out that he's been lying to his readers. It is so clear to me and anyone with half a brain, that he was going to reveal the truth and Norman Hicks had to stop him. It's open and shut."

"Not to the police it's not. And not to Oliver, either. He says that Seymour was as keen to keep the secret as Norm. He doesn't believe either one wanted the truth to come out."

"Hang on a minute. Are you saying that Oliver *knew* that Norm was the real writer, and didn't tell me?! How long has he known?!"

Roxy scrunched her face up tighter. She hadn't meant to let that cat out of the bag. "I don't know ... a few months maybe."

"A few months! And he didn't say anything. To anyone?"

"There is such a thing as client-agent confidentiality," she said, defensively, but he wasn't buying it.

"That's nonsense! They weren't even his clients anymore. That was important information, Roxanne. Once he heard about Seymour's death he should have come forward with that. He should have told the investigating officers."

"Well maybe he did, we don't know that."

"I know that," David said elusively. "It would have made my job a great deal easier. I would have got my scoop out earlier and they might not have been so quick to release the body. Now my story's dead in the water." She heard him release a huge sigh. "Apologies again, Roxanne, I don't mean to take this all out on you but I just hate to think a killer might be getting off scot-free."

"I understand that, really I do. But I doubt the police would be releasing the body if there was any hint of foul play. Your theory about Norman Hicks is a good one, but it's obviously wrong." There was mute silence at the other end. "Anyway, back to more important topics, like your book ..." She was trying to lighten things up, maybe even elicit a tiny chuckle out of the man, but he was clearly still brooding. "The funeral's on tomorrow morning, so can we meet up for our interview either in the afternoon or Friday morning, instead?"

"Um ... tomorrow afternoon should be okay," he mumbled, sounding distracted. "Um ... around fourish maybe."

She agreed and they hung up. Roxy then spent the rest of the day trying to focus on David Lone's book, but his words kept flying through her brain: *"I just hate to think a killer might be getting off scot-free."*

She thought about this. What if David was right? What if Norman Hicks was a killer and now, thanks to bodgie police work, was getting away with it? She shuddered a little, and then, remembering she was about to spend a morning with him, felt suddenly buoyed. Most people would be jittery at the thought of time with a potential killer, but not Roxy. The funeral was her chance, she realised, to check out Norman Hicks up close and personal, so she could decide for herself.

She couldn't wait.

A rumbling stomach caught Roxy's attention and she glanced up from her screen and out to the view, which was darkening by the second. Time had gotten away from her and she'd barely eaten all day, so she padded into her compact kitchen and towards the fridge. She opened the door reluctantly, knowing only too well what little nourishment she would find inside. It was just as she suspected. She padded back to the loungeroom and put in a call to her favourite Thai restaurant.

"Timmy, hello, yes, it's Roxy ... I'm great, thank you. Just after my usual. Yep, Pad Thai, vegie this time. Thanks, Timmy, appreciate it."

She hung up and then stepped back into the kitchen and towards a small wine rack by the fridge. She reached down and smiled. If there was one item she was never short on, it was a decent bottle of merlot. She made sure of that. She pulled out a 2011 Coonawarra, unclasped the top and poured some into a Moroccan tumbler from the cupboard.

As she sat sipping the wine and listening to a Billie Holiday CD, she realised she hadn't yet asked anyone to Max's party. Part of her wanted to invite Gilda, and part of her didn't want to give Max the satisfaction.

He could source his own flings, thank you very much.

She briefly considered David, but decided against it. *What if he got the wrong idea?* He was flirtatious enough, without the extra provocation.

Perhaps she should turn to her usual escort for times such as these. Roxy lowered the volume on her stereo, scooped the phone back up and called Oliver. A night out could be just what he needed. She'd lock him in now, then sort out the details at tomorrow's funeral, or at least, that was the plan. Unfortunately, Oliver wasn't at home and his mobile number went straight to voice mail. Roxy didn't bother leaving a message but she did wonder where he was and why everyone in the world had a social life except for her.

The downstairs intercom buzzed loudly and she jumped, surprised by her own jitteriness, then grabbed her purse and headed down several floors to retrieve her takeaway from the smiling delivery guy. As she climbed up the stairs, the first nutty scent of Pad Thai wafting towards her, she knew, deep down, that no wild night out would ever replace this as one of her favourite occupations.

******

A few hours later, across town, an occupation of a very different kind was under way. The man exhaled long and hard, his body dripping with sweat, adrenaline coursing through his veins. He prodded the corpse again and a tentative smile slunk across his face.

He was astounded that he had actually done it. It had been easier than he had imagined and something else, too. Exciting. My God, it had been exciting! He wasn't expecting that.

The exhilaration of the kill had now replaced any feelings of remorse. He felt strong, powerful, all conquering, and he didn't want it to end.

In fact, it wasn't over yet. He had so much more to do, just like the last one. He took a deep, settling breath, grabbed the gardening shears and got to work ...

CHAPTER 9

Roxy could feel a trickle of sweat beneath her dress and she shifted uncomfortably as she cranked open the car window. She was in Oliver's beat-up, old Holden, on the way to Seymour's funeral, and she wondered as they drove whether air-conditioning had even been invented when this vehicle was designed. She glanced across at her agent who also looked sweaty, but then he always looked sweaty, and he was now whistling into the wind, clearly unperturbed by the soaring heat. While she had donned her most demure black dress for the occasion—think Audrey Hepburn meets Grace Kelly, with a string of pearls and some kitten heels thrown in—Oliver looked like he'd chucked on the first bowling shirt he could find. Matched with scruffy black jeans and a fedora, he didn't exactly look like your average mourner, but then again, she doubted this was going to be your average funeral.

While the Holden creaked and groaned and made a strange rattling sound that Oliver insisted was perfectly normal—"cha-chaa-clunk" followed by an agonising squeal, then "cha-chaa-clunk" again—Roxy began fanning herself with an old *Rolling Stone* she had located on the backseat. It wasn't working.

"Are we there yet?" she asked and he glanced over at her with a crooked grin.

"What are you? Five? We'll get there when we get there. Just chill."

"It's hard to chill in this noisy old furnace."

"Watch it! This car is vintage I'll have you know. Some people pay good money for old Holdens."

"Yes and some people also buy Celine Dion albums. Doesn't make it right."

"Ouch! What's buggin' you today?"

She sighed, kept fanning. "Nothing, sorry. Just didn't sleep well last night. Kept thinking about the Seymour case and—"

"What case? There's no case."

"Well, David thinks—"

"Forget Davo! He's a sensationalist. That's why he gets paid the big bickies at the Tele, but unfortunately for him, this story is over. Kaput. He has to let it drop. So do you."

"Fine," she said, opening the magazine and immersing herself in a story about an indie rock band called Ghost Mountain. There was something about the name that had her intrigued.

Eventually Oliver turned into a gravel courtyard and pulled the car up beside some others in the front of a large sign that read Halloson Crematorium. Beyond it was a monolithic brick building where a large crowd had gathered. Oliver put the Holden into park, extinguished the spluttering engine, and leaned back against the vinyl bench seat. For a moment they both enjoyed the quiet while Roxy wondered whether the damage to her eardrums was reversible.

He leaned back in his seat and stared at her. "You cool?"

"I wouldn't use that word exactly," she said, peeling her dress off her back and reapplying some lipstick. "But yes, I'll be fine. Come on, we're running late."

Roxy opened the car door and stepped out. Oliver followed and they began walking towards the largely young, almost exclusively black-clad crowd that were milling around, kissing and commiserating. One or two were dragging on cigarettes and several were laughing, as though it were a garden party and they hadn't a care in the world.

At that moment a very short, very fat man with tufts of red hair and splotchy white skin that had been squeezed into a black, unironed suit, stepped out of the crowd and began waddling towards them. A woman with purple streaked hair and a long, flowing black dress called out to him but he ignored her completely and headed straight for Oliver, grabbing him by one elbow and dragging him away from the group. Roxy followed.

"Jesus fucking Christ, Horowitz! What the fuck have you done to me?!" he hissed and Oliver looked taken aback. "You see yesterday's fucking news or what?!"

"Yes, I did, Norm. Look, I'm sorry, mate—"

"Don't fucking 'sorry mate' me, you fucking prick. You *should* be fucking sorry. David Lone's one of yours, right? You spill the beans on me? Give him the inside goss?"

Oliver shook his head vehemently. "No way, mate, I wouldn't do that to you, told you I wouldn't, and I didn't. I'm very big on client confidentiality. Just ask Roxy here, she's one of my clients. I don't know how he found out, honest I don't."

Norman Hicks whipped his eyes across to Roxy who was pretending to be very interested in the bush beside her.

"Roxy?"

She looked up. "Yes, Roxy Parker. My condolences—"

He ignored her and whipped back to Oliver. "It's a fucking joke. I was going to break the story when I was good and ready. Jeese Louise, it's a fucking disaster." He took a deep breath through flaring nostrils and Oliver cringed, ready for the next onslaught, but Norman's sneer instantly subsided. "Anyway, you good? Haven't seen you for a while. All good at work, that kind of thing?"

Oliver shrugged and Roxy stared at him, speechless, as Norm rubbed his pudgy hands together.

"Okay, better get back to it. The wake's at Venus's pad afterwards. Just get the details from her."

And with that he waddled off towards another group of mourners gathered to one side.

"Bloody hell," said Roxy. "Dave's right, he's as nutty as Seymour."

Oliver nodded. "But at least Seymour had an alien abduction to blame for his mental health issues. Oh, looks like they're moving inside. Don't forget to switch your mobile off so it doesn't ring in the middle of the service. That's all we need."

Oliver began moving towards the crematorium which had now swallowed up half the congregation. Roxy located her phone and began changing her profile to silent. As she did so she glanced at the mourners ahead of her and noticed several had turned to glare at them.

"I'm not sure we're the most welcome people here today, Olie," she whispered, catching up to him. "We could be centre stage at the next funeral if we're not careful. Should we quietly slip away?"

"Nah, don't worry about it. Norm's always like that. Up and down. Don't take it to heart." Then Oliver stopped and turned back to Roxy. "Speaking of which, if you see Davo let me know and we'll get him out of here fast before he gets a crucifix through his."

David Lone was smart enough to avoid Seymour Silva's funeral and Roxy just hoped he had the good sense to also stay clear of the wake back at Venus's pad, wherever the hell that was. Roxy didn't attend the wake, insisting Oliver go it alone. She had questions to organise for her interview with David that afternoon, and she was feeling suddenly ill-prepared.

The ghostwriter had done hundreds of interviews in her time, but oddly enough, had never actually interviewed another interviewer, especially not one as accomplished as David Lone. She wanted to get it right because if she didn't, he'd be the first to know.

After peeling her sticky funeral frock off and showering, she slipped into a fresh, 1950s-style cotton dress that was lighter and more colourful, then sat at her desk and began to work.

After a good hour, Max's face suddenly flashed through her brain and she sat back with a thud. *She'd completely forgotten to ask Oliver to his party.*

Roxy glanced at her screen clock. It was almost 2:00 p.m. She tried calling but Oliver was still not answering and she was starting to panic. She left a message and tried to focus on her work again, failing miserably.

"Come on, Oliver," she said aloud, only too aware she was talking to herself, and not caring one bit. It had become a daily habit after years of living alone and she had given up trying to break it. She didn't mind sounding like a loony, there was no one to hear her after all. "Ring me!" she implored. "Riiiiing meeeeee!"

Glancing back at the ticking clock, she sighed. She needed to lock in a date for Max's party, and fast. Perhaps she'd better ask Gilda after all. Turning up like a Nigel No Mate was worse, she decided, than turning up with his next potential conquest. Besides, she had a feeling Gilda wouldn't go for Max's type.

"You mean that hunky photographer friend of yours?" Detective Superintendent Gilda Maltin asked a few minutes later when Roxy had rung and been transferred to her office phone.

She slumped back in her seat. "Yep, that's the one."

"Oh I'd love to go. Is he seeing anyone?"

She slumped even further. "Don't know."

"Really? I thought you two were besties."

"No, not so much anymore."

"Right," said Gilda. "So, what are the deets? To the party, I mean."

Roxy filled her in, arranging to meet earlier at her place

for a pre-party drink.

"That'll settle your nerves," Gilda said and Roxy bristled at this.

"Nerves? I haven't got any nerves."

"Yeah, right."

Gilda was too perceptive for her own good, although it no doubt helped enormously in her role as the North Shore's head detective.

"Course you don't," she said and then, "Oh, hang on a minute." There were muffled voices at the other end and after a few minutes Gilda said, "Sorry, sweets, gotta go. We've got another nutter on the loose, keeping us all on our toes."

"Oh?"

"Yeah, grisly homicide."

"Sounds interesting."

"To you, I'm sure it will be! Can't talk, got to get back to it."

Gilda said a hurried good-bye and Roxy felt a sudden pang of regret. She liked Gilda, had enjoyed their occasional catch-ups because she was easy company and fun to be around. But that was the whole problem. They were two traits Max also adored.

Roxy was beginning to wonder whether she'd just hammered the final nail in the coffin of their once vibrant relationship.

Speaking of coffins, Roxy glanced around. Perhaps the news channel would have some coverage of Seymour Silva's funeral—she had noticed a few reporters there—or maybe there'd be details on the homicide Gilda had referred to? She flicked on the TV and waited patiently while an excruciatingly dull stock market report droned on. Perhaps it wouldn't be quite so dull, she decided, if she actually had some stocks to report on. She was about to get up and make a pot of coffee when a familiar face appeared in a small window on the screen behind the anchorwoman.

Roxy's heart dropped.

She grabbed the remote control and zoomed up the volume: *"Gardening Guru William Glad found dead this morning in the grounds of his sprawling northern suburbs mansion,"* explained the anchorwoman, a middle-aged ashen blonde with barely there spectacles and a stern look on her face.

Oh no, thought Roxy. Dear old William. His cancer must have caught up with him at last.

Or had it?

She realised there was something strange about this news story. The wording was all wrong, and what was a dying man doing in the grounds of his sprawling mansion anyway? He should have been safely tucked up in his sick bed. She ramped the volume up even further.

"Glad, aged sixty-six, had been battling cancer for some time and leaves behind a daughter, Erin, and five grandchildren. Police are currently at the scene, investigating, and we'll bring more to you as this story unfolds."

As the anchorwoman moved on to the Syrian crisis, Roxy sat back, stunned.

That wasn't an obituary, it was a news item. It must be the homicide Gilda had mentioned. She worked in the northern suburbs where William had lived. Cancer deaths didn't usually warrant police attention she thought, and then sat forward.

"Unless ..." Roxy chewed her lip. She hoped William's daughter hadn't done anything silly. Perhaps she was an advocate of euthanasia? "I'd better call Oliver again."

She grabbed the phone and redialled his mobile number. This time, thankfully, it picked up.

"Olie, it's Roxy. Are you okay? You haven't been answering your phone."

"Stupid me, I turned it off at the funeral and forgot to switch it back on," he replied, his tone flat. "When I finally did, I had three calls from Erin. Distraught. Been at her place ever since."

"I'm so sorry, I only just heard myself. "

"Yeah, it's terrible stuff."

"Is there anything I can do?"

"Nope, nope, nothing any of us can do. Look, let's talk tomorrow, okay? I'm still with her now, it's gonna be a long day."

"Of course, sorry, I'll call you tomorrow. But, Olie?"

"Mmm?"

"You sure you're okay?"

A pause. "I'm not the one with gardening shears through my head, Roxy."

And with that the phone clicked dead.

CHAPTER 10

"Ay, it doesn't sound verra good to me," agreed Loghlen O'Hara in a lilting Scottish twang as Roxy sat across from him at his inner-city café, the sun slowly fading outside. It was Thursday afternoon and she was waiting for David to show up for their first official interview. He was already fifteen minutes late.

Lockie's Café had always been one of Roxy's favourite cafés and she was glad she'd decided to meet David here instead of his place or hers. She really needed an old friend this afternoon, and Lockie was certainly that. She'd known the gangly Scotsman for over a decade, he'd even helped her with one of her books, and she'd always admired his mellow temperament and quiet optimism, which was why his comment surprised her.

Sure, Roxy knew a set of gardening shears through the skull was suspicious, but she'd half expected languid Lockie to suggest otherwise.

"It's not like you to be thinking the worst," she replied, eyeing him slyly. "I thought you'd try to tell me it was some dreadful accident or something. I must be rubbing off on you."

"Just tellin' it like it is."

"But why would someone murder a dying man?"

He scratched his orange, pork-chop sideburns while considering this. "I guess burglars and nootters don't know ye're dyin' of cancer when they break in and kill ye for the silverware. Couldn't give a toss. In fact, maybe they knew he was dyin' and realised he'd be easy prey. Then, he tried to have it out with them—on the lawn did ye say?—and they gave him what for!" Roxy stared at him open mouthed and he laughed. "Sorry, been watchin' too much *CSI*."

"You? Television? I didn't even know you owned one. What about your painting?"

"What paintin'? Nae, I'm as dried up as me old brushes. Can't seem to find inspiration these days."

Again, Roxy was surprised. She glanced around the café. It was decorated with the remnants of past inspiration: a grotesque yellow sunflower on one wall, a Mona Lisa look-alike on another, all for sale and few ever making it out of the café. But what he lacked in talent he made up for in enthusiasm. Or at least he used to.

"Are you okay? Something on your mind?"

He continued caressing his sideburns for a few seconds and then laughed, the old Lockie returning momentarily. "Ay, I'm fine. I do carry on like a big girl's blouse, dinna I? So, what ye havin' this time?"

"Just get us a weak latté, thanks. It's late and I'm waiting for someone."

"Not ye mum?" He couldn't hide the alarm in his eyes.

"Christ no. It's not Sadist Sunday yet, is it? No, I'm just waiting on ..." she hesitated, not quite sure how to describe David Lone, then said, "a client."

"Ooooh, sounds mysterious!"

He nudged his bushy eyebrows up and down and then returned to the counter to make the coffee himself, while she settled back into her seat checking her watch again. Mr Lone was now officially twenty minutes late.

"Hey, there," David said a good five minutes after that,

striding up to her table and landing a quick kiss on one cheek as he deftly slipped into the chair opposite her, placing a satchel on the table as he did so. "Have you ordered?"

"Just a coffee. You're late."

He stared at her as though waiting for her to make her point, so she let it drop. Instead she said, "Have you heard?"

"That I'm late? I didn't know it was breaking news." He glanced up at her annoyed expression and smiled. "Sorry, that's a bit lame at this time. Yes, of course I've heard about William Glad, that's exactly why I'm late. I'm on it."

He reached into his pocket and produced his iPhone which he checked before placing beside the satchel. He clearly couldn't live without the gadget and she forgave him this. He was on the job, after all.

"In fact, I've just come from the paper now," he said. "They need a statement from Oliver so I haven't got a lot of time. Let's just go through the basics and I'll head over to his office after this. He's at Erin's now, but will meet me there soon."

"Tell him to call me if he needs any help. He sounded dreadful earlier."

"Why wouldn't he? He's now lost two of his old clients."

"Yes, but surely that's a coincidence?"

David blinked a few times and was about to say something when Lockie appeared with Roxy's coffee and a menu in hand. After ordering an espresso, David rechecked his phone.

"Listen, if you need to run off now, I'll understand—" Roxy began but he cut her off.

"Hell no! We're definitely going ahead with my book. I can multitask if you can. Besides, you're the one doing all the work, not me, which is just as well, because this story is going to keep me very busy. I can tell already, it's going to be *big*."

"So what is the story then, on poor old William? The TV report made it sound like there were some suspicious circumstances, and then Oliver mentioned something about gardening shears."

"He told you that, did he? I'm still trying to work it all out and no one's giving too much away at this point. Never do this early in the game."

"It's hardly a game, David."

He frowned, looking disappointed with her. "Just a figure of speech, Roxanne, you mustn't take offence. This is what I do, I don't mean to sound voyeuristic."

"No, no, no." She shook her head, cranky with herself now. "And I don't mean to sound judgmental, sorry. Besides, I'm one to talk. I take an interest in murder and I don't usually write about it for a living. At least you've got that excuse. So, what do you think's happened?"

He sat back and rubbed a hand across his jawbone. "I don't know exactly but something's up for sure. The old man obviously didn't die of cancer, and what was he doing in his backyard anyway, especially at that time of night?"

"Yes, I thought that seemed strange, too, but he was a gardening nut. Perhaps he was taking one last stroll when he fell onto the shears? He was pretty shaky on his feet, after all." She knew it sounded ridiculous and the look on David's face confirmed this.

"They think he died around midnight. Bit late for a sick man to be out and about. Anyway, there's too much police action over at his place for that. I just swung by there and there's police tape, the works. They refused to comment, of course, but it's pretty obvious that something is up."

She thought about this. "But why would someone want to kill a dying man? Unless of course it was assisted suicide."

"A pretty brutal way to help him die, I would suggest. No, Roxanne, I have a really strong hunch about this one."

"You and your hunches," she said, eyes rolling.

"Hey, my hunches usually make me a lot of money."

She had to concede that point. "So what do you think?"

"I think it's linked to Seymour Silva's murder."

Roxy sat up straight. She hadn't expected that. "The sci-fi writer? Really? What's William's death got to do with him?

Don't forget they still say Seymour killed himself."

"They say a lot of things, doesn't mean they're right. No, I believe both deaths are connected." He paused while Lockie returned with his coffee and disappeared again. "Seems to me that someone is killing the great writers of Sydney."

Roxy almost laughed then checked herself. The expression on David's face was totally sincere. "That's very catchy," she told him, "but aren't you getting a little ahead of yourself? Even if Seymour Silva was murdered as you predict—and the police certainly dispute that—it still doesn't connect to William. As far as I could tell, they didn't exactly mix in the same circles. Apart from Oliver, I doubt they had anything in common. Surely it has to be a tragic coincidence?"

David picked up his coffee cup. "I don't believe in coincidences, Roxanne, and you can put that in your book." He took a sip and placed the cup back down. "Look at the facts: Two successful writers have been murdered in just five days—"

"You keep forgetting, Seymour's death was ruled suicide."

"Semantics," he said, brushing her off. "What, you think the cops never get it wrong? I always knew his death was suspicious and now there's been another one, in less than a week. It rings alarm bells. At least it does for me. I believe Norm did it, and I think he's guilty of killing William, too."

"Norman Hicks? Are you serious?!"

"Completely."

"But why Norm? I mean, sure, he might have had motive to kill Seymour, I'll grant you that. But what possible motive would he have to kill an old horticulturalist? Did he even know William?"

David shrugged. "I'm still working all that out. But I *will* link them, you'll see." Then he flashed her a confident smile. "Don't look so worried, Roxanne. This is what I do best. You should be taking notes. You're getting to watch me in action."

His arrogance was astounding and would normally put her off, but he was absolutely right. There *was* a certain thrill in watching a top investigative reporter in action, and it would make great copy for their book. She studied him for a few minutes, crunching on the side of her coffee cup, then asked, "What other links do you see?"

"Well, as you said yourself, they both work or *worked* for Oliver Horowitz."

She felt her stomach lurch. The thrill was starting to wane. "Hang on, you're not saying Oliver is somehow involved?"

He took another sip of his coffee and then dabbed at his lips with a serviette. "I'm just talking about the commonalities. There are several as far as I can see. Both writers were once on Oliver's books. Both were very successful in their chosen genres. Perhaps there's a begrudging wannabe writer or publisher or agent out there?"

It wasn't completely unreasonable, but she still couldn't quite buy it. And she was usually a big fan of conspiracy theories. "So, you think there's some psychopath out there bumping off genre writers? Sounds a tad sensational, even for you."

"I'll take that as a compliment, shall I?" He grinned at her, his blue eyes twinkling. "Anyway, if there is a psychopath out there slaughtering writers, Roxanne, I can guarantee you, I'm onto it."

"Oh that makes me feel so much better," she said, offering him a wry smile. "Have you spoken to the police at all?"

"Tried to, but as I said, it's always a pointless exercise, at this stage. 'Early days in the investigation', 'Keeping an open mind'—all the usual clichés. They're e-mailing us a statement this evening." He glanced at the phone again. "I doubt they'll have much to say."

"And Oliver? What are you hoping he has to say? God, I hope he knows to keep his mouth shut."

David frowned. "I'm not out to lynch him, Roxanne, but he *was* William's agent. I'd be a hopeless reporter if I didn't speak to him. He'll just tell me what I already know, he last saw William at my film launch, spoke to him via phone the following day, yada yada. Look, I'm treating Oliver fairly, but I need to do my job, too." Sensing her distress, he added quickly, "Don't worry, I won't write anything incriminating. I'm on his side, you know that. That's the great thing about reporting on this—I can find out what's really going on, help him out. I can be at the centre of all of this, and that works in everyone's favour."

"But aren't you supposed to be impartial?"

"Jesus, you can't have it both ways." Now he looked exasperated with her.

"I just worry about poor old Olie, that's all. Things were going so well for him, he just doesn't need the grief. Look, do you think we can drop it for now and just get on with your book?"

He glanced at his watch. "Yes, we're going to have to, I've only got twenty more minutes to spare."

"Then let's make tracks."

She reached down to her handbag under the table and pulled out a digital recorder and a small note pad and pen. As they polished off their coffees, the two writers tried to douse all thoughts of grisly deaths and gardening shears, and got down to the business of David Lone's biography. There was only time for a few background questions and Roxy learned that David had been brought up an only child in a "fairly average" middle-class family from the Adelaide 'burbs. His parents, he told Roxy, had had him late in life and were not that interested in the whole parenting gig, preferring to lavish their attentions on each other, so he had largely brought himself up. His dad, an electrical engineer (with a gardening fetish), had tried to push David into law or medicine, "some snooty vocation", but David had resisted, more interested in a glamorous and creative career. He'd first applied to NIDA, a world-famous acting school, and when that failed, had settled on a journalism course. "But it's books that really excite me," he said, suddenly checking his iPhone again.

Taking this as her cue, Roxy put her recorder away and pulled out her own smartphone, clicking on the diary application. "Okay, then," she sad. "I'll let you run away, but you owe me a decent interview, soon!"

He laughed and promised her that. They then knuckled out their schedules for the next month. They decided to meet at David's home office every day for the first fortnight, starting from the following Monday. After getting David's "side of the story", Roxy would then branch out and start interviewing his friends and family. David reached into his satchel and produced a plastic folder bursting with newspaper and magazine articles that he had either written or were written about him.

"So the newsmaker becomes the news," she said idly as she flipped through them.

His lips broke into a dazzling smile. "Well, just for a while, at least. I've put them in chronological order. Nothing too substantial, just some reviews—all good of course—and society gossip pages, including last Friday night's preview."

"Oh?" Roxy glanced up. "Did I rate a mention?"

"I'm afraid not. But Oliver's in there. There's a particularly embarrassing snapshot of him with Tina Passion, both looking legless. Must have been towards the end of the evening, that one."

Roxy located the picture and laughed. Tina Passion was wedged into something tight and metallic, both arms slung around Oliver's neck as she planted a sloppy kiss on one of his cheeks. It was clearly her favourite part of his anatomy and she seemed incapable of leaving it alone. For his part, Oliver looked semi-comatose, his eyes half closed as though he were about to pass out. Roxy guessed the photographer had caught him mid-blink. Or at least, she hoped he had.

"Oh dear," she said. "Not his best look."

"Those two are getting pretty cosy. Are they an item?"

She shrugged one shoulder. "He wishes, she's a little less forthcoming. Plays him like a fiddle but he keeps going back for more." She crinkled her nose at the thought. To her, Oliver was like a pudgy, older brother, not someone she wanted to imagine in an intimate situation, especially with someone as trashy as Tina. "What else have you got for me?"

David produced a separate piece of paper with half a dozen names and numbers typed neatly in a row. "Here's a secondary list of people you might want to contact, including some old girlfriends."

Roxy's eyebrows shot up. "Ex-girlfriends? Really? You want me to talk to them?"

"Of course. I'm good friends with all my exes, you'll see. No one has a bad word to say about me."

"That's dull," she said, scanning through the list.

One name looked vaguely familiar and she was about to comment on it when he said, "Just because they don't have a bad word about me doesn't mean they won't have some juicy gossip." His own eyebrows twitched several times mysteriously. "You'll find a few of my old teachers in there, too. Make sure you talk to Mrs Porter, she was my senior English teacher at high school." He pointed halfway down the page. "She always had such faith in me."

"Excellent. That'll make good copy—living up to your favourite teacher's aspirations." She glanced through the list. "No mention of university. You said you studied journalism. Which school did you go to and is there anyone there worth interviewing there?"

"No," he said quickly. "Don't worry about that. I studied at Southern Cross Uni at Lismore, up on the far north coast. Complete waste of time."

"Really? Why?"

He shrugged. "Really lame course. I dropped out early, found the whole thing extraordinarily dull. I was rearing and ready to go in the real world by then. Got a good job on a Wollongong paper soon after that, the number's there. They might have some of my early articles they can scan and send you."

She saw a contact for the *Illawarra Mercury* and nodded. "Cool. But maybe there's a chapter there, about how disappointing university was for you? Or something?"

"There's nothing there," he said firmly. "Honestly, I don't want you wasting your time with that."

So she let it drop.

After they'd finished and paid their bill, Roxy dragged Lockie to one side and gave him a quick hug. "You take care, okay?"

"Always," he said, then shook David's hand. "Nice to meet ye, David, always good to have another writer aboot the place. Drop in any time for a coffee, eh? The next one's on the house."

"Thank you," David said. "Okay, Roxanne, I'll catch you at my place Monday afternoon for the first interview, yes?" She nodded. "I'd better run, don't want to keep Mr Horowitz waiting."

"Hang on a minute." She turned back to Lockie. "Give us a couple of your almond friands, Lockie, that might cheer Olie up." She paid for them and handed them to David.

"With my love," she said, and watched him dash away, hoping as he did so, that he went easy on their agent. But she knew deep down that he was too good an investigative reporter for that.

CHAPTER 11

Friday morning was as dull and dreary as an old dishcloth. Thick clouds clung to the sky, threatening to unload, but Roxy didn't let that put her off as she slipped into khaki trousers, tank top and Converse sneakers, and headed outdoors to fetch the morning papers. She used to subscribe to every newspaper she could get her mitts on and then, with the advent of the Internet, happily viewed them all online, until she realised she was turning into a hermit. Without a paper to go out and purchase, she could go days, once even a full week, without ever leaving her apartment. This didn't worry her nearly as much as everybody else. Her mother was constantly horrified by her solitary lifestyle and couldn't understand for a moment why she didn't rent with others "like a normal thirty-something".

"Because I don't need to rent, Mum, I own the place, remember?"

"Then get a lodger in!"

"And stick them in the pantry? This is a one-room apartment, the size of a shoebox, and I'm not talking boots."

"Then buy something bigger."

"Would love, to! Got a spare six hundred grand?"

Her mother always glanced away at this point, money a topic she felt extremely uncomfortable discussing. Roxy guessed it had something to do with her own guilt. Since Roxy's father had died of cancer when she was just a girl, Lorraine had sold their family home and moved into posher, pricier yet far smaller digs in the well-heeled suburb of Lane Cove where she and Charlie were fast going through the inheritance. Roxy wanted to tell her now as she often did that she couldn't give a toss about the inheritance—would give it up in a heartbeat to have her dad back—but she didn't bother. Lorraine never seemed to hear her.

Even Max used to wonder at her hermitic existence. It was the reason he instigated their regular Thursday "sanity dates" at Pico's—to get her out whether she liked it or not. But those days were long over, too, and Thursdays now passed with little more than fond memories for Roxy. It had been months since she and Max had shared beers and banter together.

Roxy shrugged off the encroaching blue and headed down the street to her nearest newsagency, a tiny sliver of a shop between a steamy Laundromat and a Chinese takeaway. It was run by a gregarious Greek guy with an enormous nose and a hearty appetite, judging from his pregnant belly, and he spent most days standing outside his shop, not so much to summon trade as to free up space inside. Costa greeted her warmly (and why wouldn't he? She spent a small fortune here each week) and threw in a free, chocolate Freddo Frog for good measure.

"You spoil me," she said with a laugh and he laughed along as he handed her the papers.

Back in her apartment, Roxy slipped off the sneakers, made herself a plunger of fresh Papua New Guinea coffee and two slices of Vegemite toast then padded into the lounge room. She spread the newspapers out on the floor, grabbed her scissors and the scrapbook, and began to work her way through them.

The lead story in the *Herald* was something political and there was just a small image of William Glad on the top, urging you to turn to page five. They clearly didn't have the scoop. That honour was David's alone, and his story took up the entire front page of the *Telegraph.*

To call it sensational was an understatement. It led with details of William Glad's death and she lapped the words up like a hungry Labrador. According to David's "sources", the gardening guru had not just been found dead in his own sprawling garden, between the banksias and the bottlebrush, he had been murdered with gardening shears and a pot plant left, dumped on his stomach. It contained a small Wollemi Pine, a recently discovered species that that was once thought extinct. David wrote that it was left there "like a calling card from the devil" and "as a warning, perhaps, to all those who are past their use-by date".

She felt herself recoil, and not just from David's hammy one-liners.

How cruel and inhumane! she thought. *What kind of animal does that to a dying man, and to a sweet dying man at that?*

As she continued reading, she saw that David had done as he had promised, strongly indicating that there was a link between Glad's death and that of Silva's just five days earlier. There was no mention of the fact that Silva's death had been ruled a suicide.

A separate section titled, *"Last Writes"* and sub-titled, *"Two famous authors dead in less than a week!"* featured headshots of Glad and Silva and a breakout box listing so-called "similarities" between the two deaths. This included the fact that they were both famous in their own genres and had both once worked for the writers' agent Oliver Horowitz. As far as she could see, the only other mention of Oliver was a quick, polite statement of condolence that shed him in a good light. He came across as nothing more than a grieving agent, and she was glad of that. She kept reading.

David went on to say that someone was "clearly targeting genre writers", and to prove the point, he was leaving a different calling card at each murder scene. According to David, Seymour Silva had been deliberately marked with an "X" across his wrists, to indicate the science-fiction genre, while the once-extinct Wollemi Pine had been left as a reminder of the horticulturalist's own inevitable demise.

This secondary story ended with an ominous warning. *"Who will be next?"* David wrote. *"Will a famous cooking writer be found gassed in his own oven? Will our greatest comic book artist be discovered drowning in black ink? When and how will this horrific story end?"*

Roxy sat back with a thud. Did David really believe there would be more horrific murders? And did he truly suspect that another writer would be next?

The phone's sudden shrill caught Roxy off guard and she yelped, then took a deep, steadying breath and picked it up.

"You reading it?" Oliver's voice was almost chirpy at the other end.

"Yep, sensational stuff. Haven't got to the *Herald's* story yet."

"Don't bother. They know nothing. Just playing catch-up. Nope, Davo's The Man."

"He doesn't really believe there's a psycho serial killer on the loose, does he?"

"Don't know but it sure makes great copy."

"Makes me on edge, is what it does."

"Think you're next on the list?"

She scoffed. "I don't think I sell enough to warrant murdering, but I do think David is tempting fate. He could be putting ideas in crazy people's heads."

"Nah, he's just stirring the pot. But you have to give it to him, both deaths were very suspicious, especially poor old William. The pot plant and all that. It does look like someone is leaving some kind of message."

"Where does he get his inside goss? Is it Kay or does he have someone at the copshop in his pocket?"

At his end Oliver shrugged. "Again, don't know, don't

care. The point is he gets it. He's a bloody champion reporter, probably Australia's best. This book of his is going to be a best seller for you, Roxy, the man is getting quite a reputation. You're going to make a motzer." He laughed. "So am I now I mention it."

She didn't laugh along, didn't want to think about that now and wondered at Oliver's ability to. He was supposed to be an old friend of William's.

As if reading her mind he said, "Look, I'm as cut up about old Will as you are, Rox, but this is an important story and we want to get to the truth, right?"

"Well now that you cloak it like that."

"I was just speaking to Erin, actually. She's devastated, of course, but she also wants some good to come from this."

"Oh yeah?"

"Yeah, well, we're thinking of bringing out his back catalogue after all. William had a bunch of old gardening guides that haven't been published in a decade, we might dust them off and get them out there. Show the world that William is certainly not past his use-by date!"

She felt a little nauseated suddenly. "Capitalising on his death, are we?"

"Hey, don't be like that. We're celebrating a great Australian horticulturalist. And his family's all for it."

"But will his books even be relevant today?"

"Jesus, Rox, you sound like old William himself. Nature doesn't change too dramatically no matter what the doomsayers predict. Winter plants are winter plants, spring are spring, and that's still the same. So his books will do well. Channel Nine is already dusting off his old gardening programs, can't see why we shouldn't do the same. Of course, we'll wait 'til things settle down a bit, and then Erin and I will make it happen."

Again, she was surprised by his capitalistic take on the gardening guru's death, such a switch from the dispirited man she spoke to just yesterday, but she guessed that it was Oliver's way of dealing with it all. So she let it drop.

Again, he seemed to catch her reticence through the phone. "Listen, Roxy. We all miss the guy, deeply, but thanks to Davo, the cops will find out what's happened to William and they'll put the bastard away. And while they're doing that, we'll celebrate him and his amazing work. So don't let it get to you. Okay?"

She muttered something and hung up, but still she wondered at Oliver's buoyancy and wished she could bounce back as quickly. Two famous writers were dead, and David was predicting another gruesome murder. No best-selling back catalogue was going to change that.

CHAPTER 12

The next twenty-four hours were spent doing what Roxy hated doing the most—cleaning her apartment, shopping for groceries and ticking off her weekly chores. Eventually she found herself with enough free time to focus on the Saturday papers, which she had placed like a lure, just out of reach until the domestic duties were done.

The apartment gleaming, cup of peppermint tea in hand and Nina Simone belting out the blues on the stereo in the corner, Roxy grabbed the *Telegraph*, dropped down onto her sofa and began to read. This time, David's article was not only sensational, it was verging on defamatory. According to him, the police had now uncovered an "alleged link between William Glad's homicide and Seymour Silva's manager Norman Hicks".

Roxy's eyes popped. *What link?* It had her enthralled. *What had David found?*

She kept reading but there was nothing more, nothing to back up his startling assertion, and she imagined Norman reading the same copy, his pale face bursting red with rage. It was a very damning statement and she hoped David Lone knew what he was doing, and had good lawyers on his side.

"I hope he knows what the hell he's doing," Oliver repeated an hour later as he reread the article on Roxy's coffee table.

Her agent had dropped around briefly, hoping to drag Roxy to an afternoon movie before his "hot date" with Tina Passion that night, but she put him off. She had much more important things to do, like working out what to wear to Max's party.

"You and Tina should come along after your dinner date," she said. "I'm sure Max would love to see you."

But he wasn't interested. "No way, José. I'm finally getting Tina to myself and I'm not prepared to share her."

Roxy laughed. "Well, good on you and good luck with that one! What time are you meeting up?"

"Oh we're having a late dinner. Her bloody father's still in town, so she can't get away until about nine-ish."

"That is late. So what's the story with this father of hers? I gather you have some history?"

He scratched his double chin and cleared his throat. "Yeah, Lorenzo—that's the father—he hates my guts. God knows why."

"There must be a reason. I mean, you're annoying at the best of times, but hate's a pretty strong emotion."

He stared at her deadpan. "You're hilarious, you know that?" She shrugged. "I don't know what Lorenzo's problem is, but he always avoids me like the plague when he comes to town. I did run into him last time, though, and it wasn't pretty. Called me a scumbag and told me to fuck off."

"Yikes."

"I know. Embarrassed the shit out of poor Tina, and she doesn't embarrass easily, that one. Look, I figure it's just 'cause he's Italian. You know what Italian dads are like. Super protective. He'd be jealous of any bloke in Tina's life." He pulled himself up. "Rightio, I'd better bugger off if I want to catch this flick. Have fun tonight, eh?"

"You too, and good luck with Ms Passion."

She saw him out then headed straight to her wardrobe

where she found herself staring glumly into it again, wishing suddenly that she had heeded her mother's advice and bought something exciting and new. Roxy hadn't wanted to stand out at Max's party, or look overly keen, and she realized now there was no chance of that. Her entire wardrobe, she decided, was frumpy and forgettable. She groaned. Why did it matter so much? It was just another party.

Or was it?

She didn't let that thought develop, simply refocused on her clothes and began to pull pieces out.

Two hours, ten wardrobe changes and at least one hissy fit later, Roxy opened her front door to Gilda Maltin who was looking stunning as always.

"You look gorgeous," Gilda said, sweeping a quick glance down the tight black jeans and white dinner shirt Roxy had settled on. She'd tied the white, cotton shirt in a loose knot at the front and added dripping silver chains, hoop earrings and strappy black heels, but she didn't feel gorgeous, especially now she'd caught sight of Gilda.

As always, the policewoman was a knock-out. Her former pixie cut had grown out a little and her golden-blonde hair was now worn longer and tussled around her face. Her skin was tanned brown, she had a lot of smoky eyeliner on, and her petite figure was clad in a body hugging jersey dress that dropped down from one shoulder provocatively, and was cinched at the waist by a thick, black belt.

"You are the one who looks gorgeous," Roxy said, pecking a kiss on her friend's cheek and showing her in. As she did so, she wondered, yet again, how someone so sexy survived in the misogynist world of the police force. If Roxy worked with a bunch of burly blokes, she imagined she'd tone it down a lot, preferring trousers and minimal makeup. Not Gilda, and tonight she had amped it up even further.

"This ole thing?" Gilda said in a Southern drawl and stepped inside, producing a bottle of champagne as she did so.

"I know your fave is merlot, but tonight we celebrate!"

"Oh?" said Roxy, closing the door and stepping into the kitchen to fetch glasses. "Anything in particular or are we just celebrating life?"

"Life, love, whatever comes our way."

Gilda popped open the champagne cork with a cheer then poured the sparkling liquid into the glasses Roxy had placed on the bench. She handed one to Roxy, took one herself and raised hers high.

"To love!" she said.

"Actually, I'd prefer to toast life, if that's all right with you. It's been a fatal week for writers."

"You're referring, of course, to William Glad."

"And Seymour Silva. David Lone thinks the two deaths are connected."

Gilda raised a plucked eyebrow skyward and stared at Roxy for a few seconds, leaning across the kitchen bench. "I can see you're going to try to squeeze some valuable information out of me."

Roxy laughed. "Would you expect any less?"

She shrugged, grabbed the bottle and proceeded to the living area where she dropped down into Roxy's bright, cushioned sofa, patting the seat next to her. "Okay then, let's get this out of the way. So you read today's article or do you have some sort of inside track with Mr Lone?"

"Actually I'm writing his life story, as we speak." This took Gilda by surprise so Roxy added, "We've got the same agent, Oliver Horowitz. So ..."

Gilda nodded and thought about this for a few seconds, slowly sipping her champagne. "Hmmm," she said eventually. "This changes everything."

"What do you mean?"

"I mean I can't tell you a bloody thing. You're too close, my dear."

Roxy scoffed. "You can trust me, Gilda, you know that."

"It's David Lone I don't trust."

"You know him?"

"Know him? I've had to lock horns with him on several occasions. Not my cup of tea. Excuse the mixed metaphors."

"Really? What's wrong with David?" She was feeling protective of him, suddenly.

"Well, it's nothing a bit of heavy duty insect repellent won't fix. He's a like a relentless mosquito, that man! I've only ever dealt with him a few times before but now he's practically camped out at the office trying to get the inside goss on the William Glad homicide."

"So you're investigating that?"

"Not me, specifically, but some of my colleagues are, it's in our jurisdiction. And I have to say, Lone works his charms well. At least one of them has been leaking information to him, he knows way too much for my liking."

"Or maybe he's just a very good investigative reporter," she said and Gilda narrowed her blonde eyebrows.

"I can see he's worked his charms on you, too, missy."

"It's just business. I never mix the two."

"Fantastic philosophy. And nor should you! So, tell me, what other hunks are worth devouring at this soiree?"

"Hang on, not so fast. We hadn't finished discussing William Glad."

"Really? I thought we had." She batted her eyelids innocently.

"Come on, give me something. I won't mention anything to Mr Lone, I promise. I'm just curious, that's all. David says there's a direct link now between William Glad's murder and Seymour's agent, a guy called Norman Hicks."

Gilda sighed. "I guess it's okay. It'll be in all the press tomorrow so ... Yes, David's right, there is a direct link. And God knows how he found that out. But it's been tarnished."

"Sorry?"

She sighed again. "Okay, this is off the record and you never heard this from me, right?" Roxy nodded firmly and Gilda scowled at her briefly. "Well, we found the murder weapon, the gardening shears that killed Mr Glad."

"I didn't realise they were missing."

"Well they were and they showed up Thursday afternoon, in the back of a certain motor vehicle. You will not believe whose."

Roxy's jaw dropped. "Norman Hicks?"

"Norman Rodney Hicks," Gilda confirmed, swallowing some champagne and looking like it suddenly tasted of acid.

"So there is a connection, then, between the two deaths? That's extremely damning for Norman."

Gilda held her glass out for Roxy to refill. "Not necessarily. You see, Mr Hicks is a very lucky man. He happens to have an ironclad alibi for the time of William Glad's murder on Wednesday night. So unless he paid someone to do it, and we're still looking into that, he's off the hook."

"That's a pity. What's his alibi?"

"Oh, some dinner party at his place, seven equally creepy sci-fi types to vouch for him. The party went late, finished up around 2:00 a.m. There was no way Mr Hicks could have snuck off and killed William Glad then returned. Not without being noticed. It was a pretty intimate affair and he was the host, after all."

"Damn it. So how did the gardening shears end up in Norm's car, then?"

"That's the million dollar question. Would've made our lives very easy if we could have pinned it on Mr Hicks. Now we have to look at scores of people who were at that blasted funeral."

"Funeral?"

"Yes, well, if Hicks is innocent—and no one's saying he is yet, so let's not get too carried away—then my people believe the shears were probably planted in his vehicle the morning after the homicide, during Seymour Silva's funeral. Couldn't have happened any earlier. Mr Hicks had his car in his lock-up garage the night before and only removed it to drive directly to the Crematorium on Thursday morning.

There's little chance anyone could've snuck it in earlier. So they either planted the shears during the service, or maybe later at the wake." She turned in her seat. "You were there, I believe?"

Roxy nodded. "Just at the funeral. I went along with Oliver, then he dropped me home and he went on to the wake. But there were dozens and dozens of people there. You'll have your work cut out. Anyone could have slipped out during the funeral and done it. Was the car unlocked?"

"'Fraid so."

"And does David know all this?"

She nodded. "Of course he does, he knows everything. I tell you, he's like an insidious insect. So, as I say, it'll be in all the papers tomorrow, hence the reason I'm being such an unbelievable blabbermouth. Now," she scooped up her glass and held it high again. "Enough talking shop, already! No more mention of death, murder, suicide or anything remotely like it. Promise?"

Roxy rolled her eyes, pretended to scowl and then laughed. "Fiiiine, let's just focus on pretty things like butterflies."

"Oh, darling, I think we can do better than that! Tell me about sexy Maxy. You still keen on him or what?"

Roxy shrugged. "We're just friends, always were, I honestly don't know why everyone carries on about it."

"I'm not carrying on. He's too cute to be wasted on the likes of you anyway. But you didn't answer my question. I know you're just friends, but are you *keen* on him?"

Roxy blushed and glanced away. She didn't understand why talking about Max was so difficult for her. She realized, then, that it was probably because she no longer had any idea how she felt about him. Once upon a time she could clearly say he was a friend, nothing more. Now, well, she didn't know what to say, so she glanced back at Gilda and shrugged again.

"I honestly don't know what I feel anymore. I'm a bit messed up."

Gilda smiled. "I love messed up! Makes life much more interesting."

"No wonder you're a cop then."

"That and the chance to carry a big, fat gun. So, you never answered my earlier question. Any other gorgeous men at this do?"

"I'm sure there'll be a few. If I know Max, he'll have all the beautiful people swanning around him."

"Then *we* should fit in beautifully. Come on, drink up, we've got a party to go to!"

CHAPTER 13

Roxy and Gilda stepped out of their taxi in front of the large Darlinghurst warehouse that served as Max's home and photography studio and stared at it for a few seconds. Roxy reapplied a little lip gloss, tossing the tube back in her handbag, straightened her black fringe down, then took a deep breath and led the way in, past a crowd of people who had gathered outside, smoking God knows what. As they walked along the stairwell and through the open doors, she wondered how Gilda dealt with the obvious drug scene at Sydney parties, but decided not to ask. She probably feigned ignorance, and it wasn't like she was the straightest matchstick in the box.

Once inside, it was clear that Max's party really was awash with the beautiful people. Whippet-thin models loitered at every glance, trendy stylists and makeup artists hung close by, as did all manner of thespians and bookish types. Unlike David's film preview earlier in the week, this crowd was less "A-list" and more "underground cool" with hipper hairdos, weirder body piercings and more original tattoos. Watching them glide about in a mixture of bright, lollipop coloured jeans, dark leather and vibrant mini dresses, half of them with non-prescription black specs on, Roxy felt even more boring in her oversized man's shirt, and wished she could go home and change. Again.

As if responding to her earlier thoughts, Gilda whispered, "Listen, at these kinds of dos, I see no evil, hear no evil. Frankly I just don't want to know. And if anyone asks, I'm a public servant, got it?"

Roxy laughed. "Got it. Now shall we get a drink?"

They made their way to the open-plan kitchen which Max had transformed into a bar and where a sinewy black man was struggling to keep up with the orders. They eventually clinched a glass of wine and began to slowly circle the room, looking for the host.

"I want to get this out of the way," Roxy told Gilda.

"He's not a dentist, Roxy, you should lighten up."

"It's just that I haven't seen him for a while. It's a bit awkward, that's all."

"What's awkward?" a familiar voice asked behind her and Roxy turned to find Max standing there, a wary smile on his lips.

Unlike his guests, Max looked like he hadn't even bothered to change clothes for the event. His checked cowboy shirt was rumpled and his black jeans well creased. As usual, his messy hair flopped across his face, and he was brushing it back now with one large hand while the other reached out to Roxy.

"Hey Parker, how are you?" he asked.

Before she knew what she was doing, Roxy had wrapped her old mate in a bear hug and they stood there, holding each other just a second longer than normal, Roxy wishing that the rest of the world would just bugger off for a while. She felt safe, she felt warm, she felt Max suddenly pull away. He seemed uncomfortable and glanced across at Gilda, offering her one of his breathtaking, heart-stopping smiles.

"Hey Gilda, glad you could come."

Gilda stepped forward and gave Max a quick kiss. "Thanks for inviting me. This is quite the par-tay."

He looked around the room, bemused. "I'm not quite sure how it got this big. I think we can blame my sister for that." He turned to Roxy. "You heard Caroline's in town?"

"Caroline? No, I had not. How long's she around for?"

"Too long. She's doing some real estate course."

"That must make your parents shudder."

Roxy had never met Caroline, but she knew that Max's folks were old hippies. They'd fled office jobs and moved to Nimbin in the 1960s to join a commune and veg out, in every sense of the word. Despite this bohemian upbringing, or perhaps because of it, Max didn't have a hippie bone in his body (don't get him started on dreadlocks and djembe drumming), but he did have a laid back nature and a general disinterest in wealth, consumerism and keeping up with the Joneses. Caroline, it seemed, had no such qualms.

"Oh yeah, she's the black sheep in our family now. But, well, Caro could sell ice to the Eskimos so she'll be a very rich black sheep one day. Actually, I'm a bit over her to be honest. She's high maintenance, you know how I hate that."

"Is she staying *here*?" Roxy suddenly remembered that throaty woman's laughter in the background, last time she had spoken to Max, and she felt foolish. It must have been his sister. Relief quickly replaced folly and she cheered up considerably.

"Yep, hopefully not for long," he was saying. "She needs her own digs. She's exhausting the crap out of me. Hyperventilates if she stays in more than two nights in a row, and God knows how many blokes she's brought back with her. I can't keep up."

"Cramping your style, is she?" Roxy asked jokingly, but the wounded look that was now crossing his face made her instantly regret it. She quickly changed the subject. "So, have you been getting a lot of work lately?"

"Um ... yeah, the usual stuff. You know how it is. Too many anorexic models and diva fashion editors to count. Honestly, I think I need a career change. Hey, listen, I'd really love for you to meet Caroline." He looked around anxiously. "Can't spot her just now." He turned back to Roxy and studied her for a moment. "You look beautiful."

His unexpected compliment threw her and she blushed crimson red just as a shriek of laughter came from near the front door. Max swung around.

"Argggh, more people are flooding in, I'd better go say hello." He turned back. "Have fun, guys, help yourselves to more drinks, and let's try and catch up before the night slips away from us. Good to see you again, Gilda."

Gilda waved him off and then turned to her friend who was staring after him looking melancholy.

"Like two ships, passing in the night …" she murmured, then clicked her wine glass against Roxy's. "Come on woman, you heard the man—it's time to have some fun! Now, where shall we start?"

She glanced around the room then pulled Roxy in the direction of a group of black-clad men at one end. Roxy rolled her eyes and followed like an obedient puppy but was secretly glad she'd invited her friend along. If there was one person who was guaranteed to get her spirits up, it was the indomitable Gilda.

In fact, thanks to Gilda, the night would turn out to be a complete disaster.

CHAPTER 14

As the party got into full swing, a DJ now pumping out tunes from a turntable in the corner, Max found his way back to Roxy's side and she felt a flutter of excitement. They were standing to the side of the makeshift dance floor and he quickly pulled her and Gilda away.

"In case someone tries to make me dance," he said, shuddering. "Can't bloody stand dancing."

"I hate it too," announced Gilda and he smiled.

"Really? I would've pegged you for a dancer."

"God no," she said, launching into a long and embarrassing story about a recent dance floor incident at a Police Union Ball.

Max found it hilarious, and proceeded to grill her about her life on the beat. He was soon so caught up with Gilda that Roxy began to feel like a spare tire. Useless and neglected.

Was Max playing some kind of game? she wondered. *Or was he suddenly, genuinely fascinated in the policewoman and her entire life story?*

As Max prodded Gilda with endless questions and laughed uproariously at her every joke, Roxy recalled his invitation, suggesting she bring the policewoman along. It tugged at her heartstrings. Was Gilda the real reason she was invited along? Or, worse, the *only* reason?

"Okay, it's official, I am stalking you," came a deep voice beside her and Roxy looked around to find David Lone standing there, two Coronas in hand, one with a sliver of lime in the neck of the open bottle. He thrust that one towards her.

"Looks like you need it," he said. "Having a bad night?"

She laughed him off, unconvincingly, and gladly took the bottle. "Just not really in the mood, I guess."

He glanced towards Gilda and Max who were now so deep in conversation they barely registered his arrival. Something flickered across his eyes. She couldn't read it but he seemed to be reading her now, like a book.

"Come on, I know how to cheer you up. I want you to meet someone."

Taking her hand, David led Roxy away from Max and Gilda, and towards the back of the warehouse to a small lounge setting where a few people had gathered around a table bursting with candles, cheese platters and a motley collection of glasses. Sitting in the middle of the group was a stunning blonde with a vivacious smile. She looked up at David and then across to Roxy, her smile deepening.

"Roxy Parker, I presume?" she said, jumping up to embrace the writer in a warm hug. Roxy was taken aback and the woman laughed. "I recognize you from Max's photos! I'm Caroline, the prodigal sister."

"Of course you are, sorry," Roxy said, marvelling at the woman before her. She was nothing like her brother. This sibling looked like she'd just stepped out of one of his cutting edge fashion spreads—her '80s-inspired royal blue dress clashing with bright yellow beads and stilettos. It was bold and garish and should not have worked, but on Caroline's tall, skinny frame, it looked sensational. She had a small tattoo of a rose bud on the back of her right shoulder, and bright, jangly bangles on both wrists. Roxy guessed she liked to dance, and often.

"How long have you been in town?" Roxy asked.

"Long enough. I can't believe Max never introduced us. I thought you two were inseparable."

"Yeah, well ... So how do you like living in Sydney?"

Caroline clapped her hands together, the bangles clashing loudly. "I love it! Although Max is *such* a bloody bore. Good thing I don't have to rely on him for my fun!"

She slipped one arm in David's and he smiled.

"So how do you two know each other?" Roxy asked, an unsettling feeling flooding her stomach. She wondered suddenly if they were a couple, and why this should matter. Lone shifted a little and Caroline laughed.

"Ooh, he hates this topic," she said. "You might want to take notes."

"No I don't," he replied. "In fact, you're on the interview list for my new book, Caroline. You can tell Roxanne anything you like."

She laughed. "Oh it's nothing major. We went out for about five seconds back in our university days, in Lismore."

Roxy relaxed considerably. "Of course, I did see your name on the list! So, you both studied at Southern Cross? That's close to where your parents live, isn't it, Caroline?"

"Yes but puh-lease! I didn't live with them in their crazy old yurt. I moved into town, where it's much more civilised."

David scoffed. "You call that dump you lived in civilised?"

She slapped him hard on the arm. "I loved that dump! It was right on the river—"

"A flood plain," interjected David.

"And the rent was soooo cheap."

"*Because* it was a flood plain."

Caroline laughed. "True, that and the fact it was haunted."

Roxy's eyes widened. "Haunted?"

"Oh, I'd forgotten about that," said David. "What was the story again?"

Caroline reached down to the table to retrieve a champagne glass and took a quick sip. "Well, we'd heard that somebody had drowned to death in the old bathtub there once upon a time." She looked at Roxy. "The place was like a hundred years old so I'm sure it had more than one skeleton in the closet. Anyway, that bathroom was definitely creepy. Definitely something dodgy in there."

"Dodgy?"

Her eyes widened dramatically. "Yes, a presence! The blinds on the window would fly up whenever I was in the bathtub and ..." She turned to David. "Do you remember Jacko? That was my flatmate, a sweet, nerdy kind of guy—well, he swears he came home one night to find the bathtub filling with water." She paused for effect. "But there was no one home!" She mock shuddered. "Creepy."

David laughed. "He made it all up, Caroline, you know that. As for the blinds, I'd say Jacko was perving on you. You were a looker back then."

"*Back then?!*" Caroline grabbed a pillow from the sofa and lobbed it at David's head. He ducked. "Anyway, I'm not the only one who thinks the place is haunted, Roxy. They've never been able to sell it. Last time I looked it was derelict."

"That's because, once again, people, it's on a flood plain," said David. "Plus it's a dump."

"Oh I like the haunted story much better," Roxy said, laughing. "See, David, *these* are the kinds of stories we want for your book, especially if you ever stayed over. Caroline, prepare yourself, I'll be grilling you further about all this."

"Consider me a lamb chop and grill away," she said, grabbing a packet of cigarettes from the coffee table and pulling one out. "Do you mind?"

Roxy shook her head. "So what did you guys study at university, anyway?"

"Arts," Caroline said as David picked up a candle from the table and held it out to light her cigarette. She dragged on it for a second then blew a long plume out while saying, "A giant waste of time, eh, Mr Lone?"

David shrugged, not answering.

"You didn't like the course, either?" Roxy said and Caroline laughed.

"Like it? I loved it! It was just our Mr Lone here. He upped and left halfway through. Not even a word good-bye! He's just lucky we'd broken up by then, or I might have taken it personally." She squinted her eyes at him as she blew a plume of smoke in his direction.

Roxy glanced at David and he said, "Don't give away all my secrets, Caroline. Roxanne's getting good money to investigate me, we wouldn't want to make her job too easy now, would we?"

"My lips are sealed," she replied.

"No, you have to tell me, why'd you leave so suddenly, David?"

"Oh she's exaggerating. I just left uni and moved to Wollongong. End of story."

"Left uni *mysteriously*!" Caroline amended and his smile deflated.

"This is such a boring topic, Caroline."

"Not to me, it's not," insisted Roxy. "I'm supposed to be writing your life story, remember?"

"Not tonight, you're not. Tonight, you're supposed to be letting your hair down and having fun. It's a party, remember?" He raised his beer to hers and she clinked it back before taking a long sip.

Caroline smiled at them both. "Do what he says, Roxy, or you could be sorry ... Ohmigod! That's not Jason, is it? Jason Morrison?!" Caroline squealed and then stubbed out her cigarette, blew them both a kiss, and dashed across the room, her champagne glass in hand.

David laughed. "Well, that was Caroline. In full flight as usual. She's a laugh, right?"

"A barrel of them," Roxy said. "She's so different to her brother."

David's eyes narrowed. "Yes, Max. I don't know him at all, to be honest. Caroline invited me tonight." He studied her for a few moments. "There's obviously history there for you."

She took a swig of her beer, feigning nonchalance. "What do you mean?"

"I mean you and Max. What's the story?"

"Nothing. Well, nothing very interesting."

"Did you go out once?"

"Oh, no! No, nothing like that!"

She was trying to sound casual but it was clear from his raised eyebrows and hint of a smile that she wasn't pulling it off.

His smile suddenly looked forced and he said, "Speak of the devil."

Roxy glanced around to find Max walking towards them, one hand extended towards David.

"It's David Lone, right? Friend of Caroline's? I'm Max."

"That's right," David said, shaking it back.

There was an awkward moment of silence and for the life of her Roxy couldn't think of a thing to say. Both men seemed to be eyeing each other off and she wished badly that Caroline would return to lighten the mood. Finally, Max spoke.

"I'm off to the bar, see if I can't get myself a drink at my own party. Don't like my chances. Anyone want one?"

He glanced from David to Roxy and back again. They both indicated their Coronas and he glanced again at Roxy, giving her an inscrutable look before striding away.

David turned to Roxy. "He always like that?"

"Like what?"

"Dark and brooding like he's Mr fucking Darcy," David scoffed. "Excuse my French but I loathe photographers, they think they're God's gift when all they're doing is taking a few happy snaps. Not rocket science. All you need is a decent digital camera these days."

"Oh Max is all right," she said and his frown softened a little.

"Sorry, I know, he's a friend of yours." He paused.

"Maybe more by the looks of it."

David's eyes swept across her face and she shook her head vehemently. "No way, David. I told you before, there's nothing going on there."

"That's not what Caroline told me. She hinted at some kind of history between you guys."

"We're just friends, we've never been anything more."

He weighed this up for a few seconds then shrugged. "Good. You'd be wasted on him."

She didn't know what his beef with Max was, but she did know it was time to change the subject. "So, what's the latest on the William Glad murder?"

Now it was David's turn to look uncomfortable. He took a long swig of his beer. "I wish I could tell you. The story gets more confusing by the day. I find one clue and then I hit a brick wall and everything falls apart. I'm at a bit of a loose end to be honest, and I just don't know what to report anymore. Maybe I've been barking up the wrong tree all along."

For the first time since the story broke, David did not look at all confident.

"Okay, so you don't know who did it. But tell me this," she paused to sip her own beer, "do you honestly believe what you wrote? Do you really think there'll be another death? Another writer murdered?"

He mulled this over for a while. "I don't know, of course, Roxy, but I do worry. Sure, Norman Hicks might be innocent, but there is an obvious pattern even if the police refuse to accept it." He stared at her strangely. "Sorry, this is a pretty morbid subject. Are you okay?"

Roxy's head was spinning a little and she gave it a shake. "Yeah," she said, placing her bottle down on the table. "I think I've had enough grog for one night."

He stepped towards her protectively. "Do you want to get some fresh air?"

She nodded and he led her away from the party and out onto the street where she leaned against a brick wall then bent over a little and took some deep breaths.

"You don't look too hot," he said. "I shouldn't have given you that final beer."

She shook him off. "No, it's my fault. This always happens when I mix my grapes with my grains. I've had champagne, red wine, now beer. It never does me any favours. I'll be all right in a few minutes."

"Good." He produced a set of car keys. "Then let's get out of here, go somewhere quieter."

Roxy looked up. "Really? You want to desert the party already?" She looked at her watch; it was only 11:00 p.m.

"Well, you look like you've had enough. I just thought ..." He broke off, looking suddenly embarrassed. "I just thought we could spend some quality time together, that's all."

David gave Roxy another of his intense, piercing stares and she felt for a second that she could get lost in those blue eyes, but something held her back. She shook herself out.

"I feel a bit rude, David, taking off so early, and leaving Gilda on her own."

"The policewoman? She can take care of herself, believe me."

"Yeah, Gilda tells me you two have locked horns."

"Well the police force needs a bit of accountability. They act like us journos are only there to annoy them but they forget we're the ones who crack half their cases. They'd be nowhere if it wasn't for me ... and *you*, now I think of it. Didn't you solve one of Gilda's cases for her?" She raised one shoulder nonchalantly. She wasn't going to take all the credit for that one. "They should be thanking us, not trying to avoid us."

"She's not avoiding me. Gilda's a good friend of mine."

"Well she hates me, I can tell you that for a fact. Can't believe you brought her here. She can't be much fun to have around."

Roxy disagreed. "Actually, she's great fun and I don't think she hates you at all. She gets that you have a job to do." He looked as though he didn't believe her. "Either way,

I'm not ready to leave the party yet. Sorry."

"Is it the party you don't want to leave or is it Max?"

She glared at him. "David, I already told you, we're not going out. Not that it's anyone's bloody business."

"You're right, sorry." He held his keys out and pressed the button on top. A sudden beeping sound and a flash of lights came from a nearby car, a gleaming black BMW. "Think I might head off."

"Come on, David, don't be like that. I promise you, we can avoid Gilda and Max if you feel that way."

He shrugged, his eyes clouded over. "Nah, you go in, I'm not really in the mood anymore."

"Really?"

He shook his head firmly this time. "Yeah, but you go. You look a bit better now, anyway."

She shrugged and left him standing in the gutter beside his car, looking forlorn while she chastised herself all the way back in.

What was wrong with her?! she wondered. *Why couldn't she just skip off into the night with the hunky and successful writer guy?*

Perhaps it was because she wasn't quite finished with the "dark and brooding" photographer bloke. Roxy had finally realised that she needed to talk to Max, and she needed to do it tonight.

No more games, she promised herself. It was time to put her heart on the line.

Back inside, Roxy noticed the music was now pumping and the lights were a lot dimmer. She looked around for several minutes, trying to find Max, and eventually, across the dance floor she saw him, fleetingly, before the revellers swirled to block her view. She craned her eyes, peering through the writhing bodies, trying to catch him again.

Ah, there he is!

He was leaning against a wall right up the back and she smiled, raised one hand in the air to wave, hoping to get his attention, when she realised something and dropped her hand back. He was standing very close to another woman, their shoulders touching and his head leaning into hers. He was whispering something in her ear but she couldn't quite make out who it was in the darkness. She watched him for several seconds, mesmerised, then felt her heart lurch as she recognised the woman he was talking to.

It was Gilda Maltin.

Roxy watched them for a few more minutes, debating whether to walk up and interrupt them—*I mean, how much more of Gilda's life story did the man need?*—when Max suddenly took Gilda's hand and lead her gently away from the party, and up the back stairs towards the mezzanine level.

Towards his bedroom.

Roxy gasped. She let out a tiny, agonised groan then turned on her heel, and fled into the night.

****

The clock reached midnight. How appropriate, he thought, the perfect time for this little princess to turn into a pumpkin. But he had a much better fairy tale ending in mind for this writer, and from his coat pocket, retrieved a large, shiny red apple. He placed it to the side while he reached into his gym sack, pulling out a tiny bottle of strychnine and a large syringe. As the woman lay unconscious on the floor beside him, he injected her with the poison straight into the eye, and then refilled the needle and injected a little into the apple. He had to wait several hours for death to take hold, her body writhing and buckling, her face spasming, her eyeballs popping, her mouth foaming up, but he tried not to watch.

Fortunately, there were plenty of trashy books around to distract him. They weren't much chop but they could certainly kill an hour or two. Eventually, when she had stilled, her last gasp now echoing across the fashionable polished floorboards, he placed the book aside and felt for her pulse.

Nothing.

His own pulse skipped a beat. He had done it. My God, he thought. It gets easier each time. He snapped himself out of his reverie and pulled out a cloth, wiping her frothy mouth clean, then reached for the apple. Placing it between her lips, he forced her perfect white teeth down upon its soft flesh and tore a good mouthful from it. Then, leaving that small piece in her mouth, he placed the rest of the apple in one manicured hand and splayed her body out neatly across the floor. He surveyed the scene carefully, making sure everything was in its place. He felt a momentary pang of regret, but it was too late now. It was his only option, he knew that. He'd stuffed the first two up very badly. He wasn't going to stuff this one up, too.

Besides, this writer would be missed the least.

Then he slowly collected his things, noticed the book he had half finished and pinched that, too, before silently slipping away.

CHAPTER 15

The sound of beating drums and screeching violins woke Roxy from a deep sleep and she sat up with a start, her head pounding, then looked around the room and felt the headache intensify.

Where the hell was she?

She glanced down to one side and spotted a man's naked body entwined in the sheets, and reached a hand to her mouth to stifle a cry. She felt her stomach lurch. She grappled for her glasses, which, blessedly, were sitting on a table to her right, and wedged them into place, then snuck another quick look.

Oh my God. It was David Lone.

Roxy glanced around nervously, realising now that she was obviously in his bedroom. On the bedside table there was a selection of photos of the writer posing next to film stars and politicians, and on one wall she spotted a promotional poster for *The Supermodel Diaries.* She looked down at herself, slightly relieved to see her shirt and underwear still in place, but wondered where her jeans, shoes and handbag had got to, and why the bloody music was blasting so loudly. It took her another moment to realise the din was coming directly from her head, an aching, screeching migraine.

Roxy crept out of bed as quietly as she could manage, towards what looked like the bathroom. Ah yes, a very large, blindingly white bathroom. She softly shut the door, stepped across to the toilet bowl and threw up. Then threw up again.

She winced, flushed the toilet, and then staggered to the sink where she splashed cold water on her face before glaring at her reflection.

Oh, Roxy, what the hell have you done?

There was a soft tap on the bathroom door.

"You okay in there?" David called out and she swung around, startled.

"Yes ... yes ... I'm fine," she managed to croak, her head throbbing with every word. "I'll just be a minute!"

"Take your time. I've put your jeans by the door. I'll see you out in the kitchen."

"Thanks!" she sang, trying to sound casual but coming across stressed out.

She swung back to stare at her reflection again. Her hair was tufted up at the back, her eyeliner was so smudged she looked like a raccoon, and her lips were puffy and cracked. She glanced around, then quietly opened the bathroom cabinet and looked inside. Thank God for metrosexuals, she thought, grabbing a bottle of cleansing milk and dripping a little into one palm before scrubbing her face clean. She washed the cream off, then found some moisturiser and applied a little, perking her skin up. Next, she squeezed a little of his toothpaste onto one finger and brushed it over her teeth, rinsing her mouth thoroughly before sweeping her fingers through her hair, calming it down.

"Not your best look," she said quietly to the mirror, but it would have to do.

She opened the door, retrieved her jeans and slipped them on.

Out in the kitchen, Roxy found David wearing nothing

but a pair of baggy blue and white checked Calvin Klein pyjama pants, hard at work on a gleaming gas stove. He was cooking something, and had already prepared a cup of coffee from the espresso machine on the marble kitchen bench. The kitchen, like the rest of the house, was enormous and kitted out with the very latest in appliances including a four-door, stainless steel fridge, matching stainless steel dishwasher, and an induction oven that almost took up half a wall. There was an oversized silver clock hanging on one wall, and a large pantry half hidden behind white doors.

"You want that one?" David said, turning towards her and indicating the cup.

His hairless chest was tanned and boasted a chiselled six-pack, and she tried not to stare as she dropped onto a black leather barstool at the other end of the kitchen bench.

"God yes," she said, dragging the much-needed cup towards her. "What're you cooking?"

"Spanish omelette. It's my speciality." He raised his eyebrows a few times, smiling widely, then turned back to the stove.

He looked like he was having great fun and she wished she could say the same. Sipping her coffee and watching him cook, his back muscles flexing as he did so, Roxy tried to stop ogling him and get her thoughts together, to remember how she had ended up in David Lone's bed.

All she drew was a blank.

David leaned down into a cupboard and produced two oversized white dinner plates, then placed two pieces of French bread on each plate, a slice of omelette and a fork. He sprinkled some spinach leaves over the top and some cracked pepper, then pushed one towards her, pulled a second stool from underneath the bench, and sat across from her, digging in hungrily.

Roxy took a small mouthful and was sure it tasted great, but she couldn't stomach anything today. The orchestra in her head had died down, but her stomach was now playing a game of killer volleyball.

"Come on," he said. "Eat up. It'll do you some good."

She took another bite and then dropped her fork back down. It was no good. Nothing was going to take this hangover away. She sighed, took a deep breath then asked what needed to be asked.

"Um ... what happened?" He looked up at her blankly, the fork suspended near his lips, so she added, "Last night. What happened? Exactly?"

He dropped the fork back down. "You don't remember anything?" She shook her head and he looked incredulous. "Nothing *at all*?"

She scrunched her lips to one side. "Sorry, not really, no." She hesitated. "Did we ...?"

"God no!" he said and then added, more gently, "I wouldn't do that to you, Roxanne. You were in no state."

The volleyball game calmed down a little. "So what happened then?"

"Well," he took a quick forkful of egg, "we were at Max's party and you'd just brushed me off."

"I do remember that bit, which is why I'm a little surprised to be here."

"Yeah, well, that makes two of us. About two minutes after you left me whistling in the wind beside my car, you came running out and demanded I take you home. If I remember correctly, you said something like, 'Take me back to your bed or lose me forever.'"

"No?!" She blushed and dropped her head in her hands, unable to look at him. "I am sooo sorry."

"Don't be sorry. It was very flattering, actually. Although I think it had more to do with Max than my wily charms."

She peeked through her fingers at him. "Max?"

"Yep, you were a bit hysterical. Kept ranting and raving, something about 'bloody Max' and 'that bloody policewoman bitch' and how they could 'go lock themselves up for life' or something to that effect."

She moaned louder. "Oh God. I am so sorry."

He laughed. "Don't worry about it. You were quite

hilarious. We headed off and then you suddenly changed your mind and suggested I take you dancing to Bar 11."

"We went to Bar 11?!"

"No, I could see you weren't quite yourself, so I nixed that idea and brought you back here where you proceeded to work your way through my wine collection—polished off my best bottle of Pinot Grigio if you must know." He indicated an empty bottle by the recycling bin in the corner.

"I drank the whole thing?"

"Well, with a little help from me." Now he was indicating two enormous wine glasses that had been rinsed and were resting beside the sink. "Then you suddenly noticed it was 2:00 a.m. and freaked out, said you needed to get home, pronto, like you were going to turn into a pumpkin."

Roxy had a sudden flash of memory then. She remembered the sickly tasting white wine, remembered glugging it down and giggling, and she remembered suddenly staring at that ridiculously sized clock in the kitchen, the enormous '2' zooming out at her, freaking her out. She wasn't an owl at the best of times and 2:00 a.m. was way past her bedtime. She vaguely remembered attempting to leave, but her memory was clouding over again.

"By this stage you couldn't actually walk," David explained, "so I refused to let you go. I put you into bed instead." He paused. "Oh, and if you're wondering why I wasn't gentlemanly enough to sleep on the couch, you can blame yourself for that. I tried to—" His eyes swept across to the open-plan lounge room where she spotted a rumpled pillow and blanket that was sprawled across an enormous, cream suede couch—"but you kept insisting I share the bed with you. I tried sleeping out here a few times but you kept coming out to drag me back, so I eventually gave up and we both just went to sleep."

"So there was absolutely no ...?" She cut off, blushing again.

His eyebrows nudged a little again. "Well, there was a teeny bit of smooching for a while there before you passed out. You don't remember that at all?" He looked a little disappointed and she felt dreadful.

How could she forget that? She shook her head. "I'm so sorry, David."

He shrugged. "Oh well, your loss." He stood up and tried to smile but couldn't quite manage it, and she felt like a fool. She had led the poor man on, and she had obviously done it to spite Max.

Her heart lurched again as scraps of memories came flooding back.

Max and Gilda.

Gilda and Max.

She wasn't sure what had happened exactly, but something *had* happened, she knew that for sure. Had she seen them kissing? Were they holding hands? Then she remembered. It came back to her with a sudden whoosh and she realised now that it was worse than that.

Max had taken Gilda into his bedroom. It was game over.

Roxy felt queasy again, jumped up and ran back to David's bathroom where she hovered over the toilet threatening to throw up. Nothing came this time so she eventually gave up, rinsed her mouth out and returned to the kitchen. On the way back she noticed what looked like a spare bedroom, but was clearly a gymnasium. There were weights of varying sizes scattered around, a fancy, multi-speed bike machine and a very high-tech looking treadmill. No wonder he was ripped, she thought, padding back to the kitchen.

David was now clearing away the plates, stacking them in the dishwasher, and looked up at her as she approached.

"I had no idea I'd drunk so much," she said, peering at him apologetically through her fringe.

He smiled. "You must have, you were pretty plastered. Even before we got back here."

She cringed at the words. "Sorry, it's not usually my style, not at all. I can't remember the last time I felt this bad." Then she remembered David's film preview, and that first night at Bar 11. Perhaps this was becoming her style after all.

He shrugged. "Honestly, it doesn't bother me. It was quite nice actually." He stopped, stared hard at her. "It was nice to see you let your guard down. And I enjoyed kissing you."

She crossed her arms and tried to look away, but that intensity in his eyes was back and she felt even more uncomfortable. She glanced at the clock. "Shit, it's almost 11:00, I cannot believe I slept that long. I'd better get home."

"I can give you a lift if you like. I've got to get to the office anyway."

"On Sunday? It *is* still Sunday, right?"

He laughed. "Yes it is, and yes I do have to go to work. The news never sleeps, you know that. Just give me a few minutes to shower and get changed."

As David returned to the bedroom, closing the double doors behind him, Roxy glanced around anxiously for her handbag and was relieved to find it slumped beside the front door where she'd obviously dropped it on her arrival. Thank God she hadn't lost that along the way, and thank David she hadn't been allowed to go dancing into the wee hours of the morning. She'd clearly had way too much to drink and way too little sense last night. She picked up her bag and noticed as she did so, a large wine rack against one wall. That must be the rack I raided, she thought, sweeping her eyes across the impressive selection of reds and whites. There were various brands of her favourite tipple, merlot, including a vintage bottle she could only ever dream about.

Roxy stepped towards the creamy sofa, pushed the blanket to one side and dropped down into it, feeling weary to the bone. She glanced around again. She liked inspecting other people's houses, they were always so revealing, and the revelation today was that David had a lot of money and a really good cleaner. Either that or he was a neat freak.

The sprawling, architecturally designed house was not just tidy, it was surprisingly stylish, especially for a bloke, and a bachelor at that, and she admired the high ceilings, shuttered windows and whitewashed paint job that revealed not a single blemish. The polished floorboards were so shiny she could almost see her reflection in them, and there were plush rugs, expensive looking furniture and lamps, and a gleaming red Fender Stratocaster guitar hanging like artwork on one wall. Another wall contained a faux fireplace with a mantelpiece above it, and she spotted several gleaming trophies, including David's Walkley.

Beside that stood a soaring, white bookcase and she pulled herself up to take a closer look. Unlike her own bookcase at home, which was stuffed to the brim, paperbacks wedged on top of each other and at every angle, this collection was neatly placed and separated into genres—non-fiction on one shelf, literary classics on another, and then, on a lower shelf, a more obscure collection, including several sci-fi and a few cheesy sounding romances—*Hot Enough For You* and *Lover's Delight*. She sniggered, about to inspect them further when she spotted two very familiar dust covers and reached towards them instead.

They were books Roxy had ghostwritten, so her name was not on them, and she wondered whether he even knew they were hers.

"I particularly like the one on that rich resort owner," David said softly and she swung around. "I've been following your work for a while."

"How did you know—"

"That you wrote them?" She nodded. "That's what agents are for."

"Ah, Mr Horowitz. You've got few of his here, I see."

"Not *his*, actually. He can't write a sentence. But he is generous, I'll give him that. He gave me all of those books for free."

"Oh great," she joked. "So no royalties for me, then?"

He laughed, fiddling with the collar of his shirt. "Nope, but I do promise you, this book of mine will more than make up for it. It's going to make you big, Roxanne, really big."

She smiled at his renewed self-confidence, wishing she had just a touch of it, and wondering if she'd be a whole lot more successful if she did. As she smiled at him she noticed, again, how striking his eyes were and how handsome he looked today. He had changed into a deep blue shirt, which seemed to bring out the blue in his eyes, and had combed his hair back neatly. He also looked like he'd just shaved and she caught the slight scent of something spicy.

"Do I scrub up all right?" he asked, catching her staring at him, and she blushed. This delighted him. "Come on," he said, smiling at her slyly, "let's get you back home before the neighbours start gossiping."

CHAPTER 16

Back in the relative safety of her snug apartment, Roxy swallowed some heavy duty pain killers, slipped her shoes and jeans off, and made a beeline for her bed, where she stayed, moaning to herself for hours, as much from her throbbing head as from her broken heart.

Max and Gilda.

Gilda and Max.

She couldn't stop thinking about them. A mini movie of that moment on Saturday night kept flashing through her brain—Max leaning into Gilda's ear, whispering sweet nothings then leading her gently by the hand towards his bedroom.

His bedroom!

"Agrrggh," she groaned, pulling a pillow over her head in a vain attempt to block it out.

Roxy could have handled anything, she decided, anything but that. Two of her favourite people. Now together. Now intimate. Her heart squeezed tighter.

If truth be told, she had expected it. Had even enabled it by dragging Gilda along to Max's party. So why was she so surprised? And why, she wondered, did it hurt so much?

Roxy knew the answer, of course, had known the answer for some time, but she wasn't about to admit it now. Not after Saturday night.

Throughout that miserable afternoon the phone rang several times, but Roxy ignored every call. There were two from Gilda, sounding bright and breezy, as though nothing had happened, and it made Roxy want to get up and stab her through the telephone. There was also one from Max. He didn't say much either but he did sound guilty. *And so he should!* He asked her to call and she threw a shoe at the answering machine by way of reply.

And, of course, there was one from her mum, oblivious to her pain, rattling on about her nosy neighbour Valerie, some horrendous shopping expedition with Charlie, and checking they were still on for the following Sunday.

"And isn't that atrocious Tina Passion woman with the same agency as you?" she finished off. "Such a shock about her. Valerie was a closet fan, she'll be most upset. Oh, well, call me when you can be bothered to find the time."

Roxy sat up.

What was she saying about Tina Passion?

She whipped the sheets back, struggled out of bed and grappled for the phone. It was too late, her mother had hung up. She stared at her clock radio. It was not yet 6:00 p.m. She flicked the radio on and began scanning for the news. All she could find were bad pop tunes and a cricket round up. She switched it off and dashed into the lounge room to try her luck with the TV. There was nothing on the commercial stations and the twenty-four-hour news channel was doing a story on the African famine. Growling with exasperation and the remnants of her worst-ever hangover on record, she then staggered through to the sunroom and clicked on her laptop. As it slowly whirred to life, she grew impatient, grabbed the phone and dialled Oliver's home number. His machine picked up.

"Olie, it's Roxy. Just wondering what's going on."

Next, she tried Oliver's mobile but it was switched off, so she dropped the phone back on the handset and said, "Bugger it, I'm going over."

Then she returned to her bedroom, peeled off last night's crumpled shirt, and hit the shower. Within twenty minutes, Roxy had changed into fresh blue jeans and a grey T-shirt, and was storming through the streets of Kings Cross, handbag wedged under one arm, worried look stencilled to her face. Oliver lived just a short walk from her place and a million miles away.

While Elizabeth Bay was a little shabby, it still had an elegant air, a lot like a spinster aunt who held her head high. Oliver's suburb, Kings Cross, was more your trashy younger cousin, the one who wore her skirt too short, her hair too bleached, her eyeliner way too thick. It was Sydney's main red light district and boasted more strip joints and seedy bars than you could poke a crack pipe at, but like loving family members, the two suburbs were still close, and it took just five minutes for Roxy to storm past the iconic El Alamein Fountain towards Oliver's aging art deco building.

As she approached, Roxy spotted a police car pulling up in the opposite direction, its siren and lights off. She watched as it double parked out the front of his apartment block and gasped when the back door swung open and Oliver stepped out. He didn't say anything, simply slammed the door and waited for the vehicle to drive away before turning around and stepping towards his front door.

Roxy called out Oliver's name and he spun around, a dazed look upon his face. He didn't seem to recognize her, so she stepped closer.

"It's Roxy. Are you okay?" He looked relieved to see her but said nothing. "What's going on, Olie?"

He glanced around. "Not here," he said quietly, motioning into the building and grappling for his keys.

It took him a few moments to unlock the door and she knew, for certain now, that something terrible had happened, but she wasn't about to get ahead of herself. Her brain was pounding enough as it was.

Up in his apartment, Oliver had managed to locate the coffee grinder and some beans but stood standing at the counter holding them for several minutes, so Roxy took them off him and set about making coffee, strong and black.

"I need a shower," he muttered and disappeared into the bedroom, returning less than ten minutes later, changed and a little more alert. Roxy handed him his coffee and steered him onto his bright red sofa, wishing she'd brought her sunglasses along. She didn't recall it being *this* bright.

"There's a couple of sugars in that," she said, assuming he'd need them, and then sipped her own beverage slowly, waiting for him to speak. Eventually, after several long, slow gulps, he did.

"It's been another crap day, Rox."

"I gather that."

"You heard about Tina?"

"Not really," she said, bracing. "What is it?"

"She's dead."

That was what Roxy had been dreading. She squeezed her eyes shut and asked, "What happened?"

He sighed long and low. "Don't know, but whatever happened, they think I did it."

Her eyes flew open. "Who? The cops?" He nodded, looking away. "What?! That's ridiculous! Did they actually say that?"

He looked back at her, his eyes like a wounded animal. "Didn't need to, Rox. Pretty bloody obvious. I've been in there for questioning since 2:00 p.m. Four fucking hours of the same old fucking questions."

Roxy's jaw dropped. "What sort of questions? So she was definitely murdered then? No chance of suicide or—"

"She was murdered, Rox, no question. Some bastard killed her and it's being pinned on me."

Roxy placed her cup down carefully and moved closer to him. "This is all insane. You have to tell me exactly what happened. Did you meet her as scheduled at Pico's last night?"

"Yes."

"Was she okay? What happened?"

"She was fine!" He was starting to snap now and she wondered whether interrogating him further was the worst thing she could do, but he was racing ahead. "She was great. We had a laugh, a bite to eat and then she had to go home."

"You didn't go back with her?"

"Of course I bloody went back with her! I'm not about to let a beautiful woman walk herself through those city streets! They're worse than Kings Cross, every fucking hooligan from the 'burbs comes in."

"Okay, easy. So you walked her back. Then what?"

"Then I said good night and she went up. That was it." He stopped, swallowed back his tears. "I ... I went home to watch a bit of TV then go to bed … Next thing I know I get a visit from some detectives around mid-arvo, they start grilling me with questions and then before I know it they've barrelled me into the back of their car and taken me to the station. No time to call a bloody lawyer, nothing."

"But why do you need a lawyer, I don't get it?"

He slammed his cup down and stood up. "Jesus, Miss Suspicious, you oughta get it. It's crime fiction 101. I was the last one to see her alive, I'm the first bloody suspect."

Roxy looked away, her heart sinking. Shit, she thought. He's right. Oliver read her mind and slumped back into his seat.

"I'm fucked."

"Was Gilda there? Did she interrogate you?"

"Gilda Maltin? No, why?"

"Never mind. So did they tell you exactly what happened? To Tina? How she was killed?"

"No, not exactly. But they did say it was brutal. They were aggressive, Roxy, they were asking all sorts of weird questions about how long I'd known her, what subjects I did at high school, for Christ sake!"

"Huh?"

"Exactly. Bloody weird. Wanted to know if I'd done chemistry, or something bizarre. Anyway, I should've demanded a lawyer but they never quite accused me—"

"You didn't ask for a lawyer!?"

"Didn't think I needed one. Not until the last hour, when it finally clicked. The minute I mentioned it, they terminated the interview and drove me home. Bastards." He looked up at her, his eyes watering now, his face softer. "Poor Tina, eh? Who the hell'd want to do this to her? It's just horrendous."

"And so soon after Seymour and William," Roxy added, immediately wishing that she hadn't. Yet Oliver seemed encouraged by this. His eyes were racing around in his head and he jumped up and began circling the room, round and round the parquetry floor.

"Jesus, Roxy, you're right. They have to be connected! Davo was really onto something ... There must be a nutcase out there killing writers. Which is great news ... I mean, not for the writers, obviously, but, well, I've got alibis for those other murders. Remember, I was with you, at Davo's premiere when Seymour was killed?"

Roxy smiled assuredly at him but her heart was sinking further. She didn't want to mention the small matter of him disappearing for about an hour during the screening of the movie. She'd seen him leave, herself, as did others no doubt. Roxy hoped to God Oliver had a good alibi for that time, or he really was in trouble.

"Where were you last Wednesday night, then?"

"What?"

"That was the night William Glad was killed. Where were you then?"

He seemed confused, gave his head a shake. "Um ... let me think. Wednesday night ... um ..." He glanced at his coffee cup and then stood up. "I need a proper drink."

Oliver marched into his kitchen, flung open the fridge and produced a beer. He held it out it to Roxy but she shook her head, no. Her stomach convulsed at the mere sight of alcohol. He flipped the top off the beer, took a lengthy swallow, and then returned to the living room.

"Wednesday night, Wednesday night ... That's right, I was at work quite late, catching up on some stuff, and then back here, of course. Just ate at home and went to bed."

She frowned. It was the night before the funeral. She distinctly remembered trying to call him about Max's party, both at work and at home and getting no reply. Perhaps he was too busy or tired to pick up.

"Was Sharon with you at work late? Was anyone here when you got back?"

"No, course not, I live alone, you know that."

She felt her stomach turn. None of his alibis looked good, no wonder the police were questioning him. He was also present at Seymour Silva's funeral around the time the police believed that the gardening shears had been planted in Norman Hick's car. She wondered, suddenly, how Norm's alibi was looking for Saturday night.

"You've gotta help me, Roxy," Oliver was saying, his eyes imploring. "I didn't do this, I wouldn't do this. You know that."

"I know that," she told him, reaching over and pulling him back down on to the sofa. "You need to calm down. The police are just doing their job and looking into all angles. Don't let them freak you out. Can I get you anything? Something to eat? A kebab from down the road?"

He shook his head no and polished off the rest of the beer.

"Then try and chill out, and get some sleep tonight, okay?" He looked at her like she'd just asked him to fly to the moon. "I've got some sleeping tablets at home, want me to go get them?"

"Nah, I'll be right. You get back. You don't look too hot yourself."

"Yeah I've got the hangover from hell. But that's a whole other story for a whole other time." She pulled herself up. "You want me to stay?"

He stared at his empty beer bottle blankly, not appearing to hear her.

"Olie?"

"No, no," he said. "You go, we'll talk tomorrow. Can we talk tomorrow?"

He had that pleading look again and it scared her. It was so out of character for the usually nonchalant Oliver Horowitz. He'd been acting out of character a lot lately and she didn't like it. She wanted the old, blasé Oliver back.

"Of course. I'll drop in to the office, maybe in the afternoon some time."

"Sooner, if you want, I won't be in late."

"I'll get there as soon as I can, Olie. I've just got someone I need to see first."

He looked at her puzzled but she didn't say any more, just reached for her bag and made her way to the door.

As she opened it, he called out: "Be careful, Rox! I don't want to lose any more of my writers. Not tonight."

Oliver's words shadowed her all the way home.

CHAPTER 17

It was Monday morning and Gilda Maltin did not look happy. She motioned for Roxy to enter her office, nodding at the uniformed officer who had shown her through, but her usual smile was nowhere to be seen.

"I know why you're here," she said, cutting Roxy off the moment she opened her mouth. "And there's nothing I can do, I'm sorry Roxy. But it's not looking good for your mate."

"Oliver Horowitz didn't do it, Gilda, you know that."

"I know nothing," she said. "I just follow the evidence trail and I've already had a bit of a squiz at it. It does not look good, but you didn't hear any of this from me. I shouldn't even be talking about this with you. It was bloody stupid of me to blabber on the other night. It didn't occur to me that Oliver would become a person of interest."

"A person of interest?!"

"Shit, there I go again. You didn't hear that from me."

"So you are on the case now?"

"God no, I'm too close to Oliver to be put on this case, even though the truth is I don't really know the man that well."

"Well I know him very well and he didn't do this, Gilda.

He didn't."

Gilda sighed. "Look, Oliver seems like a decent bloke in the short time I've known him. I suggest he shuts his mouth and gets himself a top-notch solicitor."

"They're charging him?!"

"I never said that, Roxy, but it won't hurt him to get good counsel."

"Can you at least tell me what time Tina died? And if Norman Hicks has an alibi for then?"

"You're hoping we can pin this back on him."

She shrugged. "You said it yourself. He is kinda creepy."

Gilda opened a desk drawer and located a half-eaten block of dark chocolate, offering it towards Roxy who shook her head no. Gilda broke a sizeable chunk off and popped it in her mouth then, chewing, glanced at her computer screen and clicked the return button a few times.

"Okay," she mumbled, "the coroner believes Miss Passion ..." She paused and stared at Roxy. "What kind of a name is that, anyway?"

"A nom de plume, I gather," Roxy said. "All the better for selling erotic novels."

Gilda blinked at this and turned back to the screen. "Right, so, Miss De Plume was murdered some time between 11:00 p.m. Saturday night and about 2:00 a.m. Sunday morning. That's now in the public domain so I can tell you that much." She wiped her mouth and dropped the chocolate bar back into her drawer. "As for Mr Hicks, all I'll say is his alibi is looking stronger than Oliver's at this stage. Not perfect, but solid enough."

Roxy scowled. "And what time did William Glad die? Got that on your screen, too?"

Her eyebrows shot up. "Glad? About the same time, I gather, why? I thought you were here about Tina Passion."

"I am. But ... well ..." Roxy blushed. *Had she just put her foot in it?*

"Don't stress, Rox, the investigators have obviously already connected those dots. In fact, I hate to say this but it looks like Mr Lone might be right. They're getting a task force together now to look into all three deaths. Reopening the Seymour Silva case. There are just too many similarities to ignore, too many common threads."

"By common thread you mean Oliver Horowitz."

She said nothing but for a woman who was refusing to speak, she had been surprisingly forthcoming.

Eventually Gilda sighed loudly. "Listen, Roxy, it's not looking good for Oliver. At least not in regards to the deaths of Mr Glad and Miss Passion. As far as I can tell he has no substantial alibi for either one, and he was at Silva's funeral when the gardening shears were planted. He had access to Mr Hick's car. He could have planted them to throw suspicion in a different direction."

"I was at the funeral, too!" Roxy said. "So were about sixty other people. Why aren't you looking at any of us?"

"The detectives will be, don't you worry about that. Tell me this, though, can you account for Oliver's time during the entire funeral?"

"Yes," she said triumphantly. "I got a lift from him and he didn't leave my sight the entire time, not even for a ciggie!" *Thank God.*

"And afterwards? At the wake?"

Roxy's shoulders drooped. He had attended the wake alone. Gilda gave her a knowing look.

"Okay, but what's his motive? Why on earth would he want to kill William, let alone Tina or Seymour? It's so insane!"

"They're still piecing it all together, Roxy, and I've told you I can't say anything."

"Please, Gilda. He is an innocent man."

For once, Gilda's lips remained firmly shut so Roxy tried a different tack.

"Surely you have other suspects? At least for the other deaths? Did you know for instance that Erin might have a motive to kill her dad?"

"And what motive might that be?"

"Well, Oliver said she was anxious to republish her father's old gardening guides, but her father had been dead against it. Maybe she killed him so she could cash in."

Gilda gave her a sideways stare. "She could do that anyway, once he died. She only had to wait another week or so, the cancer was doing its job. That's also a motive for Oliver, you know."

Roxy groaned. *Damn it, she'd put her foot in it again!*

Gilda stood up. "Come on, you need to let this one go, Roxy, you're too damn close. Just tell Oliver to get a decent lawyer and you stay out of it. Now, I really have to get on with it and you really have to get out of here."

Roxy sighed. "Fine, fine." She opened the office door.

"Before you go, though," Gilda said and Roxy raised her eyebrows. "About Saturday night ..."

Roxy knew she wasn't referring to Tina Passion's murder, and felt a white-hot heat race through her. She had deliberately tried not to think about that night and she did not want to get into it now, not with more important matters to worry about.

"Doesn't matter now," she said, and walked out.

Unfortunately for Roxy, that night was not going anywhere. When she returned to her apartment block, Max was standing out the front, his hands pushed into his jeans pockets, a sheepish look across his face. Her anger returned and she tried desperately to swallow it back down. She had no right to be angry with either of them, she knew that, they were both free agents and she had already knocked Max back, so why shouldn't he hook up with Gilda? Yet that kind of logic didn't seem to help. She just wanted to punch them both out.

"You okay, Parker?" he asked as she approached and she shrugged, reaching into her handbag for the front door keys.

"Why wouldn't I be?"

He stared hard at her. "Gonna play it like that then?"

"Play what?"

He shook his head, his own anger clearly rising. "I

thought you'd taken off with that David Lone wanker," he said and she rounded on him.

"He's not a wanker! He's more of a gentleman than you'll ever be, and what does that have to do with *anything*?"

He stepped back, surprised by her hostility. "I thought ... I just thought you two were, you know ...?"

"No, Max, I don't know."

"So you didn't go back to his place on Saturday night then?"

She blushed and it was all the answer he needed. His mouth dropped, his eyes seemed to shrink back and he thrust his hands deeper into his pockets. He looked like he'd just been kicked in the guts.

"Even if I did," she stammered, still struggling to locate her keys in her oversized handbag, "even if I did, and it's none of your business what I do with my nights, but even if I did, what's that got to do with anything? What, you think I'm sleeping with David Lone so you have to jump into bed with the first woman with a pulse? Not just any woman, I might add, but one of my best friends."

"You mean Gilda?" His eyes refocused.

"No, I mean Cinderella! Of course Gilda, I saw you—"

"Saw me what?"

She cut him off, she'd had enough and she'd found the keys at last. "A-ha!" she said, pulling them out and holding them aloft, like a trophy. "You have no right to question me and my love life when you're the one who sleeps around. You're a bloody slut, Max, you always have been and you wonder why I don't want to be with you."

She turned back to her door, her hands shaking so much she couldn't get the key into the lock. She stabbed at it and stabbed at it, but it wouldn't connect. Max gently took the keys off her and opened it up.

"I'm sorry, Roxy, but you've got—"

She didn't hear the rest of it because she had already slammed the door in his face.

CHAPTER 18

Up in the privacy of her tiny apartment, Roxy let out a loud, blood-curdling cry. Then she flung a hand to her mouth and tried to calm down. She couldn't deal with Max now, she couldn't deal with any more of this. She needed to get her head together and she needed to help Oliver. He was in deep shit and this little sideshow was insignificant by comparison.

Pushing Max's wounded face out of her mind, she marched into the kitchen to pop the kettle on. Then, realizing it wasn't going to cut it, she raced into her room, changed into a tracksuit and joggers, pulled a cap over her hair and headed out again.

For the next hour Roxy just walked. She walked and walked and walked, not thinking about anything, not letting anyone's face appear too long in her head. She just pushed them out again and kept power walking as fast as she could muster, down past Peepers and the newsagency (waving to Costa as she went), across several roads and through Rushcutters Bay Park. Exercise had always been Roxy's saviour and it did not let her down today.

By the time she got back to her apartment she was

shaking with exhaustion, sweating profusely, and feeling a whole lot better. She had purchased a bouquet of hot pink tulips on her travels, hoping they would work their usual magic and cheer her up, and so she dropped them into a vase with some water, placed them on her coffee table and hit the shower. Afterwards, she slipped into light shorts and a flowing peasant top, poured herself a glass of chilled water and sat down in front of her laptop. She needed to catch up on the latest news, yet she couldn't bring herself to switch it on, and she couldn't prevent the nagging anxiety that was creeping up on her again.

There was something about the Silva/Glad/Passion story that was worrying her; something she hadn't yet put a finger on and she couldn't work out what. She was certain of one thing, though, she didn't want it to be a story. At all. For the first time in a very long time, Roxy hadn't bought the morning papers. She didn't want to find a gruesome article that she could neatly snip and glue down in her scrapbook. Nor had she watched the morning news shows or switched the radio on. She wanted there to be no story, for the whole thing to die down and go away. She knew Oliver was innocent, the wrong man at the wrong place, but she couldn't help feeling seriously worried for him. If the police had connected the dots, the press would soon follow.

The press.

Her mind went straight to David Lone. He'd spent yesterday afternoon at work. She knew that for a fact. What had he found out? What did he know? Was he connecting it all as she had done, as the police had done? Had David noticed, for instance, that Oliver disappeared halfway through his film preview the night of the first killing? Did he know Oliver had no alibi for the second killing, and did he recall, as she did, that Oliver was taking Tina out that tragic Saturday night? More importantly, would his journalistic ethics force him to mention it?

Would hers?

That's when it struck her. That's what was niggling at the

back of her mind, what she didn't want to face. If the police asked, would she feel compelled to tell them the truth—that Oliver Horowitz had no alibi, not just for William's and Tina's deaths, which they already knew, but for Seymour's, too? Surely she must tell them about his little jaunt out of the cinema. But where did friendship and loyalty stand in all of this?

Roxy pushed her chair back, stood up and stretched her arms out, noticing for the first time all morning the stunning view of the small bay in front of her. Sailboards ploughed through the water, a small dinghy circled nearby, and the sun glittered off the rippling waves. It didn't hold her attention for long, though, she was already thinking about Oliver again. It was time to face it all head on, she decided, to fight fire with fire. She took a deep breath, picked up her phone and rang David Lone.

By Monday afternoon, David and Roxy were walking into Oliver's office, both writers now in a very different mood from the last time they had been together. They met briefly outside, and David leaned in and gave her a light kiss on the lips. Roxy felt awkward, a little embarrassed even, but concern for Oliver quickly swallowed that up.

"Feeling better today?" he asked gently.

"Better than Oliver, let's put it that way."

"Do you want to talk about it?"

"Nope, nope, we've got bigger fish to fry. I need to speak to you quickly before we see Oliver. About what you know. What you're going to print. I can't have you accusing Oliver of this. I couldn't handle that."

He frowned. "Hey, I think I've been more than fair. Have you seen today's article?"

She shook her head sheepishly. "Couldn't stomach it."

"Well, perhaps you should take a look at that first before you accuse me of anything." There was a slight edge in his voice. He was clearly hurt. "Oliver's no doubt got a copy upstairs."

"Then let's go up, shall we?"

She turned to the ground floor intercom and punched in the access code. A quick "beep" indicated it was unlocking, and David pushed the entry door, holding it open for her to walk through.

Upstairs they found Oliver at his desk as always and, as David had predicted, he had the morning edition of the *Daily Telegraph* laid out in front of him, the shaken look still firmly on his face. It was clear he hadn't got a wink of sleep last night, the bags under his eyes were bulging, his pallor now gray. Sharon sprang up from the sofa when she saw them, a look of devastation on her own face.

"Jesus, horrific news, eh guys?" she said. "She could carry on like a chook with her head chopped off when she wanted to, but jeez she didn't deserve to go like that. No way!"

"Like what?" Roxy asked.

"Oh, Davo didn't fill you in?" She raised a scrawny eyebrow at the reporter.

"I don't think she wants to know," he replied.

Sharon grabbed the paper from her boss. "I think you've read enough for one day," she said, thrusting it into Roxy's hands before turning back to David. "I hope you're gonna go easy on him. Know which side your bread's buttered on and all that."

"Oh lay off him, Shazza," said Olie. "He's a mate."

"Yeah, well, let's hope it stays that way."

She glared at David for a second and then stalked out, cursing quietly under her breath. Roxy dropped into a chair and began reading the newspaper. As she slowly worked her way through it, David paced up and down behind her and Olie sat in a trance, not really looking at anyone or anything. This was yet another front page story, and this time David's sensational prophecy screamed out from the leading headline: *"Last Writes: Who is killing the great writers of Australia?"*

That was not unexpected. He was absolutely right. Three successful genre writers were now dead; there was no avoiding that. The next line, however, was the one that really caught her eye. The sub-heading was *"The Snow White murder"*, then a few teasing lines announced that Tina Passion, *"world-famous erotic romance writer"*, had been found dead in her apartment with an apple in her hand. *"Full story: Page 5"*. Roxy licked a thumb and forefinger and flicked quickly to the relevant page where the details were indeed horrific.

Even though the police had little to say other than that they were treating the death as suspicious, an unnamed witness wasn't quite so reticent. This source revealed that a *"juicy red apple"* had been found in the hands of Ms Passion by her distraught father who had shown up to take her out for a pre-arranged brunch on Sunday morning. While results from the post-mortem examination had not yet been revealed, the story strongly indicated that she had been poisoned, most likely from the apple. Roxy turned to Lone.

"A poisoned apple. Are you serious?" He stopped in his tracks.

"What?"

"Just because she's got an apple nearby, what makes you conclude it had poison in it? Maybe she choked on it? Or maybe she just happened to be eating an apple when she was killed?"

"My sources say otherwise."

"Sources?" She thought now of some sexy young police officer slipping him secrets between shifts, perhaps even between the sheets. "But even if she was poisoned, what's to indicate that it wasn't suicide?"

Oliver sat up with a start. "Hey, she was happy as Larry when I left her, I can promise you that!"

"Olie, I'm just playing devil's advocate here, that's all."

"That's okay," David said. "These questions are valid. My sources tell me there were signs of trauma to the back of the head, indicating she'd been hit by a blunt object. They don't know—yet—whether that killed her, or the poison. But there's no way she could have hit herself, the angle was all wrong, apparently."

"Unless she poisoned herself and then fell back, hitting her head?" Roxy suggested and Oliver looked ready to blow. "Not that I think she did, Olie, honestly. I'm just trying to sort it all out in my head."

"I am telling you, Rox, Tina was in good spirits, had everything to live for. Another book coming out in just six weeks, we were at the proofing stage. She was even planning a trip to Rome to write the next one. There is no way she topped herself."

David was also growing impatient with this line of questioning. "Roxanne, you are not seriously going to try to pass this one off as another suicide or a coincidence, too? I expected better from you. Three well-known genre writers have died in the past seven days. All under mysterious circumstances." He held his palms out. "They have to be linked, don't you see? They *have* to."

She sighed, nodding slowly. He was right of course, it was impossible not to accept, but it was still hard to face especially because Oliver seemed to be caught up in the middle. David's article mentioned Oliver's name a few times, stating that he was Tina's agent, and that he was the last to see her alive, but it did not link him specifically to the murder and she was grateful for this.

"So who's doing this then?" she asked. "Do you really truly believe some crazed madman is out there bumping off writers?"

He raised one shoulder. "That's what it looks like. Have you spoken to Gilda Maltin since Sunday? Does she know anything? Anything that might help Oliver?"

Roxy shook her head. "She's a policewoman first and foremost, she wouldn't tell me anything." In fact, she had learned a lot from Gilda but she had promised not to spill the beans to David Lone, and she wasn't about to break her promise. "Anyway, she's not actually on this case."

David seemed disappointed, as did Oliver who held his head in his hands despondently. Then he sat straight up.

"Friggin' hell, Tina's dad is going to fry me," he wailed.

"But you didn't do anything, Oliver," Roxy said.

"I didn't protect her. I should have protected her."

"That's insane. You were her agent, not her bodyguard."

"I was the last person to see her alive! Maybe the killer was lurking around her apartment, maybe I walked straight past him, and didn't see him ..."

Roxy folded the paper over, then reached across and smacked him gently across the head. He looked at her aghast. "That's for being an idiot," she said. "Tina's father can not expect that you were going to watch his daughter every minute of every day. She was a grown woman for goodness sake, verging on middle age."

"Still, Lorenzo hated me. He's never gonna forgive me. Never."

"You don't need his forgiveness, Oliver, you didn't do anything," Roxy reiterated.

David coughed. "Guys, I've really got to get back to the office—"

Oliver held a hand up. "Before you do, though, Davo, can I ask you a big favour?" He glanced at Roxy. "You too, Rox."

David sighed and finally took a seat in the director's chair beside Roxy, but his right foot was tapping away madly. He clearly had a lot on his mind.

"You're both gun investigators," Oliver began, "you've proven that time and again." He looked from one to the other imploringly. "I need your help. Desperately. I need you to find out who's been doing all of this. Not just to clear my name, but to help Tina and William and, yes, even loony old Seymour."

David frowned. "I'm already on this story, 24/7. I will find out who did this, I can assure you of that."

"Yeah, but you're on it for the Tele. I want you to help me."

David's frown deepened. "What? Work for you instead of the paper?"

Oliver shook his head. "No, no, I just mean ..." He broke off. "I don't know what I mean ..."

"I'm sorry, mate, but my first loyalty is to the *Telegraph*, and to my readers. To truth," David added firmly.

There was an awkward silence. Oliver looked stung and Roxy glanced from him to David and back again.

"What does that mean?" she demanded of David. "What are you saying?"

"It means I have to stay impartial."

"So if you discover something that is not in Oliver's best interests ...?" She let the question dangle there and he shrugged.

"I'm a journalist, Roxanne. I have no choice."

Well, that's not exactly true, she wanted to say. He did have a choice and he was choosing truth. She swallowed her anger back down. He was right, of course, there was no denying that. He was a journalist. He *should* be choosing truth. She sank back into her seat with a sigh while Oliver looked mortified.

"Davo!" he was saying, waving a hand at himself and then back at David. "We're mates, right?"

David shrugged again and Roxy felt compelled to rescue him. She was also a journalist. She knew how these things worked.

"He has to do what he has to do, Oliver, you must understand that."

Oliver didn't look like he understood that at all and David stood up.

"Look, I haven't got time to argue my code of ethics with you. I'm not out to lynch anyone but I can't take sides either. I have to report what I find and I'm sorry if that hurts you." He paused. "I've really got to get back to it. Do you have anything else you want to tell me, Oliver? Anything that might help?"

The agent's anger was now bubbling over; he had lost all sense of perspective and looked like a caged rat. "Just that I didn't do it!" he wailed. "I had no reason to bloody do it! I'm not capable of killing anyone, especially someone as beautiful as Tina, or old William. No way, I did not do this thing! Tell that to your readers!"

"Easy, Oliver," Roxy said. "He's just doing his job. Come on, David I'll see you out."

As they passed through the front office, Sharon was just picking up the ringing phone and gave David a death stare that would have shaken mere mortals, yet David didn't seem too perturbed, and Roxy wondered how he managed to stay so detached. She envied him that.

Back on the street, pedestrians trudging past, the traffic roaring beyond, David took Roxy's arm and swung her gently around. His piercing eyes bore into hers, and she felt a little uncomfortable again. She hated the way he had that effect on her.

"I hate this job sometimes, you know," he said. "But you understand my predicament, I can see that. You understand what I have to do."

"Yes, sadly, I do. But Oliver didn't do this, David. You've got it all wrong."

The look he gave her then was chilling. He looked at her as though she were the most naïve little girl he had ever met. She fell back against the wall.

"My God, you really believe he did it."

He shrugged one shoulder again. "The police certainly do and I'm sorry, but I can't help but wonder. He's got no decent alibi, not one. He was missing in action for all three murders. What are the chances of that? You've got to look at the facts."

"So you know about ..." She couldn't bring herself to say it but he understood.

"My film premiere? Of course I do. I didn't miss that one. While you and I were sitting quietly watching the movie, Oliver snuck off, like a thief into the night. The police know all about it, too. There's CCTV footage showing him walking out of the theatre, about halfway through, around the same time Seymour was killed."

"He was going for a smoke."

"Extremely long smoko. According to the footage, he didn't return for forty-five minutes, Roxanne. Forty-five minutes."

She flinched. "Do the police know where he went?"

"He says he just went for a stroll, wandered about aimlessly. Another street camera caught him walking away from the theatre, in a northerly direction around the same time but there's no sign of him after that, not for that period anyway."

"Damn it."

He nodded and leaned back against the wall, his shoulder just touching hers.

"Maybe a shopkeeper or a witness recalls seeing him nearby? They could be his alibi?"

"The police are onto it, I'm onto it. But I have to prepare you, Roxanne, it does not look good."

She sighed. "Okay, what else have you got? Any CCTV cameras outside Tina's apartment?"

"Not that I know of. I do know he was witnessed leaving the restaurant with her at about 11:45 p.m., that's what the waiter tells me, and then the shopkeeper at the convenience store near his apartment spotted him there, buying a few groceries, around 12:30 p.m. Bloody odd thing to be doing."

"Not if you know Oliver. He doesn't keep normal hours like the rest of us. Okay, so what time did Tina die again?"

"The police say it was some time between 11:00 p.m. and about 1:00 a.m."

She did the math. "Enough time, then."

"Enough time."

"Shit, shit, shit! Okay, what about our gardening friend William? Please tell me Oliver wasn't spotted anywhere near William's house at the time he died."

"Got nothing there, no sightings of Oliver at all that I've heard of, which is good news, and also bad, because that leaves his alibi wide open."

"And William died around the same time, right?"

"Yes he did, between about midnight and 2:00 a.m. on Wednesday night, or more precisely, Thursday morning. That's why I think it's a serial killer. Same modus operandi."

"But *of course* there were no sightings at that time. Oliver would have been tucked up in bed, alone, trying to get some sleep."

"Still doesn't help. And as I say, the cops seem to have him pegged as suspect number one."

She groaned and turned to face him. "That's the bit that's the most aggravating! Why on earth are they even looking at Oliver's whereabouts? What possible reason would he have to kill all three writers, let alone one? It makes absolutely no sense."

David's phone beeped and he glanced down at it. "Shit, I really have to go, but we'll talk again, I promise. We'll sort through this."

"But what about your book? I'm supposed to be interviewing you this afternoon."

He shook his head firmly. "No can do, Roxanne. I just haven't got a spare minute to focus on anything but this case. I'd love it if you could keep working on the book, though, do your research, interview some people. Do you think you can crack on without me while I focus on the *Last Writes* murders?" She nodded half-heartedly, prickling at his tagline. "Good, because this is huge, Roxy. This story is too big to ignore. Hell, it's an investigative writer's wet dream, if you'll excuse my saying so. I couldn't have designed it better myself. There's no way I'm letting this one go. No way."

Roxy winced. That's exactly what she was afraid of.

Back in the office, Sharon was preoccupied on the phone so Roxy slipped past her again and into the chair opposite her agent. He had disappeared into his own gloomy world and didn't look up, so she gave him a few minutes to re-enter the earth's orbit while she mulled the mess out.

And what a mess it was.

Just one week ago, Oliver Horowitz was on cloud nine. He had a bunch of very successful, very *alive* writers who were all bringing in good money. He had book deals and film launches and was watching his authors fly up the best seller lists. She recalled that glamorous cocktail party following David's premiere, and how happy Oliver had seemed. He was finally making good money and his future looked bright.

Today, everything was bleak. Oliver's life was being dismantled in front of him and, with the likes of David Lone on the story, would very soon be dismantled in full view of the public, too. How could it not?

Unlike David, however, Roxy did not believe for one moment that Oliver could do what the police clearly suspected. Yet even she had to admit, it did not look good. If she were a cop she would be pointing the finger firmly at him. He was the common link. Oliver had no alibi for all three murders. And he was present when one of the murder weapons was planted in Norman Hick's car.

But what was his motive?

That's what she kept coming back to, and what baffled her the most. Perhaps a better question was: what was the real murderer's motive? Why would someone want to see three writers dead? These three in particular? If she could answer that, she realised, Oliver might just stand a chance.

Roxy sat quietly for a few seconds, chewing her lower lip and thinking about this. It was such a big question, however, she just couldn't get her head around it. Perhaps she needed to break it down into parts? To focus on one murder at a time.

Her mind went straight to Tina Passion and things seemed slightly clearer. She knew of at least one person who might have a motive to want to shut the erotic fiction writer up. She just needed to focus on that.

"Sorry, Rox," Oliver said, suddenly coming back to his senses. "I'm worried, really worried. The police just called. They want me back at the station this afternoon for more questioning."

Her heart sank even further. "You have to take a lawyer with you this time. No more speaking to the police, hell, no speaking to *anyone*, without one."

"Shazza's onto it."

"That includes our friend David Lone." He caught her eye. "I'd advise this of any journalist but especially one as good as David. You keep your mouth shut from now on, don't say a word to him, okay?"

He nodded slowly, the dazed look returning.

"Forget about David, I'm going to help you, Oliver, I'm going to sort this mess out. There has to be a logical explanation for all of this and I'm going to find it. But you have to trust me and you have to stay quiet. Okay?"

"Okay, okay, I won't say a word. But how're you going to do it? You already told me your cop friend is no use."

"I don't need Gilda. I need another way in and I know just the person to help me."

CHAPTER 19

Maria Constantinople was a larger than life character. Brazen, bawdy and, best of all, the editor of one of the nation's top-selling, trend-setting women's magazines *Glossy*. She could always be counted on for some back-up bucks when the ghostwriting dried up, but today Roxy was counting on her to help save Oliver's life.

Maria's office, the exact antithesis of Oliver's dingy digs—all bright lighting, plush furnishings and fashionable young things teetering about in designer heels—was certainly buzzing when Roxy strolled in and, having rung ahead, the receptionist, Trevor, wasted no time leading her past the ogling staff towards Maria's inner sanctum.

The editor's office was a spacious, glass-walled cubicle, strategically designed to keep a firm eye on her quivering minions while Sydney Harbour glittered behind her. Today, Maria was standing, staring out at that harbour, one hand on her ample hip, the other holding the latest igadget up to an ear that was dripping with an enormous silver and blue earring.

"Then tell him to shut the fuck up!" she boomed, her tone jovial and upbeat despite the language.

"Coffee? Tea?" whispered Trevor, lurking by the door.

He was a pretty young thing, clad in a deep purple, velvet suit with a white shirt, pink and lilac tie and shiny black boots. He looked a little like Willy Wonka and Roxy was about to ask for some Gobstoppers but decided against it. She'd met him several times before and knew he wasn't the jocular type.

"Coffee, milk and two sugars, thanks," she whispered back before slipping her handbag off her shoulder and sitting down in the rigid chrome and leather chair in front of Maria's desk. She wondered if it was specially planted there to make guests feel uncomfortable. If so, it worked a treat.

Maria laughed loudly, snorting suddenly, and Roxy relaxed a little. She was clearly in a good mood today. That would work to her advantage.

"Oh, he would say that! Yeah ... Yeah ... Oh, I don't give a flying fuck." She turned and stared at Roxy. "Hey, Houso, I gotta go, got freelancers to eat up."

She winked at Roxy, laughed and then clicked off, tossing the phone onto her expansive glass desk as if it were made of rubber.

"Roxy Parker, ghostwriter extraordinaire," she said, dropping into her own chair which was also leather but twice the size and extremely comfortable looking. "To what do I owe the honour?"

"Actually, it's a favour you owe, and I'd like to collect."

Maria's good mood dissipated a little. Her thin, pencilled eyebrows scrunched together. "Say what?"

Trevor returned then with a glass of espresso coffee and placed it in front of Roxy, glancing up at Maria who shook her glossy auburn locks in reply.

"Just get the door," she said, and he closed it on his way out.

"So he proved to be gay after all," Roxy said of her assistant and Maria's eyebrows relaxed.

"Typical bloody story. They come in acting as straight as choir boys, get themselves the job, then turn fairy queen very soon after. I would've sacked him if he wasn't so good at reception. Makes a mean cuppa, too."

"Plus it's nice to have a bit of eye candy about."

"I don't just want to look, Roxy, I want to *touch*."

An evil glint flickered across Maria's heavily made-up eyes and Roxy felt a shudder of disgust. She didn't doubt for one moment that Maria could be as predatory as any chauvinistic male boss, and suspected that if the poor PA had been straight, he would have been fighting her off by the end of his first week.

"Anyway, enough about my non-existent sex life," Maria was saying. "What do you want? And I don't want to hear any more about favours. I know I still owe you after setting that lunatic artist on you a while back, so just spit it out and let's call it quits."

Roxy took a deep breath. "I want you to run a story on Tina Passion and I want you to hire me to write it."

This had the editor's attention. "The slutty writer who was just found dead?"

"Yep, that one."

Maria considered this. "Can I ask why?"

"You can ask." Maria glared at Roxy, her patience clearly wearing thin, so Roxy quickly said, "It'll be a good story, Maria. She was a big seller, a regular on the social circuit. It's worth the space, I can assure you; it's going to be huge. Already is in fact."

Maria looked irked. "Since when do you tell me what to commission?"

"It's just a story suggestion, from one of your favourite freelance writers. I always give you story ideas. That's what I do."

Maria gave it some thought, clinking long, red-polished nails across her desk as she thought aloud. "Well, the girls *were* all gasbagging about Tina Passion in the tearoom this morning. Bit of a shock, eh? Plus they reckon it might be a crazed serial killer which is even more exciting." She licked her thick, botoxed lips. "So, it's a big story, I'll give it that.

I'm just not sure it's a *Glossy* magazine story. Plus it'll be old news by the time we go to print."

"My article wouldn't be all about the murder, although that would be a juicy sidebar. No, no, I would do a full expose of Tina's life, from country bumpkin to top-selling novelist. I have access to her agent, you know?"

"Oliver Horowitz? The one they think did it?"

Roxy looked horrified. "Who thinks that?

She shrugged. "That's what the girls tell me, apparently the shock jocks have been going on about it all morning."

Roxy didn't want to get into an argument, she needed to keep the editor on side so she feigned disinterest and said instead, "Did I mention full access to Oliver Horowitz?" She quickly added, "I'd also want to interview Tina's family and friends, and maybe do a quick side story on the other murders, the fact that genre writers are being bumped off."

"Ah, gorgeous, you're selling it well but like I said, crime's not really our thing."

"Hence the reason that would be a side story and the main one would be a look at Ms Passion and her incredible life. Come on, erotic fiction is so fashionable at the moment, you have to admit that. Look at *Fifty Shades of Grey*. Tina Passion is Australia's answer to E. L. James." Maria was fiddling with one enormous earring, a look of utter boredom on her face so Roxy pulled out her final ace. "Did you hear I'm doing a book on David Lone?"

The editor stopped fiddling and sat forward. "Now *there's* a red-blooded, heterosexual male if ever I saw one. Couldn't get me into his pants, could you?"

Roxy swallowed her disgust and said, breezily, "No but I could let you publish an excerpt from my book before it comes out."

"An *exclusive* excerpt?"

"All yours."

"Sold!" Maria broke into a wide smile, revealing enormous, smoke-stained teeth. Just as quickly, the smile deflated. "But I can't promise more than a double page spread on this Tina chick, I'm not really sure how much my readers care."

"I don't need any more."

Maria stared at her hard. "Why do you want this so friggin' bad? You hard up for work at the mo'?"

Roxy drained the rest of her coffee and stood up, anxious to get away before Maria started digging deeper. "I'm always hard up for work, Maria, you know that."

As she opened the door to leave, Maria called out, "Can't you at least throw in Lone's home number? His mobile?"

Roxy just laughed as she saw herself out.

Back on the street, she gave a small whoop of joy. She hadn't expected that to go so well, and she was relieved. Now she had the *Glossy* article on her list, she could do as David Lone could do and bypass Gilda and go straight to the source. Except, unlike David who was working for the gutter press and would have to barge his way in, suspicion in his wake, she had the pretence of a flattery piece for a "lovely lifestyle title" to help her get access. Or at least that's how she would sell it to Tina's family and friends. And right now she needed access very badly if she was going to help save Oliver's scalp. There was one man in particular who had some questions to answer and she was keen to make him talk.

CHAPTER 20

Lorenzo Vento had the same short, stocky build as his daughter, Tina Passion, but that's where the similarities ended. With a thick mop of greying black hair and tanned skin so wrinkled he looked like an old leather saddle, he appeared as tough as nails with none of the soft edges of his bosomy, blonde and air-brushed daughter. He had a dark checked shirt on and what looked like moleskin trousers, a battered old Akubra slouch hat in one hand, and a bulging green bag in the other, and the sneer he was now giving the press who were filming his every move suggested a man who did not court the press as Tina once had.

Roxy had not yet scored an interview, had not even tried; it was now Tuesday morning, just two days since Tina's body had been discovered and way too early to call a grieving father, even one as tough looking as Lorenzo. She would to be patient, she would bide her time, and she hoped he would appreciate that. Instead, she watched him from the TV screen in her apartment as he trudged out of his hotel, looking majorly pissed off. News cameras jostled for prime position and several reporters were throwing questions at him, their tone more salacious than sympathetic but he simply glared at them mutely, thrust the hat on his head, and stepped into a waiting car, which quickly zoomed off.

Roxy wondered where he was going, but was thankful for the media presence. Now, at least, she knew where he would be returning to—the Hotel Darlinghurst, just around the corner from her place. She wondered, too, why Mr Vento, an out-of-towner, had not been staying with his daughter, and whether he had been around during the first murder, the night that Seymour Silva had died. Roxy already knew he was in town when Glad was killed—Tina had said as much when she'd rocked up to Oliver's office the day before—but Roxy wondered about Silva. Then she wondered about a motive and her brain went all fuzzy again.

One step at a time, Roxy told herself, then picked up the phone and put a call in to her local florist, ordering a large bouquet of wild Australian flowers. Judging from the bloke's appearance, they were more his style than roses. Then she asked for a note to be attached.

"Please mark it: *With our deepest sympathies. Tina was one of the greats. Love Maria and the whole* Glossy *magazine crew.*" She didn't think Maria would mind her using her name this way, not if there was a good story in it for the magazine. She gave the address of the hotel, paid for it by credit card and hung up. As she did so, she noticed the blinking answering machine light and tried to ignore it. There were messages from both David and Gilda, but she had a horrible hunch they wanted to discuss Saturday night further, and not the part she was most interested in. Roxy didn't want to be distracted, and she didn't want to get personal, so she ignored their messages and got on with what she loved most, her work.

She turned to her computer and started a file titled "Passionate" in which to record everything she knew about the erotic fiction writer. Despite ten years with the same agent, she was slightly embarrassed to find it did not add up to much. Just like her, they were both writers and both clients of Oliver Horowitz. But one was now dead, and her apparent murder would either make her a famous figure for life or cause her to fade away into obscurity. Time, I guess, will tell, thought Roxy.

And maybe this article if I do it right.

She heard a frenzied bubbling in the kitchen and jumped up to turn off the Atomic coffee machine and finish making breakfast. Eventually, with her toast eaten and the coffee half-drunk, she picked up the phone again and dialled Oliver.

"Aww, I dunno," he said after she'd told him of her plan. "I told you Lorenzo is a cranky bastard. You'll be lucky if he returns your calls, let alone talks to you."

"Don't worry about Lorenzo. I have my ways."

"Well tread carefully, okay? I mean, it could've been him for all we know."

"Well I'm not interviewing him for his good looks, Oliver. Do you know how long he's been in town and why he wasn't staying at Tina's place?"

"Her place is pretty swish, but it's the size of a portaloo. No room, I'd say. As for how long he's been around ... Dunno for sure but ... Listen, do you really think he's our man?"

"I have absolutely no idea, really I don't. Let's not get ahead of ourselves. I just need to get access to him and then see what he has to say. He's the one who found Tina's body, after all, so he might have some pivotal information. What I need from you is some background on Tina."

"Like what?"

"Like a proper biography, and I don't mean the PR drivel she runs on her book covers."

"Hey, I helped her write that drivel."

"Toughen up, Oliver, this is serious stuff. I'll interview you properly but it'll save me time if you can e-mail me a full rundown on when and where she started writing, how you got involved, a full list of her book titles, that sort of stuff."

"Consider it done."

"Good, and e-mail me any other contacts I should call for the story."

"Like who?"

"Like good girlfriends, any relevant exes. Was she ever married?"

"Yep, twice."

"Now why does that not surprise me?"

"Hey, careful, she was a good friend of mine."

"Sorry, force of habit. Can you get me the exes' details?"

"Yeah, I can source 'em somehow. Listen, Rox, take care of yourself, okay?"

"What, you think an ex-husband did her in, now?"

"I don't know what I think anymore. All I'm saying is watch your back."

"I always do, Olie, there's no one around to do it for me."

"Should I string my violin now or later?"

"Very funny. Just get that stuff to me as soon as you can, all right? Hey, how did your last chat with the cops go?"

"Short and sweet. They just wanted to clarify my whereabouts during Seymour's funeral and wake. Don't know what that's about but—"

"What did you tell them?"

"I told 'em I was with you and then with about thirty others at Venus's place."

"Did you go outside at all for a fag? On your own?"

"Jesus, Rox, you sound like the coppers. Yes, I did, Constable, but there were loads of people out there, too. Don't sweat it, Rox, I have all the witnesses I need."

"Okay, well, good," she said, but she was sweating it. The police were clearly still on Oliver's tail and she wished they'd start sniffing around elsewhere.

Roxy said good-bye to Oliver and turned to the newspapers she had run out for earlier that morning. There would be no more avoiding this story; she was in the thick of it now.

As expected, Tina Passion's sensational murder continued to dominate the front page of David Lone's paper, as it did the other major dailies and Internet news sites. The police had now confirmed that the erotic author had indeed met with foul play and that they were looking into all angles, including, yes, potential poisoning, but they refused to comment further until the toxicology results came back. Whenever that was.

No wonder they were asking Oliver about chemistry at high school, she thought. *It must be related to the poison.*

The competing newspapers, Roxy noticed, had now adopted Lone's catchphrase and were calling this "the Snow White" murder, but Lone had moved on. He was more interested in the serial killer angle, and while the police "categorically denied" this, clearly determined to keep the public calm, David made a good case.

Today's article included yet another break-out box featuring the similarities between all three deaths, this time, with Tina Passion in the mix. The calling card for this "third tragic murder" was, according to David, a poisoned apple and it was used to symbolize "both the romantic nature of Tina's work (hence the link to the Snow White fairy tale) and women's ultimate erotic sin—the handing of the forbidden fruit to Adam".

Was he suggesting that Tina was responsible for her own murder? That her salacious, risqué content had led to this? Or was that what the murderer intended all along?

She felt a chill run through her and shuddered. In any case, David had been spot on from the start. He had insisted that Seymour Silva's death was suspicious, and no one had listened to him. After William's murder, he had intensified his insistence, begging people to see the connection, and again, this was largely rejected. Even Roxy, normally open-minded and unapologetically suspicious, refused to validate his fears. And now they had come to fruition. Roxy winced at the pun but couldn't dredge up a smile.

Tina Passion was dead, and David Lone had predicted it all along. She wondered, now, whether there was any way it could have been prevented, if only people had listened to him.

Roxy returned to the papers, methodically cutting out each article, but instead of pasting them away in her scrapbook as she normally would, she placed them in a fresh Manila folder. She would need to refer to them in her article. Then, she sat back in front of her computer and began a new document in the Passionate file. She typed several paragraphs of notes, starting with her first memories of meeting the writer to that last day in which Tina burst into Oliver's office buzzing with excitement about their impending date. Roxy remembered the way Tina had largely ignored her in deference to the two men in the room and guessed it was normal behaviour. She knew that kind of woman well. It reminded her a little of her mother—always putting men first, especially older, richer men. Roxy sniggered then, knowing only too well how horrified Lorraine would be to be considered in the same sentence as the trashy writer. Yet, it was women like her mother, or at least her mother's neighbour Valerie, who lapped up Tina's semi-erotic novels.

"I'd better start with one of those," she decided, opening her e-mail account to find Oliver's message waiting. He'd sent her a list of contact names and numbers to call, and she quickly pressed reply then jotted a message of her own.

Thanks, Olie. Another favour: can you get the full collection of Tina's books together for me? I'll drop by later today to pick them up. Rox xo

He e-mailed her straight back: *You sure you don't have a well-thumbed one under your pillow somewhere?*

Not my style, she replied.

Pity, he wrote back, *might do wonders for your love life.*

What love life? she typed then added, *Good to see your humour's returned* before clicking off and getting back to work. While Roxy was using this article as her way in, she was also taking it seriously and hadn't been lying when she told Maria she needed the work. She might as well get paid while she investigated.

Over the next few hours, Roxy began tracking down the various relatives and friends of Tina's that Oliver had suggested, getting useful quotes about the forty-something's life, but also, surreptitiously, ascertaining who had last seen her and who had any idea why she had been murdered. It turned out not one of the people on Roxy's list had spent any time with Tina in the past week of her life. And no one seemed to have any idea why she had been targeted, although a cackling older neighbour suggested her writing was so bad, it could easily be a motive.

Tina's cousin Brianna, however, did have something useful to say. She was fifteen years younger than Tina, she gushed over the phone from her rural home of Moree, and had always found Tina "soooo inspirational and that!" Despite this, they had "all felt a bit sorry for her, really."

"Why?" Roxy asked down the scratchy phone line.

"Oh, just cause of her dad and that."

"Lorenzo?"

"Yeah, eh. He kinda, you know, was always naggin' her and sayin' she ought write something respectable and stuff, like he was embarrassed, but I mean what the hell was he doing with his life?! Growin' a bit of cotton! Whoopee-doo! There was nothin' wrong with what Tina wrote. We loved it. Well, Mum and me sisters did, eh? Reckon me brothers read her stuff too but they wouldn't admit it. Book reading! Ha!"

"So Tina's dad wanted her to stop writing?"

"Yeah, think so. And aw, man, he was real cut up when she went and did that *Playboy* spread." She laughed. "Friggin' hell, Tina couldn't come home for a year after that. Not that she wanted to! Why would ya wanna come to boonsville Moree when you live in Sydney, eh?"

Roxy couldn't argue with that. "Do you think Lorenzo ever tried to stop Tina from writing?"

"Dunno, but he never wanted to talk about it. Got ribbed a lot down at the local pub and that. One time someone stuck Tina's centrefold to the dunny door, well, you can imagine how that went down." There was a sudden ruckus at the other end. "Fuckin' hell, Jayden, put that digger down! Shit, gotta go, eh, kids are tearin' the place apart. Listen, you gonna quote me and all that?"

"Well ... maybe ..."

"Epic! Can't wait. Okay, better go ... Jayden ... Jaaaay—!"

The phone went dead and Roxy smiled. Thank God for awestruck younger cousins. She thought about what Brianna had said and wondered whether Lorenzo Vento had finally had enough of being ashamed by his daughter's novels. That would certainly link in with David's "forbidden fruit" premise.

It would also explain Lorenzo's aggression towards Oliver. He must have hated the agent that enabled Tina's work to get out there. *Did he hate him enough,* she wondered, *to set him up for three murders?*

It seemed like a long shot but she was short on other options. Roxy already knew from what Tina had told her, that her father had been in town around the time she was murdered, so he certainly had opportunity, and now perhaps, he also had motive. Perhaps he had finally had enough of her salacious writing. Perhaps he had placed the poisoned apple as a message to others.

Roxy thought about this some more. Being ashamed of your child's chosen profession was one thing. Killing them for it was quite another, but she tried not to let sense get in the way of a good motive.

By late afternoon, Roxy had made considerable progress on the Tina Passion article, transcribing several interviews and constructing a rough outline. Tonight she would focus on Tina's books, speed-reading the most popular ones, including the first and last ones published. There was one more book, Oliver reminded her when she trudged back up the stairs of his city office to collect them that afternoon. It was to be her tenth novel and had been finished, but was still at the final editing stage.

"Can I see the proof?" Roxy asked.

"What for?"

"I don't know, just to see where her head was at when she died. Maybe ..." she stopped.

"Maybe there's a clue in there somewhere—pointing to the suspect?"

It was another long shot but she was growing increasingly desperate. No one seemed to have any idea why Tina had died, and even her father's obvious disapproval didn't seem a strong enough motive.

"Well, we only got two proofs mocked up," he told her. "Tina had one but there's no way you can get into her place, the cops have it sealed, and I sent the other one to her editor for a final read. I can see if I can get it back."

"That'd be good. I do think it's important."

"Fine, I'll hassle her for it. But you have to promise not to publish any of it, not until I get her dad's permission. He hates me enough as it is. I'm going to have to avoid him at the funeral. Speaking of which—"

"Of course I'll be there. When is it?"

"Actually there won't be a proper funeral for a while, it's still a murder investigation at this stage, but friends of Tina's are holding a memorial service in Gibson's Park near her place Friday lunch time, and it'd be great if you could come. I'm not sure I'll be the most welcome person there. Be good to have some support. I can pick you up—"

"No, no, no," she said quickly, "my eardrums are still recovering from our last trip together. I'll make my own way, thanks. So what about William Glad? When does he finally get laid to rest?"

"Not sure. Coroner still won't release the body, but Erin thinks it might happen later this week. No plans for a memorial service, not that I've heard of anyway. Then again, Erin probably won't invite me."

"I know the cops are snooping around, Oliver, but surely Erin knows you didn't do it."

He shrugged. "She's acting a bit strange, although she is

still talking to me at this point, so I guess I should count my blessings."

"So what's happening with those gardening guides you were going to release together? Weren't you—"

He held a finger to his lips. "Shhh! Don't even go there, okay?! The cops have been asking all sorts of questions about that, like it could be motive or something."

Roxy's heart sank. She had said something to Gilda about this, and now felt responsible, but Oliver was pointing the finger firmly back at Erin.

"She's been blabbing to the cops, acting like it was all my idea. Traitor."

"Do the police believe her?"

"I don't know, hope not. But it's just crazy. I mean, I wouldn't kill the old man for some bloody gardening books. I'm not that hard up for sales."

Roxy agreed it was crazy and let it drop. She got to her feet and gave him a quick kiss before trudging off with Tina's novels in a green bag by her side.

That evening, Roxy went through Tina's collection, first reading the back cover blurb for each one. She didn't know what she was looking for but she was hoping that maybe there was a Snow White-style plot amongst them, something to work from. Yet nothing leapt out and she decided that she really needed to get her hands on that final book, the one in the proofing stage.

The phone rang shrilly, and noticing it was from the *Glossy* offices, she quickly picked it up. "Hello, Maria," she said and the older woman cackled.

"You're gonna love me. I just got that hunky friend of yours a gig."

"Sorry?"

"Max Farrell can do the photos, for your Tina Passion story. He charges like a wounded bull these days but I reckon it'll be worth it."

She felt her heart stop. She gulped. "I don't think that's

necessary, Mari—"

"It's done, darls! My Art Director's already had a quiet word and he's on it. Says he'd love to do it and awaits your call. Just let him know when you tee up the interviews and he can tag along and get the snaps. We want it a bit photo-journo like, not too stiff, black and white, bit moody, that kind of thing. Okay, gotta go, but you can thank me later for that one."

She hung up and Roxy gulped again. Max Farrell. *Damn it, now there was no more avoiding him.*

CHAPTER 21

"You're avoiding me," David Lone said, his blue eyes sparkling mischievously.

"Am not," Roxy replied defensively, aware she hadn't returned his calls for two days. "I've just been busy, you know that."

He laughed. "You're so easy to bait."

"I'm not fish, David."

"And there you go again. Hook, line, sinker ..."

It was late Wednesday night and they were seated at the bar of a Kings Cross hotel. David had rung several times to ask Roxy out and eventually, feeling wired, she had agreed. But only if they met close to her place.

"And only for one!" she had told him, but was already onto her second merlot. New habits die hard. The bar, Glenda's, was one of the least seedy in the area, with moody lighting and plush lounge chairs, but Roxy didn't want to get too comfortable so had opted to stay perched on stiff stools up at the counter. She no longer trusted herself, at least not around David Lone.

"So what's the latest?" she asked and he held his head to the side.

"I'm not sure I should be revealing anything to you. We're competition now, aren't we?"

"Hardly. I'm just doing a lifestyle piece on Tina. It's a monthly mag, David, any info I put in about her death now will be old news by the time it sees the light of a newsstand." He relaxed a little at this. "You're ferociously competitive, you know."

"It's how I got to where I am now."

"And where is that exactly?"

"Sharing a few drinks with the sexiest writer in Sydney," he replied as she rolled her eyes.

"You really do aim to make a girl uncomfortable, don't you?"

"What? By complimenting her? Most women lap it up."

"Well, I'm not most women."

"I'm beginning to work that one out."

She crossed her legs and stared into her wine glass. "So ..."

"So?" he echoed.

"So what's the latest on the infamous Snow White murder?"

"So this is why you agreed to meet up? You want to grill me?"

She smiled sweetly. "Just for a little while. I am an Australian writer, after all. Finding out the latest might just save my life."

"Gee, I hope you're not next on the hit list. I can think of quite a few writers I'd bump off before I got to you!"

Her smile dissolved. "You think he's going to strike again?"

His own smile deflated as well. "I certainly hope not. I'm sorry, I really shouldn't joke about this. It's not at all funny, is it? Okay, what can I tell you, you've read the papers yourself. They're all such sheep, aren't they, the press? They would have called it Tinagate if I hadn't come up with my great line."

"So the apple really was poisoned?"

"Yes it was. According to my sources, strychnine may have been used, that's still being verified."

"Strychnine? How very Agatha Christie!"

"I know. Tina had also been struck from behind as we thought, by a large metal object. Killed first and then the apple placed in her mouth."

"So did the poison kill her or the blow to the head?"

Someone called out David's name and he glanced around and waved. It was a pretty young thing, someone Roxy vaguely recalled from a reality TV show, and she was smiling at David flirtatiously but he ignored her and turned back to Roxy.

"The poison ... I'd say, but we don't know for sure, yet."

"Why would someone do that? Do you really think it's to leave a message?"

"Absolutely. And for dramatic effect. But then who knows what's in the mind of a serial killer."

Roxy felt a slight shudder. "So do you think this person is a sicko or is there some kind of motive?"

"There's always a motive."

"Not always. Plenty of people do kill in the heat of passion."

"Yes, but this was clearly planned. Orchestrated to the last degree. Maybe the first death was spontaneous. Not the next two."

"So, then, what was Oliver Horowitz's motive?"

He took a long sip of his wine and then placed it down and turned his stool around to face her.

"You need to look at the facts, Roxy, you need to put your emotions aside."

"I find that hard to do," she said glumly and he nodded.

"Fair enough, but it's vital you get some perspective. And it's vital, for just a few minutes here, that you let me play devil's advocate. You're usually good at that but now it's my turn, okay?" She nodded reluctantly and he held up a finger. "Let's consider the first death, Seymour Silva. Did you know the police are now backtracking on the suicide verdict?

They're reopening the case?" She nodded again. "So, Seymour Silva, what possible motive would Oliver have to kill that poor man? Well, there was the small matter of him sacking Oliver as his agent a few weeks before he died."

"That was months earlier and Oliver blames his manager Norm for that. Not Seymour."

"So he says. And it was just six weeks earlier, actually. Ask Oliver. Perhaps he was still so angry and wanted to teach him a lesson? What better lesson than to kill the goose who laid the golden egg? Norm's books were hot property thanks to Seymour and his supposed alien abduction. That was the drawcard. With Seymour dead, Norm was just another writer. Think about it, Roxy, Oliver had kept their dirty little secret for years and instead of repaying him, they go and ditch him, say they don't need him anymore. That's got to cut." He paused. "So maybe Oliver got cutting ..." He indicated his wrist and slashed it left and right. She gave him a withering look. "Sorry, I'm getting carried away." He held up a second finger. "Now to William Glad's death: Oliver's motive there is very clear."

"How so?"

"Don't you recall, he told us himself, he had been begging old William to release his back catalogue for years. A very lucrative back catalogue, I might add. Now Glad's out of the way, Oliver and Erin are free to do just that."

She shook her head furiously. She had already thought this through. "It's nonsensical, David. William Glad was dying. Oliver knew that. Erin knew that. Why murder him when he'll be dead in a few days anyway? Then you can publish anything you like."

He flashed her a confident smile. "Ah yes, but did you know William had asked his daughter to arrange a bedside meeting with his lawyer before he died?" The look of surprise on her face was all the answer he needed. "It never came to pass but you've got to wonder what that was about. Maybe William was going to change his will and *insist* the books never be published, maybe they had to kill him before he did it."

"How do you know about the lawyer?"

He tapped his nose, saying nothing, and held up finger number three. "Now to Tina Passion, the third murder. That motive, I'm sorry to say, is as old as the bible. Older even."

"Oh?"

"Love, of course. Unrequited love to be more specific. The worst kind of love. That one you can't dispute."

"Oh, come on, David, I know Olie had a soft spot for Tina, but—"

"A soft spot? The guy had a hard-on, was gagging for it, and she played hard to get. Oliver must have been sick to death of her games, her constant teasing. You and I saw it for ourselves, that last time she came to his office. So he took her out to dinner, walked her back to her place, tried his luck yet again and yet again she laughed him off. That's really got to hurt. He's unbalanced as it is by now, having killed two other writers for money and revenge. So he follows her in, tries to have his merry way. When that doesn't work, he hits her over the head and then plants the poisoned apple to make it look like a serial nutcase."

She was growing increasingly frustrated by all of this. "So where did Oliver get poison from? Out of his back pocket? No way, that death was clearly premeditated, you just said so yourself. Somebody took time to arrange that one carefully, to source poison, an apple ..."

"Maybe it was a crime of passion as you call it, then he left, fetched some poison from his place or from the convenience store. The shopkeeper already said he bought a bunch of stuff."

"But there's no proof he bought poison! Or even an apple for that matter. Besides, if it turns out to be strychnine, isn't that tricky to get these days? From what I've read, it's banned almost across the board. It's not 1940 and available as rat poison at every supermarket."

"Who knows, but you still can get it, I think, if you're clever, and Oliver is pretty clever. He might have had some at home. He could've fetched it from his place and returned to Tina's to make it look premeditated."

She laughed then, feeling the ridiculousness of what he was saying and a little relieved, too. It was so outlandish, surely the police would see that.

"Well, that's how I see it," David said, moodily, "And it's how the public will, too." He looked away and took a long gulp of his drink.

There was no laughter now. "You're not?" she said. "You are not putting all of that in tomorrow's paper. Tell me you are not?" She yanked his arm and he looked back at her.

"Not quite, I can get my butt sued, you know that. The lawyers have amended a few things, but that's the general gist."

Roxy pushed her stool back and stood up. "Unbelievable!"

He stood up, too. "Hey, Roxanne, don't be like this."

"Like what?"

"I thought you understood, this is what we do, this is how we get our headlines."

She shook her head at him. "This is all conjecture. Your theories sound absurd to me. You haven't convinced me at all. Where's your evidence? Where's your proof?"

"I'm not saying he did it, I'm just throwing suggestions around."

"In a national newspaper that will kill Oliver's career, if it doesn't kill him first. You need to go to your office and pull the presses. Now!"

He shook his head. "It's done, Roxanne. It's too late."

"Then we're done, too," she said, reaching down to collect her handbag. He tried to grab her hand but she shook him off.

"Come on. This is ridiculous."

"Maybe it is, but Oliver is more than my agent, he's my good friend, and I thought he was your friend, too. I thought you'd have some heart. And I thought you were going to come to me first."

"I tried to. I called you yesterday, you didn't phone me back, remember? So I'm telling you now."

She cringed. He was right. She had ignored his calls for forty-eight hours thinking only about herself, her embarrassment over her behaviour Saturday night. Perhaps if she'd swallowed her pride, she could have had time to stop David's toxic article.

As if reading her mind, he said, "The story's not as bad as you think—"

"It better not be, David, because if you hang him out to dry, I'm done. With you, with the book. I'm done."

She stormed out, leaving him looking perplexed behind her. But she didn't care. She was furious with the way things were working out. She knew now that she had to accelerate her investigations, she had to help Oliver and she had to help him fast. No more pussy footing around.

It was time to call Tina's father.

CHAPTER 22

Lorenzo Vento was not at all what Roxy had been expecting. Yes, he had a gruff exterior and yes, he was clearly ashamed of his daughter's chosen profession, but he was polite enough and eager to please when she finally sat down in front of him over a cooked breakfast at the small café on the ground floor of the Hotel Darlinghurst. Keen to "set the record straight" he'd been thrilled when she'd called that Thursday morning offering her condolences on behalf of *Glossy* magazine, and requesting a face-to-face interview.

He hadn't heard of *Glossy* before receiving the flowers but that didn't seem to matter. He was just happy that somebody—*anybody*—wanted to write something positive about his daughter. And that's exactly how Roxy had sold the interview to him, as a "celebration of a much-loved Australian icon". She left all mention of her relationship with Oliver out of it. She didn't want to muddy the waters or turn him off.

"At last, a somebody understands!" he'd said in his thick Italian accent, and suggested they meet for breakfast at his hotel in twenty minutes.

It was sooner than Roxy had expected and she had

scrambled to throw something suitably conservative looking on, grabbed her digital recorder and raced down the three blocks to where he was staying.

"I leave a this afternoon, so you are in luck," he told her as she slipped into the booth across from him and ordered an espresso coffee. She normally liked her coffee weak and milky, but spotting the small espresso glass before him, decided to play every card she could get her grubby mitts on. So espresso it would be.

She noticed, too, that he had several of Tina's books in a green bag beside him, and this surprised her. She thought he would have burned them all by now.

"You're not staying for the memorial service?" Roxy asked and he shook his head firmly.

"Oh no, no, no. This is not a really for me. This is for the young ones. My memories of my Christina, they are in a here." He thumped his chest with a closed fist. "And in a here." He tapped his head with one calloused finger. "And they are at Christina's home, Moree."

Roxy nodded, wondering what Tina would think of all that, including his use of her full name, and whether it made her cringe but she kept that to herself and just smiled.

Oliver had already sent Roxy a full dossier on Tina and her father, and she knew from what she'd read and what she'd gleaned from interviews with other family and friends, that Lorenzo had migrated from Sicily, in Southern Italy, before Tina was born to set up a cotton farm in rural Moree. His Italian wife had not lasted long, running off with the local butcher, a younger Australian guy called Mitch, which scandalised the small rural community at the time, and turned Lorenzo into a fanatical moral crusader for life. Unluckily for him, his daughter had more of her mother in her than he liked, and despite his endless protests and lectures, she had forged her own path, fleeing Moree at just seventeen years of age and starting a life of "loose living" in Sydney ever since.

Today, Lorenzo did not want to talk about that side.

Instead, he was keen to tell Roxy all about the Tina of old, or, more correctly, the young Christina, a girl he described as "devoutly Catholic" and "innocent through and through".

With their breakfast in place, Roxy got straight to it, pressing play on her recorder and beginning the interview process. She did not feel disingenuous, nor did she feel like a fraud. She *would* write a flattering article about Tina Passion, that bit was true. But if, along the way, she could gather more information about the murder and potentially save Oliver's bacon, that would be an added bonus.

For the first twenty minutes or so, Roxy let Lorenzo ramble on about his "*bellisimo* baby girl" and her "innocent childhood". He had his own agenda too, she could see that. He wanted to absolve himself of any blame, not so much for the manner of her death as for the way in which she had lived. He went to great lengths to emphasise her love of Jesus and of her good grades at school.

"She such a sweet girl," he said, not for the first time, "so innocent, so *good*."

She let him continue in this vein a little longer than she normally would but it couldn't go on too much longer. She glanced surreptitiously at her watch. Max would be here in twenty minutes, or at least she hoped he would. Unable to face the call, she had sent him a text message on her way to the hotel, alerting him of her impromptu interview and asking him to show up in an hour to take the photos. She hadn't received a reply so hoped he was free and available, but she couldn't think about that now. The real reason she was here was to get some information, and it was time to get on with it. She took a deep breath and then gently steered Lorenzo to the present, and to the week of his daughter's murder.

"You've been in town for the past few weeks," she said softly. "That must have been a privilege to spend Tin ... I mean Christina's last days with her."

He looked up, frowned slightly. "Yes, I come a week ago last a Saturday. I had not a seen Tina for many months, so I come a to Sydney to see her. To tell her to come home." He looked down. "Always she say no." He looked up at her again. "If only she had come a home ... Maybe she would ..." He choked, looked away again.

Roxy let him gather himself while she added it up. If he was telling the truth, Lorenzo had arrived the morning after David Lone's premiere. The morning *after* Seymour Silva died. She felt disappointed and then suspicious.

"And you drove all the way down from Moree? Or do you fly?"

"I like to drive. I can not a stomach the airo-planes. This is not for me."

"Wow, that's a long journey, and such devotion to see your daughter. How long does it normally take you? To drive down, I mean?"

"It's not so far. Eight hours, depending on the traffic. That's why I drive through the night, not so much traffic at night."

She wondered if there was much traffic the night he drove down and if there were any witnesses or CCTV footage of him on the highway. Or had he had snuck off earlier and arrived into Sydney on Friday night, in time to kill Seymour, then pretended to show up fresh on Saturday morning?

Then she wondered, yet again, as she watched him chew slowly on his eggs and bacon looking like a man whose heart had been crushed to smithereens, what possible motive this sad old man would have for killing his own daughter, let alone two relative strangers. A loathing for her books and her agent did not seem strong enough. It was time to get serious.

"I have to ask, Mr Vento, so please don't be upset, but did you know the other two writers who recently died?" She braced herself but he didn't seem at all perturbed by this line of questioning, almost as if he had been expecting it.

"I do not know this man Silva, and I do not know the gardening man. They are strangers to me," he said. "And I do not think they have anything to do with my beautiful Christina."

"What *do* you think?"

He pushed his plate away and leaned back in his chair. "I think some crazy man has done this. Some sex-crazy fan has tried to have his way with my beautiful Christina and she has fought a back and she has been killed."

Now his anger was rising and she knew what was coming. He launched into a tirade about erotic fiction and how "poor, foolish Christina" was dancing with the devil each time she published a book. He kept glancing down at the books by his side, and back again. "And don't a start me on Oliver Horowitz." He humphed. "The police they think he did it and, okay, so I don't believe a this, but let him suffer!"

Roxy did a double take. "You *don't* think Oliver did this?"

"No, no, no. Not this Oliver Horowitz." He almost laughed. "He too weak for this. He is a spineless poofter but he not killer."

It was the nicest thing anyone had said about Roxy's agent in days, and she smiled. She also wanted to tell Mr Vento that Oliver was not the gutless wonder he had created in his head; he was a good man, an honest man, a man who had such a soft spot for Lorenzo's daughter he would have killed for her in fact, but now was not the time or the place, so she let it pass She almost told him, too, that she was one of Oliver's clients, just like Tina had been. She had a nagging feeling that she should 'fess up, that it would come back to bite her one day, but she took the gutless option and stayed quiet.

She would eventually come to regret that.

"Mr Vento, you said that you think your daughter was killed by a stalker or a crazy fan. What makes you think that?"

He shifted in his seat, shrugged, looking suddenly uncomfortable. "The police a, they say I no speak a, I have to keep quiet."

Not if she could help it. "Mr Vento, my article won't appear for two or three months as this is a monthly magazine and it works way ahead, so nothing you tell me can harm the case. It will be old news by then."

Okay, so this was not strictly true but she was grasping at straws. The more time she spent with Vento the less she was convinced of his guilt. Which left her with a big fat zero. He looked at her as if he didn't believe her, then he smiled—a craggy, kindly smile.

"I tell you because I like you. You good girl." She gave him her most pious smile in return. "When I find Christina ..." He stopped, choked a little, a tear swelling in one eye. "When I find my beautiful baby girl ..." Again the tears but there was anger now too flashing across his face and Roxy placed one hand gently on his to urge him on. "Lots of her books have been slashed to pieces and there is one a missing."

"Oh?"

"Yes, the new one, it is gone. Tina showed me this one last a week. She was reading it, she called it something like a evidence?"

"A proof? That would have been her proof copy."

"Yes. I look a everywhere for it. I hope to take it away so that Oliver man can not make more money from it, but it was a gone. And I am happy. I hope it never comes back. Now he cannot publish it and destroy my baby one more time from the grave."

Again, not strictly true. The editor had a copy, so did several computer hard drives, but she wasn't about to tell him that. She wanted to get hold of that book now more than ever. If Lorenzo was telling the truth, then the murderer had clearly stolen it.

Why? Was there something in that book that gave him away?

She made a mental note to ask Oliver about it when she got the chance.

The tears were welling up in Lorenzo's eyes again and she glanced at her watch. Max was due any minute now and she had so much more she wanted to ask.

"And why do you think all of this indicates a stalker?" If anything it seemed to implicate a father who was dead set against her books.

"This is not all. The police they tell me there was one strange number that was calling Christina's house all that night, leaving no message, but calling, calling ..."

Now this was interesting.

"Can they track the call? Do they know who it was?"

He shook his head sadly. "No, it is not a number that we know. It is not my number. It is not a number for any of her friends. This is why I think it is a stalker who wanted my baby girl and when he couldn't get her, he destroyed her."

Just then Max arrived. *Great timing,* she thought crankily, she had so much she still wanted to ask, but it was clear that Lorenzo was getting weary so it was probably just as well. She stood up as Max approached the table, clutching his camera bag, and made the introductions while the two men shook hands.

"Thanks for coming on such short notice," she said and he nodded quickly before pulling her aside.

"So how do you want to work this? Lighting's not real great in here. Can I take him outside?"

No small talk, no chit-chat, just straight to it, and she didn't blame him. The last time Max had tried to talk to her she'd slammed the door in his face.

"You're the expert, do whatever you think's best." She turned back to Lorenzo. "How much more time have we got before you need to head off? You've got quite a drive ahead of you."

"Hornsby is not so far."

"Oh, you're not heading back home to Moree today?"

"No, no. I go to stay with my cousin, Fabio, he has a big house in Hornsby. I cannot stay here for any longer as it is too expensive for me."

"So how long are you staying with him?" she asked, adding, "Just in case I need to check a few facts with you?"

"For a week, maybe more. I hope the police can release my beautiful baby so I can take her home." He looked at his watch. "I leave in about a one hour."

"That'll do it," Max said, opening up his camera case and setting to work.

Forty minutes later, Lorenzo bid them good-bye and returned to his room to pack up while Roxy called the waitress over to pay the bill. *Glossy* would reimburse her later. Max was also back at the table, putting his gear away, so Roxy asked, "Did you want a freebie coffee or something before you head off?"

He glanced up, shook his head then returned to his camera. The look in his eyes was not so much cold as detached, and again, she had to wear it. She nodded at the waitress who strode off to tally the bill, and watched silently as Max cleaned his lenses and placed the camera back gently into its cushioned slot in his camera case. When he was done, he clicked it shut, stood up and brushed a stray lock from his face.

"Any other pix I need to take for this *Glossy* article?"

"Well, there is the memorial service tomorrow ..."

"I'll be there, just text me the time and place."

"Look, Max, I'm really sorry about the other day—"

"Don't worry about it," he said, then he picked up the case, smiled stiffly and walked away while Roxy's heart lurched heavily, then went into freefall.

CHAPTER 23

By lunchtime on Friday, Roxy had almost finished a full rough draft of the Tina Passion article and was changing out of cargo pants into yet another demure black dress for the writer's memorial service at an inner-city park. She had been wearing a few too many black dresses lately, she thought sadly, as she slipped it on.

The park was small, just a few blocks from Tina's townhouse, and it was jammed full of people when Roxy turned up, all of them dressed brightly in vivid colours, tight, revealing clothes, and enormous flowers in their hair. She needn't have worn the dress after all, she realized, and lurked near the gate, watching as they gathered in the centre just to the side of an enormous fig tree.

Someone had placed tall bamboo poles with lurid scarlet flags at intervals around a wide circle, and the crowd were gathering there, kissing and hugging and holding hands. She spotted Oliver on one side and raised a hand to him. He said something to a tall, skinny woman with a bright magenta kaftan and flowing grey hair, and then made his way across to her.

"Thanks for coming, Rox," he said, giving her a warm

hug. "I really appreciate it."

"No worries, Oliver. Are you okay?"

He didn't look okay. Despite the bright Hawaiian shirt, his pallor was even greyer than the last time they'd met, and he looked like he'd lost weight. Dark bags hung under both eyes and they were darting around everywhere as if looking out for trouble.

"Anyone giving you a hard time?" she asked and when he didn't answer her she said, "You might have mentioned the dress code, Olie. I stand out like a virgin at a key party."

He glanced back at her, as though only noticing her for the first time and he tried for a smile. Couldn't quite pull it off. "Sorry, yes, Tina's friends all thought we should dress as Tina would like, you know, bright and cheerful, that kind of stuff."

More cheap and cheerful, she thought as she glanced around at the lurid Lycra and fake breasts, but she wasn't about to split hairs with him. Not today.

"I see Max is on the job," he said and she followed his eyes across the park to the other side where the photographer was busy setting up a tripod. At just that moment he looked up and caught her eyes, and she felt herself blush. She smiled weakly and he smiled back then returned to his tripod.

"You two friends again?" Oliver asked and she shrugged. "Well, Roxy, all I'm gonna say is life's too bloody short—that's what you need to take away from today." He looked back towards the throng who were now positioning themselves, holding hands and settling down for the ceremony, which was clearly being led by the tall, skinny woman Oliver had just been chatting to. "You going to join us? Veruna says she'll start any minute now."

"No, you go. I'll hang back here if that's all right."

"Oh shit, here comes Davo," Oliver suddenly announced. "I'm outta here. Can't believe he has the audacity ... Don't let that traitor anywhere near me." He darted back towards the main crowd.

Roxy turned around and watched as David Lone finished parking his car just beyond the gate, in a no parking zone. As he stepped out, he caught sight of her and waved.

"Hello!" he called out as he approached. "You well? You look great."

"I'm in black. Apparently it's no longer *de rigueur* at funerals." She noticed he was wearing a dark suit and wondered if he'd also missed the memo. She also noticed that he was still talking to her despite her cranky outburst at the bar a few days earlier. He clearly had a tough hide and she suspected he was used to abuse in his line of work. She decided not to mention it.

"Has it started yet?" he asked.

She craned her eyes to the circle and watched as the skinny woman held her hands up to quiet the crowd. "Any moment," she said. "So, what have you done now?"

He blinked several times. "Sorry?"

"Oliver took one look at you and bolted. Should I prepare myself for another horrible story in the *Tele*?"

"None of my stories are horrible, you should know that," he said, smiling. "No, don't worry about Oliver. He's just a sore loser, that's all."

"What do you mean? What's going on?"

He shrugged. "So I switched agents, big deal."

Roxy's eyes widened. "Really? You've dumped Oliver?" He shrugged again as if it didn't mean very much at all and she felt her temper rise. She didn't want to yell at him today, to lose control, but he wasn't making it easy. "You don't seriously think Oliver did this? You don't think he murdered three people?"

He looked at her deadpan. "If I did I'd hardly try to piss him off further by dumping him as my agent. That'd be suicide. I'd be next on the hit list." She didn't look impressed by this, so he quickly added, "Whether Oliver's guilty or not is irrelevant. This is a purely commercial decision, Roxanne. Oliver is no use to me while he's under a dark cloud. You've seen him. He's preoccupied, he's vague, he's a mess."

"Thanks in part to you!" she snapped, her anger boiling over. *So much for staying in control.*

"Hey, I'm not the enemy here, Roxanne. Don't keep taking it out on me."

She tried to calm down. "Sorry, but I just don't get it. So he's having a bad week. Why dump him?"

"It's simple. I haven't got a week to waste. I need to get on with my career, and my new agent can help me do that. It's Amy Halloran, have you heard of her?"

The name did ring a bell, thought Roxy, but it was probably because there weren't that many agents in the country.

"She's amazing," David was gushing. "Really dynamic, loads of energy. You should meet her, you'd love her. I can't believe I wasn't with her all along, to be honest. Been with her one day and she's already signed me up for a book deal on these murders. Oliver never even thought of it. Amy's keen to get your book going as well."

"Whoah! Hang on, a book deal on the murders? What, Tina's, William's and Seymour's?"

He nodded. "Yep, Amy likes my 'Last Writes' theory and has sold the idea to Penguin. I need to get the first draft to them within the month."

"But it's not even solved yet."

"It will be by then."

She stared hard at him. "What do you know? What are you not telling me?"

He smiled. "Don't you worry about that. As I say, the good news for you is Penguin also wants the book you're doing on me, so you really need to get cracking on that one, too. I'll have to make some time for you, obviously, but you have lots of names and contacts you can interview in the meantime. Start with my English teacher. As I told you, she adored me." He winked. "How long before you finish the Tina article?"

"It's almost done. Was just going to add a few notes from

today, then get it in."

"Good, then can you get onto my book? Is that going to work for you? We really don't want to muck around."

"But what about Oliver? I thought he was a partner in all this."

David shook his head firmly, raising one hand to wave at someone in the distance. "Nope, no way, Amy has looked at the contract and says we can easily cut and run. We never finished signing it properly, anyway. She suggests we sign up with her and get the book done within the month as well. Bring both books out together. Such a great idea, the sort of thing Oliver wouldn't have dreamed of. This is going to be huge, Roxy, really huge! For both of us!"

Roxy recoiled. "I don't want to cut and run from Oliver," she began and he looked at her with such disappointment in his eyes.

Just then a loud "Whoop!" came from the circle and they both watched for a few minutes as a large man began fluttering rose petals in the air while several others danced around him, singing some high-pitched song.

Bloody hippies, she wanted to say but she kept it to herself.

"When are you going to learn?" David said eventually and Roxy turned back to him.

"Learn what?"

"Learn that you have to do what's right for you sometimes." He indicated towards Max who was moving around the circle, madly taking snaps. "You let all these other people lead you on, dance around with your life. Oliver's been the worst. You should have earned a stack load more from your last two books. My new agent would have got you twice what Oliver got. They were superb stories, brilliantly written. He should have at least negotiated to get your name on them."

"I'm a ghostwriter, David, that's the whole point."

"Rubbish," he snapped and then, noticing he'd turned a few heads, dropped his tone a little. "A good agent could have worked around that. *You* wrote those books, Roxanne, not those old snobs. Your name should have been front and centre."

She was dumbfounded. She didn't care about that but he hadn't finished his lecture.

"Have you ever stopped to ask, 'What do I want? What's going to make me happy?'" He waved again at someone at the other end of the park and turned towards her, staring deeply into her eyes. "What's wrong with being ambitious, Roxy, what's wrong with making some bloody money out of all this horror?" Now he was indicating the ceremony, which was in full swing, the skinny woman warbling a woeful tune while the crowd bowed their heads mournfully.

Roxy wanted to tell him he had her pegged all wrong, he didn't know her at all, that she didn't care about money or ambition or selling her friends for any of it, but there was a small side of her that stalled. That said, "Maybe you should!"

She thought then of David's spacious home and his luxury furnishings, she thought of his glamorous film launch and his seemingly endless book deals, and she wondered, suddenly, if maybe he was right. Maybe she needed to stop standing under the shade and demand her time in the sun. Perhaps there was a grander destiny for her than a crappy little unit in Elizabeth Bay and lonely dinners with her mother and Charlie while pining for a man who just wasn't right.

"There's Tina's ex-husband, I need to get a quote," David said, oblivious to the turmoil he had stirred up inside her, and he dashed off, a digital recorder suddenly appearing in one hand.

Roxy watched him go then glanced towards Max who was still snapping away, his camera now focused on Oliver who was in the middle of the circle, holding hands with two glammed up women who might easily be men. Roxy felt suddenly deeply sad. This time it was not Tina or Oliver for whom she mourned, but herself and her confused, messed up, going nowhere life.

Tina's memorial service wrapped up after a loud and colourful hour and the motley crowd of hippies, tarts and transvestites eventually headed off to a local pub, Oliver leading the charge. Roxy told him she'd see him there later, and made her way over to Max who was back beside his tripod putting his gear away.

"Get everything?" she asked, and he looked up surprised to see her.

"Oh, Roxy, hi. Yes, I think so. You're not going to the wake?"

"I'll follow on soon enough. Just wanted to see how you're going."

"Well, I think I covered most of it. Got some good shots of the celebrant, and that fat yogi guy. Surreal memorial service, eh?"

She nodded. "I meant how are *you*. How are you going?"

"Oh," he glanced at her and away. "I'm okay, Roxy, I'm always okay."

"Good." She paused. "I'm not sure Oliver is, though."

"Yeah, he wasn't looking crash hot."

"David Lone's just dumped him as his agent. That's gotta hurt. He just didn't need that right now."

"Bastard," he said and then glanced up at her and away. "What's the latest, what does Gilda say?"

"Gilda? Nothing, I spoke to her on Monday and she wasn't giving too much away. Told me to stay out of it."

This surprised him. "She told me she's been trying to call you for days. She wants to talk to you about the case. Mull it all over."

"Really?" Roxy wondered how Max was so well informed, but she didn't want to ask and she didn't want to think of all the phone calls Gilda had left for her that she had so childishly ignored. Maybe it was time to grow up and call her back.

"I'd better get going," Max was saying. "I've got a Jeep advertorial that starts this arvo, and it's going be gruelling." He paused, coughed a little. "Um, Caroline's been asking about you, too. Thinks you're terrific. Wanted to know if you wanted to come for dinner one night. Better just do it so we can stop her nagging ... I can make myself scarce if you'd like—"

"No, of course not! I'd love to come to dinner, to see both of you."

His enormous, wolfish smile suddenly appeared and she inhaled. She'd forgotten how mesmerizing it was. "Great, how about Sunday night? You free?" She nodded and he said, "See you then."

As he walked away Roxy finally remembered to exhale.

CHAPTER 24

The Pig's Arms Hotel looked exactly as it sounded—rough around the edges and reeking of sweat—and the clientele certainly didn't help. It seemed the entire congregation from the memorial service had descended upon the pub, and Roxy struggled to get inside, let alone find Oliver. Eventually she gave up and wandered around the side to the beer garden, which was quieter, with a small bar set up on one side. At least she could grab a drink while she waited for things to settle down inside.

As she ordered a merlot and watched the barman, a young British backpacker, clumsily pour it into a ridiculously small glass, a pudgy man with a shock of orange hair approached the bar. She recognised him instantly. It was Norman Hicks. Seymour Silva's manager.

He recognised her too.

"Roxy, isn't it?" he said and she nodded, taking the fat, hairy hand he was extending to shake. He asked the barman for a Guinness and turned back to her. "Fucking terrible mess all of this, eh?"

She agreed it was. "Do you think it's all linked?"

"The three deaths?" He shrugged. "Who the fuck

knows?! Maybe, maybe not. It's working great guns for that tosser Lone, though. I hear he's got a book deal out of it. Lucky turd."

Her eyebrows shot up. "Good news travels fast. How do you know?"

"Amy Halloran's my agent, too, or didn't you know that?"

That's right, she thought, *Oliver had mentioned it a while ago. No wonder Amy's name rang a bell.*

Aloud, she said, "All I know is, Oliver used to be your agent and David Lone's. Now everyone seems to be deserting him."

"Like a stinking fucking ship," Norman agreed, unashamedly. "But remember I left him first. I get the credit for that."

Roxy had had just about enough of all this Oliver-bashing. He was just metres away, inside the hotel, for God's sake.

"I like Oliver, thanks very much," she said, "and, unlike the rest of you, I won't be deserting him any time soon."

Norm looked her up and down with a snide smile. "Don't get your fucking knickers in a knot, sweetheart. You do what you've got to do. It's your funeral."

"He didn't kill anyone, Norm!"

"Tell that to the pigs. Besides, I left him long before this mess started."

She took a calming gulp of her wine and then asked, "Why did you leave Oliver? Were you afraid he was going to reveal your little secret? Tell the world that Seymour was a fraud?"

"Nah, deep down I knew he wouldn't say a thing. If there's one thing I'll give Oliver, he's loyal. Nope, Amy came to me. Had a much better deal, that's all there was to it."

Roxy stared at him. "Really? She approached you?"

"Yep, lotsa motsa." He rubbed his fingers together as though playing with cash. "She's got shit-hot US contacts, too. Oliver can't compete with that." He took a long drag on his stout, some froth hanging on to his upper lip. He wiped it away roughly.

"What are you going to do now that Seymour is gone?"

"Onwards and upwards! I've got two more books about to come out. Amy says they're more marketable now than ever. Seymour's death was the best thing that ever fucking happened to us."

Roxy's blood ran cold and she was glad when he turned away and plunged back into the main pub. *What a hideous human being*, she thought, *so unperturbed by Seymour's death, and by Oliver's bad luck*. But her mind was quickly racing past Norm to Amy Halloran, the new agent.

Her name was cropping up a lot lately.

Roxy had a sudden thought. She took another mouthful of her wine then followed Norm inside. When she'd caught up to him, she tugged at his arm and yelled through the noise, "Hey, Norm, you couldn't set me up with this Amy woman, could you?"

He turned around with a knowing smile.

CHAPTER 25

Saturday morning dawned hot and stifling. It was true beach weather and Roxy hoped that was exactly where everyone was headed. She didn't feel like running into anyone today, least of all anyone related to Oliver Horowitz. She was meeting up with his competition, Amy Halloran, and she didn't want word to get back to him.

Oliver was super-sensitive at the moment, and with good reason. Roxy had received another early morning wake-up call from her agent, and he was distraught. The police had not only issued a warrant to search his home and office last night, they had torn both places apart.

"I don't know what they found, Roxy, but it's not good. It's not fuckin' good."

She sat up in bed, trying to kick-start her brain. She needed a coffee. Badly.

"What's happened?"

"They've asked me in for more questioning, told me to bring my solicitor again."

"Shit. Okay, have you got one? Did Sharon organise a good one?"

"Yeah, he's all right. It's Thomas Ronson, he did a good

job for a client of mine a few years back. He's meeting me in there in an hour. I've got to go."

"Just quickly, before you do. I need to finish the *Glossy* article on Tina. Did you ever track down that missing book?"

"Book?"

"I'm sorry, I know it's so trivial at this point, but it might help. You know, you said there were only two proofs made up. You were going to get one from her editor."

"Oh shit, Roxy. With all of this, I've completely forgotten. Can I give you the editor's details? Can you contact her yourself?"

"Of course," she said, reaching for a pad and pencil. Oliver rattled off the name, number and e-mail address.

"The book is called something like *Lover and Joy*, something like that. Can't bloody remember."

"Okay, I'm onto it, don't worry about that."

"Worry? I'm beyond worrying, Roxy. I'm fucked."

"Just take deep breaths, Olie. I'm sure everything is going to be okay."

But she wasn't sure, she had never been less sure of anything in her life, which is why she'd wasted no time calling Amy Halloran. She desperately needed to crack on with the case and she was becoming suspicious that this omnipresent agent had something to do with it.

For her part, Amy had not sounded at all surprised to get Roxy's call and had agreed to meet that morning at Lockie's Café. In fact, she was already sitting at a table up the back of the room when Roxy arrived, and she checked her watch. This one was punctual.

Leaping out of her chair, Amy thrust one rigid hand towards her, a toothy smile on her face. She was stick thin with long, black hair that had been straightened so stiffly, it looked brittle and ready to crack. She was wearing bright red lipstick and, despite it being the weekend, a similarly coloured suit with a lacy white camisole underneath. There were pearls in her ears, an iPad on the table in front of her, and what looked like a leather briefcase by her side.

"Roxy Parker, hello at last!" she said. "Soooo exciting to get your call! I've been watching your work for years!"

Roxy smiled brightly back. "Hi Amy, thanks for meeting me."

"The pleasure's all mine!" she cooed, dropping back into her seat. "Now, where is that fabulous Lockie? I just love him, don't you? We need to get you sorted with a coffee." She glanced around frantically and Roxy waved her off.

"I'll go and order at the bar. Have you ordered yet?"

"Yes, I'm having tea. Get yourself whatever you like, it's my shout!"

Roxy strode across to the coffee machine where a young woman with deep blue spiky hair and multiple nose piercings was hard at work on a latté.

"Hey, Rox," she said, glancing up, "the usual?"

Roxy nodded. "Thanks, Fenella. Where's Lockie? Out the back?"

She nodded behind her. "Yep, hiding in the bat cave. Go and lure him out with your temptress ways." She raised a pierced eyebrow provocatively.

"I will later, Fen, I'm having a very important meeting now." She nodded towards the back of the café where Amy was watching them closely. Amy waved brightly in return, and Fenella looked at Roxy and gaped.

"I was wondering who dragged Miss Perky in. That's why Lockie's hiding out. She talked the poor guy's ear off. It's just, like, all so *exciting*!"

Roxy laughed. "Now, now, Cat Woman, put the claws away."

Back at the table, Roxy took the seat across from Amy and smiled. "You didn't sound too surprised to get my call."

"*Au contraire!* I was *extremely* surprised to hear from you. I know how fantastic Oliver Horowitz is. Such an *amazing* agent!" The words were positive; the look in her eyes said otherwise.

"Yes, he is amazing," Roxy said. "Which is why I was surprised to hear David Lone has switched camps."

Amy brushed a hand down her long black hair, as though checking for wayward strands. "I have to be honest with you, Roxy. I love Oliver, we all do. He's such a sweet man. But I am *slightly* more ambitious than him, that *has* to be said. My clients like that about me, everybody does. Let me see if I can remember what Peter Carey said only last month ... Oh yes, he said, I've got 'cash gushing through my veins'. I love that! Hilarious. He's hilarious, I must introduce you some time."

Name dropping—another thing that Roxy despised. She ignored this and said, "Is that what you promised Norman Hicks, as well? More money? More famous fellow clients? Or did you try a different sales pitch with him?"

Amy snapped her lips shut and considered this for a moment. "I never discuss my client negotiations with other potential clients." She smudged her lips into a wide smile. "You are a potential client, I gather? Is that what this is all about?"

Roxy leaned back in her chair just as Fenella appeared with her coffee and a teapot and cup for Amy. "Thanks, Fen," Roxy said, taking a small sip. Fenella gave her a conspiratorial grin before she loped away. "Actually, Amy, I'm here to set the record straight."

"Oh?" Amy batted her eyelids as she carefully poured herself some tea. She looked as innocent as a lamb. It was time, Roxy decided, for the slaughter.

"Yes, I'm working on behalf of Oliver, actually, trying to work out who the hell is trying to frame him."

The innocent lamb look wavered, but not for long. "How do you mean? Exactly?"

"I mean, Oliver Horowitz didn't kill Tina Passion or William Glad or Seymour Silva but someone sure wants it to look that way."

Amy gently patted her hair and batted her eyelids again.

She was so good at that. "Why would someone want to do such a *hideous* thing?"

"That's what I want to know. Any ideas?" Again, the madly batting eyelashes, so Roxy tried a different tack. "Seems to me that at least one person stands to gain by Oliver's demise."

"Oh? And who would that be?"

"Another agent, I'd say. Another *more ambitious* agent with *cash gushing through her veins*."

Amy had stopped batting her eyelashes. She placed her teacup down with a thud. Her smile was gone and she suddenly looked about ten years older. "If you are insinuating I had anything to do with any of those deaths, or with trying to frame Oliver Horowitz for them, I think you are not as smart as I gave you credit for."

"Ouch," Roxy said drolly.

Amy stared at her for a few icy moments. "I have no wish to see Oliver in trouble but I do have to say this: if Oliver is losing clients, it's because of Oliver, not me. He just doesn't have what it takes to play with the big boys. He's small fry. There, I've said it. I can't help it if his clients eventually work it out and come to me."

"Except *you* keep approaching them. You approached Seymour and Norm, and stole them from Oliver. You approached David, not the other way around. And, if I recall correctly, you also tried to steal Tina Passion away."

Her jaw dropped and she rolled her eyes like a Year Nine school girl. "Oh my God! *Stole* them? Listen to yourself! They're not inanimate objects, you know? They came of their own free will. I have a much better deal I can offer writers. I'm gutsier, I'm more determined, and I get results."

"Did you ever give that sales pitch to William Glad? Did you try to steal him from Oliver as well?"

"The gardening writer?" He eyebrows shot upwards. "No, why would I? He was well past his use-by date."

Now where had she heard that line before? "Charming," Roxy said. "He's dead, you know."

"Of course I know. What? Are you seriously trying to blame that on me now as well?"

"I'm just trying to piece it all together and you seem to be popping up a lot lately."

"Because I'm *extremely* good at what I do. That's all there is to it. And if you could see past your own blind loyalty, you'd sign up with me as well."

"No thank you."

"Then I guess this meeting is over," Amy announced, reaching for her iPad and briefcase and pushing her chair back. She stopped suddenly and said, "Just be careful with that blind loyalty of yours, Roxy. It might come back to bite you in the butt one day."

Roxy's eyes widened. "Is that a threat?"

Amy shrugged, placed the iPad in her case and stood up. "It's a warning, that's all. As far as I can see you're on the wrong side, Roxy Parker. The wrong side indeed."

And with that she swept out of the café.

Roxy stared after her for several minutes, thinking about what she had said, then picked up her cup and made her way to Lockie's office, a small cluttered room at the back of the café with the words Head Honcho painted in black across the door. He looked around, slightly alarmed when she entered and she laughed.

"It's only me, relax."

He exhaled. "Thank goodness. Miss Perky left yet?"

"If you're talking about Amy Halloran, then yes."

He shuddered dramatically. "She's a nooter, that one. Comes in from time to time, actin' like ma best friend. Gives me the willies. All slick and slimy like. She'd sell her mother for a free packet o' crisps, I would'nae put it past her."

"Yes, well I think that's what appeals to her clients so much." She slumped down in the office chair in front of his desk, placing her cup on top. "But not me, Lockie. In fact, quite the opposite. I think she just threatened me."

"Oh bloody hell, why?"

"Don't know, but I think she's dodgy. They go on about

Oliver being the link, but this Amy woman is also linked, at least to Seymour, whom she stole from under Olie's nose. And now she's pinched David Lone from him as well, the snake."

"But how does tha' tie in with the other murders?"

Roxy chewed on this for a moment. "Not sure, but she's obviously ruthless, unashamedly so. It makes me wonder if she'd be up for destroying the competition if she had to. I mean, how far does her ambition go?"

"As far as murder, ye think?" He raised his bushy eyebrows and she shrugged again.

"I don't know, Lockie, I just don't know."

"Well, be careful, eh? Whether it's Amy or someone else, someone really is killin' writers out there. Hate to see ye next. You're ma favourite writer in Sydney."

"Aw shucks, thanks, Lockie."

"So how is Oliver? I hear he's bein' held for questionin'."

"Bloody hell, that's only just happened. Who'd you hear that from this early in the morning?"

He looked at her like she was clueless. "Who'd ya think?"

"So Amy knows all about that already."

"Ay."

"I wonder where she gets her information."

"Didn't ye say she's now reppin' David Lone?"

She groaned. *Of course, she now had her finger firmly on the pulse. Was that her intention all along?*

"Have ye spoken to Gilda lately? Surely she can fill ye in on all o' this?"

Roxy considered this. He was right. Max, too.

It was time to call in the big guns.

CHAPTER 26

Half an hour later Gilda was strolling into the café, bedecked in a short, white summer dress and wedged sandals, a sun hat in one hand, a beach bag in the other, a black bikini just visible beneath her dress.

"I was on my way to Bondi in case it's not bleedingly obvious," she said. "You got me in the nick of time."

"I didn't think you guys ever got a day off."

"Now, thanks to you, I don't."

Lockie appeared and she ordered a chocolate milkshake before taking the seat that Amy had recently vacated. She stared hard at her friend, waiting.

"Thanks for meeting me," Roxy began and Gilda nodded, glancing around.

"At least you didn't front up to the station this time. Much more discreet."

"I'm sorry I haven't called you back. I've been ... busy."

"Busy? We're all busy, Roxy." The edge in her voice was obvious and it spoke of hurt feelings and disappointment.

"Okay, sorry, I've been slack. And I've been avoiding you because I don't want to talk about Saturday night. About you and Max."

That seemed to thaw the ice and Gilda's voice softened. "So we won't talk about Saturday night. For now. So why did you finally phone me back?"

"We need to talk about Oliver." She leaned forward, dropped her voice a little. "You have to tell me what's going on, why are the police questioning him again?"

Gilda sighed. "I really shouldn't be saying any of this ..."

"I won't repeat this to a soul, I promise. I just need to know. He'll tell me eventually anyway, you know that."

"How well *do* you know Oliver?" Gilda asked, taking Roxy by surprise. "It's just that the evidence is looking really bad for him."

She felt her stomach drop. "Like what?"

"Like a lot of stuff I can't tell you."

"Come on, Gilda, like what?"

Gilda considered this for a few minutes, her mind clearly wrestling with itself while Lockie handed her the shake. She thanked him, took a few sips and then said, "There's a phone."

"A phone?"

"A cheap-as-chips, buy-anywhere mobile phone. They've traced it back to the phone calls both William Glad and Tina Passion received not long before they were killed."

"So?"

"So they found it in Oliver's office."

She shrunk back. "No way!"

"Way. Big, whammy, whopping way. It had been hidden in a pot-plant by the door. Know the one?"

She nodded, trying to get her head straight. "Someone must have planted it there. Excuse the pun."

Gilda gave her a cynical look. "What are the chances?"

"I don't know, but the chances of Oliver being a murderer are even less!"

Roxy tried to get her head around that. It was obviously the reason the police had hauled Oliver back in today. Someone must have put it there, but who? And when? Had Amy been to see Oliver recently and planted the evidence?

Had Norman Hicks? Or Lorenzo?

"They're dusting the phone for fingerprints but at this point it looks clean, which is suspicious in itself."

"The very fact that it was in Oliver's office is suspicious," Roxy railed. "Even if he did use that phone, he'd hardly hide it in his own bloody pot-plant for your lot to find."

Gilda shrugged. "You'd be surprised how stupid most crims are. You give them way too much credit."

"Have they considered anyone else? What about Norman Hicks or Amy Halloran, agent extraordinaire?"

"What about them?"

Roxy told Gilda her theories and, as she did so, she could tell Gilda was trying very hard not to scoff. "Amy could have killed all those writers to draw suspicion to Oliver and steal his clients away."

"She already had Seymour Silva, remember? Why kill him?"

Roxy thought about this. "Maybe that was a separate thing? Maybe he was threatening to reveal the truth, that he wasn't the real writer, and Amy was terrified it would destroy Norman's book sales and her commission, so she shut him up. Only the truth came out anyway. So then she had to kill William and Tina to make it look like someone else. Someone like Oliver."

Gilda slurped on the milkshake and smiled. "Okay, that's a theory. A pretty bloody crap one, but it's a theory nonetheless. What's Norman Hick's motive?"

"Exactly the same, in fact, they could have been in it together. He kills Seymour to shut him up and then has to kill the others to throw suspicion elsewhere. Oliver's such an easy target. Everybody thinks agents are dodgy. He *must* have done it." She paused, groaned. "I know, I know, I'm even having trouble buying it."

Gilda sat forward. "What about your friend David Lone?"

"What about him?"

"Do you think he could have done it?"

This surprised Roxy and she tried to think. "If you mean does he have it in him, I don't think so ... I mean, I don't know, but I doubt it. In any case, it's irrelevant. He couldn't have done it. For starters, I was sitting a few seats behind him during his film premiere. There's no way he got up and murdered Seymour quietly while that film was showing. I would have noticed, so would the gaggle of admirers he had around him at all times."

"Yeah, we've already ascertained that. I'm wondering about the other two, though. His alibis are less concrete for those ones."

Her heart sank. "I don't know about William's murder, but I'm his alibi for Tina." She didn't want to believe David capable of such a thing but she would believe anything to get Oliver off the hook. At this point throwing suspicion elsewhere seemed like his only salvation. The problem was, Gilda was way off.

She told her about last Saturday night, blushing as she recalled how drunk she had been and how she had ended up at David's place. She did not explain the reason she'd run screaming into David's arms, did not want to get into that now, and Gilda didn't seem to need an explanation.

"So *you* were with him all that night?"

"Yep, from about eleven-ish when we left the party to about eleven the following morning."

Gilda thought about this. "I wonder why he didn't say that then."

"What do you mean?"

"Well, the detective in charge, Frankie, has already questioned him and he refused to say who he was with on Saturday night. Just said he went home after the party with someone and it was none of their business. Didn't seem important, so they didn't stress the point."

Roxy considered this, and felt instant remorse. It was clear David was protecting her, and here she was trying to stick him in it. "Well that's very gallant of him, but the scarlet woman was me. I was with him. All night."

"And was he any good?"

"Sorry?"

She laughed. "I'm messing with you, Roxy, don't answer that."

"Hey, I was joking about the scarlet bit. We didn't ... it's not like that ..."

Gilda smiled again. "It's none of my business, Roxy."

"Seriously, there is no *business* to speak of. I got terribly drunk, passed out and woke up with a hangover you wouldn't read about."

"I don't remember you drinking that much," she said and Roxy sighed.

"I don't either but I polished off an entire bottle of Pinot Grigio back at his place, apparently, which certainly didn't help."

"Pinot Grigio? That's not your style."

"Tell me about it, especially when he had some top bottle of merlot in his wine rack. See what happens when I'm unfaithful to my merlot? Seriously though, why would you ask about David? What possible motive could he have?"

Gilda slumped a little in her chair. "I don't know. He's annoying the crap out of me. Isn't that motive enough?"

Roxy smiled. "Afraid not. Do you have any other suspects? Is there anyone else I should be looking at?"

"You shouldn't be looking at anyone, Roxy. I told you before, stay out of it."

"Is that why you've been calling me?"

"Sorry?"

"I don't think you want me to stay out of it, at all. I think you want me to keep sticking my nose in. Otherwise you'd be avoiding me, not trying to talk to me. You know what I'm like. You know I'll wheedle info out of you."

Gilda looked impressed. "You really do have the mind of a detective. I keep telling you, you're wasted in your line of work. Wasted! You should sign up to the force."

"That doesn't answer my question."

"Another detective tactic. Okay, okay, you got me. Off

the record, yes, I do secretly hope you keep at it. It's the reason I've been calling you trying to get you aside. I'm taking sneaky peeks to see where things are at and I'm with you on this one. I don't think Oliver's got a devious bone in his body, let alone a violent one, but the evidence says otherwise so we have to play it very carefully."

"What can I do? How can I help? I have another theory, you know?"

She told Gilda about Tina's dad, about his pathological disapproval of her books and of Oliver's involvement with them. "He could have set this all up to get back at both of them."

"And you think he's a killer?"

She deflated. "No, spent a few hours with him the other day and I think he's a sweet old man who's pining for his daughter."

"That's what Frankie says, but first impressions aren't always spot on. Not every murderer comes with the word 'hate' tattooed across their knuckles. We can't always pick them. Tell me more about this Lorenzo guy."

Roxy smiled suddenly, enormously relieved to have Gilda on her side, and lighter for it, too. She proceeded to tell her friend all about the interview with Lorenzo and the things that Tina's cousin Brianna had said. But, like her, Gilda did not seem convinced.

"What's very annoying about this case," said Gilda, "is how all over the place it is. Sure, Lorenzo might have killed Tina that night after yet another argument about her books. As you say, another novel was coming out, perhaps he'd decided enough was enough. Great, that's sorted. Problem is, how does that explain William's macabre death? Let alone Seymour's?"

"Maybe they're *not* connected?" suggested Roxy. "Maybe David Lone is barking up the wrong tree."

Gilda shook her head. "But we have the phone. That's linked to two of the victims. And there are plenty of other connections between them, like you said—Oliver, Amy,

Norman, not to mention the gardening shears. It's like a giant maze, one path leads to another but then meets a dead end at the next."

They both sighed loudly together and sipped their drinks.

"Have they confirmed what the poison was yet?" Roxy asked and Gilda nodded.

"Strychnine, which is telling in itself."

"Yes," said, Roxy, her eyes widening. "That must narrow it down considerably. I mean, how many people have access to that kind of stuff?"

Gilda shrugged. "Sure, it's difficult to get hold of these days, but not impossible. And it does lend some weight to your Lorenzo theory."

"How so?"

"Well, from what I can ascertain, while it's been banned from most domestic poisons, Rat Kill, that kind of stuff, it is still used in some rural areas, to keep down feral animal populations."

"Do they have a feral animal problem on cotton farms in Moree?" Roxy asked and Gilda gave her a knowing smile.

"There's something you might want to look into. In any case, it works to Oliver's advantage because they have to connect him to a strychnine supply and so far they haven't been able to do that. There was nothing at his house or office."

"Here's hoping they don't. Listen, maybe we're looking at this all wrong. Maybe it's none of those people. Maybe it's a failed writer, or agent or a total stranger, a lunatic serial killer that's randomly targeting writers for the thrill of it. It happens."

"Yes, but usually there's some reason, some trigger. And it doesn't explain the shears, how they ended up in Norman Hick's car, or the phone—how that ended up at Oliver's office. To me, the phone is the most telling clue because it shows that whoever used that had access to Oliver. That's why I don't think it's a stranger, but anything is possible, I guess."

"So what happens now?" Roxy asked.

Gilda scrunched her lips to one side. "I wish I knew. From the police side, they're awaiting fingerprints from that blasted phone and the results of a bunch of other DNA tests—hair samples, that kind of thing. But that may come to nothing. As you know, they're talking to Oliver today, I just hope he doesn't give them any more reason to arrest him."

"They won't arrest him! Surely?"

"Could well do, Roxy, so prepare yourself."

She didn't know what that meant. Should she start baking a pie to hide a file in?

Gilda stretched and stood up, readjusting her bikini strap under her summery dress. "Now, if you'll excuse me, I have a spot of sun-baking to do. But you and I are not finished, missy."

"God no, we have to stay in touch over this, I'll Google strychnine and see what I can find."

Gilda held her head to one side. "I was referring to the party on Saturday night. I have some stuff I need to tell you, about Max."

Roxy's stomach lurched again. "It's just not important now—"

"That's what you keep saying, but it's not true, Roxy. I know you're worried about your agent, but you've got to keep your own spirits up, too. And I think you need to hear what I have to tell you."

Roxy winced. She didn't want to hear that Gilda had spent a romantic night with her best friend, Max. She didn't want to hear that Gilda had fallen for Max and he for her. That they were terribly sorry, that they hoped it wouldn't ruin anyone's friendships. She didn't want to hear any of it. Not now. Not ever. But she was weary to the bone and she was in avoidance mode, so she said, simply, "We will talk, soon, I promise."

That placated the policewoman for now. "Roxy, you have to watch your back, okay? I told you I didn't believe there was a crazed serial killer, but I don't know that for sure so don't take any chances. Someone is clearly targeting writers, and we don't know why. You still got that alarm of yours?"

Roxy nodded, feeling uneasy. Gilda was referring to the personal security alarm she had bought on eBay a few years earlier. She carried it in her handbag most of the time, trusting that its piercing siren would scare potential attackers off. "Keep it on you, day and night. Don't answer the door to strangers, and don't take any chances."

"This is not making me feel any better," Roxy told her.

"Not intended to. You can feel better when Oliver's off the hook and the nutcase who's doing this is safely locked up behind bars."

And on that cheerful note, they bid each other farewell and Roxy watched Gilda as she departed. Then she grabbed her things, hugged Lockie good-bye and also left.

She didn't really feel threatened but decided that Gilda was right about one thing at least. She needed to get home and get organized because if Oliver Horowitz was officially arrested, she'd need more than a freshly baked pie.

CHAPTER 27

The phone call came sooner than she expected. Roxy was just steering her VW Golf down Elizabeth Bay Road to her apartment block when Oliver's number came up on her mobile. She pulled into a bus zone and picked up.

"Oliver, where are you? Are you okay?"

A long, weary groan. "No, Rox, I'm not okay. They're arresting me, under suspicion of murder. Whatever the hell that means."

It meant he was in serious shit and Roxy echoed his groan. "That's insane, Oliver, completely insane. Where are you now?"

"Police headquarters, waiting to go through the fingerprinting process."

She felt nauseous. "Can I come and see you? Is there anything I can do?"

"No, don't bother, no visitors allowed."

"And your lawyer?"

"Thomas is here. He's trying his best, but it's not looking good. He says I could be held in custody for the entire weekend."

"What?!"

"Might not be able to make bail 'til Monday, if at all."

"Oh for God's sake."

"Don't stress too much, Roxy. I'll be okay. But I just need to know that you're out there, doing what you do best."

"I'm looking into this, Oliver, I will find the truth." She told him about her morning meeting with Gilda, omitting all mention of Amy Halloran. She didn't want him to feel any more threatened than he already felt.

"Well, I'm glad Gilda is helping," he said. "Hey, I can't talk long. I just wanted to tell you I'm okay and ask if you can go to my office on Monday and help Shazza man the phones and maybe get a press release out, categorically denying these charges, that kind of stuff. If I don't get on the front foot with this, my client base is fucked. You know David Lone's already taken off?"

"Yeah, well, I'm beginning to realise that David Lone only worries about David Lone. Of course I'll help Sharon and we'll calm this whole thing down, but you'll be out on Monday and you can do all that yourself."

"Oh, shit, they're hassling me to hang up. Thanks for everything, kiddo."

He sounded like he was giving his last good-byes and she choked back a sob. "Take care," she told him as the phone clicked quiet.

Roxy sat for a few moments, shocked that it had got to this and more determined than ever to get organized. She took a deep breath, checked the rear vision mirror and pulled out onto the street again. She needed to get home, finish the Tina Passion article and get that off her To Do list. Then she needed to sit down with her trusty journal and start making sense of what appeared to be completely and utterly senseless.

Three hours, two cups of coffee and a plate of noodles later, Roxy stood up from her sunroom desk and stretched like a cat. She had finished the Tina story and e-mailed it off to Maria at *Glossy*, and had then gone on to make some notes in her journal on the Oliver Horowitz case.

She had also *Googled* the words "Strychnine" and "agricultural use" and come up with some very interesting information. While most people now needed a special license to possess strychnine for their own use, the Department of Agriculture did use strychnine-treated grain bait to control an oversupply of emus in some rural regions across the country.

She wondered if there were a lot of emus running amok in the plains of Moree.

Chewing on the thought, she padded into the living room, flicked on the TV, and sat down on the sofa with her journal. The bulletin would start in ten minutes and she hoped Oliver's face would not appear on the screen, but she wasn't about to hold her breath. Instead, she opened her journal and started reading through it, when a soft knock on the front door made her look up with a start.

Somebody had got into the building without being buzzed in from below. She felt a tremor of fear rush down her spine along with Gilda's words, *"Someone is clearly targeting writers. Don't answer the door to strangers, don't take any chances."*

Her legs felt like lead suddenly as she stepped off the sofa and towards the door. She didn't have one of those peek holes, so could only ask, in a faltering voice, "Who is it?"

A young woman's voice came back, strong and upbeat. "It's Caroline!"

Now a wave of relief rushed over Roxy followed quickly by pleasant surprise. She unlocked the door and swung it open to find Max's sister standing on the doorstep, a bottle of wine in one hand, a small grocery bag in the other. She was wearing a pair of billowing silky pants in a bold floral print, with a strappy blouse and stilettos, and had scooped her long hair up into a high ponytail, pink gloss on her lips.

"I come bearing gifts!" she said, stepping in and planting an air kiss beside Roxy's right cheek.

"How did you get through the front door downstairs?"

"Oh, easy peasy! There was some old bloke heading out,

I sweet talked him into letting me in. May I?"

Roxy waved her through, then glanced outside before relocking the door and leading the way to the small kitchen. There she fetched wine glasses while Caroline reached into the bag and produced creamy King Island Brie, seaweed crackers and olives. Roxy found a platter and handed it over so Caroline could arrange the snack, and they returned to the living room in time to catch the 6:00 p.m. news. Roxy pushed the now wilting tulips aside to make room for the platter, then picked up the remote control and increased the volume.

Oliver's arrest was the leading story but Caroline did not look surprised. "Gilda already rang Max," she explained. "He's still on the Jeep shoot, so he asked me to drop by. See if you're okay."

Roxy melted a little. "That's sweet."

"That's Max," Caroline said, giving her a pointed look before turning back to watch the screen.

A very young, very glamorous reporter was gushing about the latest "enthralling development in the Snow White murder", as though she'd never heard anything so exciting. Roxy wanted to scream at her, "There's human beings involved in all this, you imbecile!" But she bit her tongue and bit into some cheese instead.

According to the imbecile, "local identity and celebrity agent Oliver Horowitz was being held for questioning in relation to erotic novelist Tina Passion's recent murder." A very dated photo of Tina appeared on the screen followed by the embarrassing paparazzi shot from David Lone's film launch—the picture of Oliver looking heavily intoxicated beside her. They couldn't have found a sleazier, more predatory shot and she wanted to scream again, but at least there was no connection suggested between the two earlier deaths. Thank goodness for small mercies, she thought, turning the sound down as the anchorwoman reappeared and moved on to other stories.

Caroline studied Roxy carefully, chewing on the top of

her wine glass. "Dreadful stuff," she said eventually. "And I gather from your expression, they've got it all wrong."

"Absolutely, Caroline, my agent didn't do this."

"I believe you, darling, Max tells me you've known him forever and he's a good bloke. So what can we do, Max and I? How can we help?"

Roxy chewed on her own glass and tried to think. "I don't know. I've been racking my brain, trying to make sense of all this. Three writers dead, no really obvious motives, at least not consistent ones for all three." She placed her glass down and grabbed her journal, opening it up and pointing to her notes. "Have you got a second, for me to go through it with you? I'm still trying to get my head around it all."

"That's why I'm here, baby," Caroline said, slipping her heels off and scooping her legs up underneath her. "What've you got?"

"Okay, well, I know two people who might have had motive to kill the sci-fi writer Seymour—his manager and his agent. But neither has a real motive to kill William Glad, the gardening guy, or Tina. I know that Tina's dad *might* have had reason to kill *her*, but why would he want to do away with Seymour and William? Even Erin, William's daughter, might have killed her dad if she thought he was going to forbid her publishing his back catalogue, but—"

"Hang on, back catalogue," said Caroline. "What do you mean?"

Roxy explained about William's refusal to republish what could amount to very profitable gardening books. "I believe that Erin really needs money. She's a single mum, a brood of kids. Maybe she got desperate. But again, why kill Seymour and Tina? Why would Erin want to hurt them? It's soooo frustrating!"

Caroline agreed. "A real Bermuda triangle."

"Yes, that's exactly what it is. And poor Oliver's drowning in the middle of it all. He has the terrible misfortune of being the one and only common link."

"Well, that and the fact that a dodgy mobile phone was

found in his possession."

Roxy looked up. "Gilda tell you that? Yeah, well, it wasn't in his possession, it was stashed in a pot at his office." She jumped up. "That's what I can do next. I need to talk to Sharon and I need to talk to her now!"

Ten minutes later, Roxy found Caroline by an open window, finishing up a cigarette. She fetched an old saucer-cum-ashtray and handed it to her and then they both returned to the sofa, Roxy feeling even more deflated. She'd managed to hunt down Oliver's receptionist at home to discuss just who could have planted that phone, but Sharon had been adamant.

"Sorry, love, but not one of those people have been into the office in the past week, not one."

"Not Tina's dad or Amy Halloran or Norman Hicks? What about Erin, William's daughter?"

"Nope, haven't seen her since before William kicked the bucket. Oliver met her at the house but she never came in here, or at least not that I know of. 'Course, that's not to say they didn't pop in after hours, or break in. But then we would've noticed that."

"Yes, except most of Oliver's clients have the code to that street entrance door, they could easily have let themselves in the building and hidden it one night."

Sharon disagreed. "We still lock our own internal office door upstairs when we leave. That's an old-fashioned lock. So unless they had a key ..."

"And who has the keys?"

"Just me and Oliver, love, no one else."

Roxy growled. "Damn it."

"Yeah, love, not friggin' good," Sharon said. "You've spoken to him?"

"Yes, he sounded terrible."

"And who wouldn't?! Oh, Roxy, who's doin' this to him?! This is such a stitch up!"

Roxy told her she didn't know, but she was going to try

to find out and that seemed to make the older woman happier. Still, as she slumped back down next to Caroline and took another long sip of her wine, Roxy wondered whether this case was beyond even her natural sleuthing talents.

"More wine?" Caroline asked and Roxy held her glass out.

"Thanks. I really needed this."

"You might need it even more in a minute."

Roxy looked at her, bemused. Caroline held up her iPhone. "Max just texted me. The shoot's done. He's on his way over."

Roxy felt a wave of panic rush through her and then took another larger gulp of wine while Caroline watched her closely.

"When are you two going to get your shit together?" she said finally.

Roxy scowled. "I don't know what you mean."

"*I don't know what you mean*!?" she said mockingly. "Honestly, Roxy, I've been watching you two from afar for years, it's exhausting!" She hesitated and then changed tack. "I have to ask: are you and Lonesy, well, are you really together?"

The cocked eyebrow indicated she found the whole idea ludicrous and Roxy felt suddenly defensive. "If you mean did I end up back at his place last Saturday night? Then yes, yes I did."

The eyebrow rose even further. "Damn, I thought Max was just being neurotic as always." She hesitated. "Listen, Roxy, David Lone can be a charmer, I know, he charmed me once, but—"

"But you're here to tell me your brother is a much better match?"

"Max is a good guy, Roxy, and he cares for you deeply."

"So deeply that he keeps running into the arms of every other woman he can find?"

"What women? He's been single for the past six

months—that has to be some kind of record for him."

"Are you sure about that?"

"Sure I'm sure. He broke up with some airhead chick called Sandra ages ago, and he's been pining for you ever since. Can't look at another woman, it's all Roxy this, Roxy that. No offence or anything, but it's getting a bit tired. Can you help me out and give him a second chance?"

Roxy stared at her, perplexed. "So what's Gilda, then, a practice run?"

Caroline's eyebrows dropped this time. "Gilda? The policewoman?"

"Yes. They got together at his party, or didn't Max mention that?"

"No," she said, looking slightly miffed, "no he did not. Are you sure? That's not the impression I got."

"Well that's Max for you. If that's what he calls pining, then, no thanks, I'll pass."

Caroline gave this some thought and was about to say something when the buzzer screeched indicating there was someone downstairs.

"That was quick," she said, glancing at her luxury silver Tag Heuer watch.

Roxy jumped up and pressed the intercom. "Max?" she said.

"Ah, no, actually, it's David," came an unexpected voice. "Can I come in?"

Oh God, she thought, glancing at Caroline, panic-stricken, but the other woman was already up and grabbing her heels and bag.

"I'll leave you to it then."

"Caroline, about David. I don't think you understand—"

She held a hand up. "Not my biz, babe, you're a grown woman. But I will text Max on my way out, try and put him off coming over. I'm not sure now's a good time."

The look on her face was one of dismay and Roxy felt awful. She wanted to set the record straight, but she also needed to talk to David, to see if he had more information that might help Oliver. There was no time to waste.

"Don't worry," Caroline was saying, reading her incorrectly. "I won't tell Max that David's here. I don't need to break his heart any more this week. He hasn't exactly warmed to the bloke."

"Thanks, Caroline. I can still make dinner tomorrow night ... if he's ... if you ...?"

"See you then," she said and opened the front door.

Caroline was about to descend the staircase when she hesitated and turned back, a slight frown crinkling her perfect forehead. "Look, Roxy, about Max. You need to know—"

Before she could finish, David was springing up towards them, two steps at a time.

"Hey there, Caroline! I didn't expect to see you here."

Caroline smiled wryly. "You know me, Lonesy, I like to get around." She turned to Roxy. "It'll keep," she said, giving her a warm embrace before heading back downstairs.

Roxy showed David in and fetched him a fresh glass so he could join her in the merlot.

As she poured the wine, he watched her quietly, a slight frown on his forehead.

"So you were expecting Max?"

She tried not to blush. "Caroline said he might drop over. Obviously not." She handed David the wine and led him back to the sofa, keen to change the subject. "Has Oliver been released on bail?"

"Yes he has, the lucky bastard. I really didn't think he'd get it. They managed to sort it out so he's not there all weekend. He'll be out shortly." He retrieved his mobile phone and placed it on the coffee table beside the tulips, then sat down. "I'm sorry, Roxanne."

She sighed long and low. *You should be sorry,* she wanted to say. He'd been a party to all of this, had helped steer the police in Oliver's direction and now, to add insult to injury, had deserted the agency. But she also knew he wasn't the enemy and, even if he was, she needed to keep him close, to find out what he knew, to help Oliver. Still, it didn't stop her from wanting to tear his head off.

She swallowed her anger down and tried to offer him a smile. At least Oliver was being released, at least he wouldn't have to spend a night in jail. Yet.

"I know you're angry with me," he said. "I understand why, but you have to understand this is not personal, it's just business."

It should be personal, she thought. Business is personal, or at least it was with her. Maybe it was a shortcoming, but she never could detach herself from her agent or her clients or the work she was writing. She took them home with her every single day, she lived and breathed them, and she would fight for them if she had to.

But she didn't say any of that either, she just asked, "Why didn't you tell the police that we were together last Saturday night?"

He looked surprised, then smiled. "You've made up with Gilda, I see."

"Yes, Gilda did tell me," she said, wondering why nothing ever got past this guy. "I want to know why. What's the big secret?"

"It's very simple, Roxanne. I didn't tell them because it's none of their damn business. And because I don't kiss and tell." She blushed despite herself. "It's okay," he said, reaching for one of her hands and turning it over in his. "It wasn't a long kiss, you didn't make a fool of yourself if that's what you're worried about. I enjoyed it, though. Very much." He'd stopped laughing and his blue eyes had taken on that intensity that unsettled her, despite herself. "I wanted to get your permission before I mentioned your name. It's irrelevant to the case, anyway, it's not like either of us is involved."

"Well, I appreciate it," she said, slipping her hand away. "So what's the latest?"

He leaned his long legs out. "They found an incriminating mobile phone."

"I heard that. Any fingerprints yet?"

"Not a one. But its very presence in Oliver's office speaks volumes. They also pulled up his computer files and found that he had looked over his old contract with William Glad, the day before he died."

She stared at him. "What does that even mean?"

"It means, he has motive to kill William. William's contract obviously stipulates the terms and conditions around publication of his old gardening guides, right? We already know that William was organizing to meet with his lawyer before he died. Maybe he wanted to change the contracts, or put something in his will about his books never being republished. But he never got the chance. Oliver must have heard about that meeting, probably from Erin, and was checking through the contract to see where he stood. Erin is already on record saying Oliver was pushing for publication really hard, insisting she try to change her father's mind before he died."

"Hang on," Roxy said. "Can we just go back one step. This so-called meeting with the lawyer. What was that about, exactly?"

He shrugged, crossed his legs over. "We'll never know now."

"What does the lawyer say?"

"He says it was never explained. William had just rung and asked him to drop over some time that week, the week he died."

"Okay, so he called his lawyer. But there's no proof he was going to change the contracts. He might have wanted to discuss something completely different. Maybe he wanted to cut Erin out of his will. Why is no one looking at her?"

Oliver gave her that "you're so naïve" look again. "Erin's a single mum with five kids. The youngest is three. You think she left them all alone to dash over and kill her beloved dad, then return home again? Do you think William really would cut his daughter off at this late stage? He loved that daughter of his."

She wondered how he knew all that but just shrugged. "I guess not."

He uncrossed his legs and sat forward. "There's one other thing I only just found out. It's really incriminating." Her heart dropped again, she braced herself. "Oliver went to see William, the night he died."

"What? Really? When, exactly?"

"It was a few hours before he died."

"How do you know this? He never mentioned anything to me."

"He didn't tell anyone but he's just 'fessed up apparently. Even Erin didn't know about it. Oliver says he was over there, saying good-bye. I think he was there trying to convince William to publish. When that didn't work, he returned and killed him."

He said it so flatly, it sparked her anger again but he seemed oblivious to this. He leaned back in his seat. "I know you're trying to find answers that don't implicate Oliver, Roxanne, and believe me I've tried, too. I wish I could find evidence that points firmly at someone else's feet. Really I do. But I have gone over it and over it, as I'm sure you have. And it's undeniable. Nobody has stronger links to all three victims. Nobody has a stronger motive for all three, than Oliver. And nobody had greater access. It's a fact."

"Not yet it's not," she said, standing up.

"I hear you had a meeting with Amy Halloran?"

His subject change surprised her. "That was to discuss Oliver's case," she stammered. "I'm not ..."

"Deserting the sinking ship?"

"No, I'm not," she said more firmly this time. "But ... well, please don't mention the meeting to Oliver. He's depressed enough as it is. I think he'll just take it the wrong way."

"Fine by me," he said. "But listen, she's a good one, Roxanne, you mustn't accuse Amy of any of this."

"Yet it's okay to accuse Oliver?"

He sighed. "I can see I'm not going to convince you of

anything."

Roxy's head was spinning now and things were starting to feel even more out of control. "I'm tired, David, can we do this another time?"

"Of course," he said, standing up. "I'll leave you alone. I really just dropped by to let you know that if you want to speak to my old English teacher, you've got to get onto it fast."

English teacher? She was confused for a second before it clicked. His book. In the drama of the past few days she'd forgotten all about it.

"The problem is, you see, she's heading off on sabbatical overseas soon so you need to get it done fast, preferably early this week. You have her number, right? Just ring and set something up. She lives up near Yamba, on the north coast. It's a bit of a drive, but I think you should go up and interview her face to face. More personal that way."

She was nodding, unable to speak, leading him towards the door before she really did knock his head off.

How could he even think about his own book at a time like this?

"Okay, then," he said, leaning in as though he were about to kiss her on the lips.

Roxy deliberately turned her head so he got her right cheek and he paused for a moment, still leaning in, and said, "Everything all right?"

"Yep, it's all hunky dory," she managed and he looked at her for a moment, his blue eyes clouded over. Then he shrugged, opened the door and headed back down the stairs.

Roxy tried not to slam the door after him. She was furious, livid, shaking with rage.

What an insensitive, horrendous, egotistical ...

She caught herself and took a few deep breaths, then reached for the dying tulips and stormed into the kitchen to dump them in the garbage disposal unit in the sink.

He's asking you to do your job, she told herself calmly. *Just like he's doing his.*

As she watched the flowers get swallowed alive by the

gurgling, spluttering sink, she realised the problem was he was doing his job too bloody well.

CHAPTER 28

Late Saturday night, Oliver Horowitz was finally released on bail, but he was not heading home. He called Roxy to tell her he was en route to Sharon's place, "out in Parramatta somewhere". His solicitor was dropping him there now.

"The press have staked out my home and office, apparently, so I'm not going to give them the satisfaction. Scumbags. Shazza has offered to hole me up for a few days until this blows over."

Roxy wasn't sure it was going to blow over. Oliver had been officially charged with Tina Passion's murder. It would only be a matter of time before they implicated him in the deaths of William Glad and Seymour Silva as well.

Of course she said none of that, instead offering, "You can always stay with me, you know?"

"Nah, too close to the action, they'll hunt me down."

Her mind flashed to the aforementioned "scumbags". Oliver was right. It would take David Lone all of three minutes to work it out. He'd be better off hidden out west.

"Listen, don't worry about going into my office on Monday. Shazza's gonna help me sort stuff from her place. She's got her laptop; thank God the coppers never thought to confiscate that."

"Is there anything else I can do?"

"Nah, nah, I just need to call my clients, that kind of stuff. Thomas is going to get cracking on our defense."

"Okay, well, unfortunately I have to head out of town this week, myself, probably Monday, to chase up some stuff for David's book, so—"

"His book? Is that still happening?"

She cringed, wished she hadn't mentioned it. "I know, it's really hard to think about something so trivial now, but he's determined to keep it rolling, and well ..."

"No, no, you have to do what you have to do, Roxy. Don't you worry about that. I'm just surprised by Davo, that's all."

"Well that makes two of us. He's certainly surprising. So, anyway, while I've got you I just need to check a few things that have been troubling me."

"Such as?"

"I've already asked Sharon this, but can you think of anyone who might have hidden that phone in your office? Anyone at all?"

He sighed. "Believe me, Rox, I've been racking my brain."

"Not Tina's dad? Or Erin? Or Norman?"

"Nope, nope, nope."

"And that hideous Amy Halloran?"

"Amy? What's she got to do with all this?"

"Oh ... I'm just wondering, crossing those Ts, you know me," she stammered.

"Right, well, no, she's never been to my office as far as I know. I barely know the woman, although she seems to have a hard-on for my clients." He paused. "Is that why you suspect—"

"Oh I don't know what I suspect anymore," she said, cutting him off.

There was a muffled conversation in the background and then he said, "Hang on a minute, Rox." A few minutes later,

Oliver said, "Look, Thomas reckons that's unimportant anyway."

"What? The phone?"

"Yeah, he says that there's no proof that mobile is directly linked to the murders. Just because it's the phone that was used to call both Tina and William the nights they died, doesn't say anything. At least that's how he'll present it to the court. It's not like it was used to leave an incriminating message. They were all just hang ups. Gonna try and get it thrown out."

She thought about that, felt a little better. "Okay, can I ask a few more questions? Have you got time?"

"Yeah, yeah, it's a bloody long drive, Roxy, plus Thomas drives like an old lady." There was laughter in the background but she was about to put an end to all that.

"You need to tell me about William Glad," she said.

"What about him?"

"Why were you looking up his contract the day he died? Why did you visit him that night and not mention it?"

There was a long pause before he answered. "I don't know why I didn't tell you that, Rox. I just had a gut feeling it would land me in it, and it has. I was right."

"It's important, Oliver!"

"I don't see why! Look, Erin had called to tell me her dad was deteriorating fast, might not last the week. I went to visit the poor bugger to say good-bye. I was there hours before he died. Around seven-ish. I was only there about ten minutes, he looked like death warmed up, was really tired, so I took off. I never returned, I promise you that."

"Do they have any evidence of you taking off? Of not returning?"

"Obviously not or they wouldn't have friggin' charged me."

"Okay. So what about the contract? Why were you looking at William's contract?"

A long sigh. "For the same reason. I knew he didn't have long and wanted to check what his final wishes were, ask if he had any plans to change it, and if not, leave it be. It turns out I never got to discuss it with him. He was too frail and it didn't feel right. It didn't feel important any more. I told all of this to the police. It just wasn't that important to me."

"David says that Erin blames you entirely for trying to push her Dad to publish his back catalogue. Says it was all your idea."

Oliver growled, "Well, Erin's a liar! It's not true. We'd all just been talking about it at David's film launch, do you remember? I wanted to set the record straight before Will died, that was all. I didn't care either way."

"But Oliver, you told me yourself, after William died, that you were looking at republishing."

"Because Erin kept going on about it. He didn't have anything in his will, so she seemed to think we had free rein. I'll tell you again what I told the police, I didn't care that much. Still don't. I don't give a fuck about that catalogue. It won't even bring in that much money, I don't know why everyone is fixating on it."

Now it was Roxy's turn to sigh. "So why then did William call to see his lawyer before he died? Maybe he was going to change his will? Maybe he just never got the chance."

"His lawyer?"

She told him what David had told her. That the lawyer had been called to William's house but never got there in time.

Oliver scoffed. "Gazza? Gazza O'Reilly? That's William's solicitor, it's also his oldest mate! Did Davo tell you that? Of course William wanted to see him that week. He wanted to see all of us, all his friends, for God's sake, he was dying!"

"So it wasn't to change his will?"

"Fucked if I know, but I doubt it. I doubt William could have held a pen up to sign anything. He was frail, Rox, and he wasn't even in that frame of mind. I saw him. He was just full of love and just wanted to say good-bye."

Oliver's voice had turned croaky; he sounded exhausted.

She was feeling that way herself and she hadn't been officially interrogated all day, let alone accused of one murder, possibly three.

"I'm sorry about all this, Oliver, you know I believe in you. I just have to ask. I need to cross my Ts, dot my Is. It's the way I do things."

"I know, I know, it's what makes you so bloody infuriating, and so bloody good at the same time. It's why I'm glad you're on my side."

"And I am on your side. Don't ever forget that. Okay, I'd better let you go. You must be sick of all of this."

"Big time. Hey, did you ever get through to Tina's editor, get that last book sent over?"

"It should be with me on Monday."

"Good. We'll talk later, but Rox—"

"I know, I know, be careful."

"Don't make light of it. I didn't do this thing, Rox, which means somebody else did. And whoever it is, he's still out there."

CHAPTER 29

As Roxy stepped out onto the street on Sunday morning and walked the three blocks down to where her car was parked in a side street off Elizabeth Bay Road, she had the distinct feeling that someone was watching her.

Bloody Oliver, she thought. He had really creeped her out last night. She looked around. There were various couples strolling along the street, a few kids mucking about, an elderly man holding onto a light pole as though his life depended on it, but none of them seemed to pay her any attention. Still, the feeling persisted.

Was she just being paranoid?

She pulled her handbag closer and continued walking while reaching for her keys and double checking her body alarm at the same time. Yep, it was still there. Still activated.

She left the main street and turned into the alleyway when something moved in her periphery and she stopped and glanced around again, fear trickling down her spine. There was no one there.

She picked up her pace and strode the few metres to her car, was just about to unlock the door when a flash of light caught her eye. Roxy swung around again and this time she spotted him, a photographer, standing close to a large council bin, a bulky camera in one hand, a look of guilt on his ruddy face.

Roxy could not have been happier. There wasn't a serial killer trailing her, after all, it was just the bloody paparazzi. They were obviously trying to get pictures of Oliver, and, failing that, anyone remotely close to him. She thrust the keys back into her bag and headed straight for the photographer whose guilty look was fast being cloaked by a kind of stubborn determination. He was thrusting his chin in the air and holding the camera at bay as though fearful she was about to wrestle it from him. No doubt that had happened many times before.

"You right?" she said, scowling.

"Yeah," he muttered, not offering any other explanation.

"I don't know where Oliver Horowitz is, if that's who you're after. But I am going to spend a very exciting hour with my mother, Lorraine Jones, at the Flower Pot Nursery, Lane Cove, if you'd like to tag along. She'd be so thrilled to see her pearls and twin set in the local rag."

He shrugged. "Just doin' my job, lady."

"Yeah, well, you're the one who has to sleep with yourself at night."

She turned on her heel and walked back to her car. By the time Roxy started the engine, she noticed that the photographer was checking his camera and walking in the opposite direction. She exhaled. While she really was meeting up with her mother that day, she didn't exactly want the paparazzi tagging along.

These fortnightly catch-ups were stressful enough as it was.

By the time Roxy got to the café, Lorraine was at a table, tapping one nail on the top of her thin, gold wristwatch.

"And what time do you call this?" she said, standing to allow Roxy to kiss her lightly on one powdered cheek.

"Sorry, I had some vermin to dispose of first," she

replied, slipping into a seat.

Lorraine's nose wrinkled up. "Rats?! Oh dear, I hope they're not out of control?"

"Me too. Have you ordered?"

"Yes, darling, and I nearly ordered for you but I know how you carry on."

Roxy ignored this, jumped up and ordered a latté and a vegie focaccia. She needed fortifying today. Not only did she have a full hour with her mother, as she'd told the photographer, but she was meeting with Max, later, and that would also require superhuman strength.

Back at the table, Lorraine launched into a long discussion about her latest renovations and about Charlie's plans for a fabulous European holiday. It pleased Roxy for once. She normally loathed small talk, but she needed a break from discussing Oliver's case and she was hoping her mother would not bring it up. Lorraine would hyperventilate if she knew Roxy was helping Oliver, and she would try to get her off the case.

After their food had arrived and was half eaten, her mother finally asked, "Is that Oliver Horowitz I keep hearing about on the news the same Oliver Horowitz as your agent?'

Roxy felt her stomach drop. So much for clean getaways. She nodded, trying to look nonchalant.

"Did he really kill three people, Roxy? Three writers?!"

"Of course he didn't, Mum!" A few people looked around and Roxy lowered her voice. "He's been accused of one murder only at this stage—"

"Oh, well, that's perfectly fine then," said Lorraine, pursing her lips.

"But it doesn't matter because he didn't do it. He's being framed."

"Framed? By whom, darling?"

She shrugged. "I wish I knew."

"Oh dear, I do hope you're staying out of it, young woman."

"You know me, Mum. Of course I'm not. I have to help

him."

Lorraine's eyes widened. "Roxanne Parker, you listen to me. You need to leave all of this to the police and you need to look after yourself."

"Mum, I can't desert Oliver."

"Yes you can, especially if he's got a penchant for murdering writers."

"Muuum ..." She looked around. "Keep your voice down. And, for the last time, he didn't do this thing. So I'm perfectly safe."

She sighed and glanced at her nails. "Well, at least he's in jail. That'll keep you safe for a while."

"Actually, he's been released, he's on bail."

Lorraine's eyes widened again. "Oh, dear, darling, that's very scary. What if he did do it? He could kill you."

"Muum!"

"No, don't you Mum me. I have always thought that Oliver man was a tad slimy. I've told you that before. He's an agent, for goodness sake. I wouldn't put it past him."

Roxy pushed her half-eaten sandwich away and stood up. "I'm not going to sit here and listen to this. I'm too busy, I've got too many things on my mind."

Lorraine leaned across and grabbed her daughter's arm. Her voice softened considerably. "I am not trying to be mean, Roxy. I am your mother, and I have a right to be worried about you. You have always had such blind loyalty to people. I don't know where you got that from but it's always been your biggest failing."

Roxy shook her free, grabbed her bag and stood up. "I see it as one of my greatest traits, Mum." She went to walk away then turned back. "And by the way, I got it from Dad."

At her car, Roxy got that spooky feeling again. This time she wasn't in the mood. She did a fast pirouette and spotted the photographer leaning forward in his car, his lens at the ready. She raced towards him while he dropped his camera and attempted to start his engine.

"You have got to be kidding me!" she screamed at him.

He hunched over, as though afraid she'd reach in the half-opened window and smack him one. "I was just checking ..." he stammered.

"Get any nice shots of Mum? She looks good for sixty, don't you think? Do you mind sending some copies to the apartment? They'll look good in the family album."

He didn't say anything so she just stared at him for a full minute before shaking her head and walking away. She wasn't really angry with the man but it helped to have a sleazy photographer around to take her growing anxiety out on, and screaming at him had felt very therapeutic. What's more, her outburst seemed to convince him she was a dead end, and he was already pulling out of the car park ahead of her and skidding away.

"Good riddance!" she screamed after him, and started up her own vehicle.

There was a sudden tap on the window and she jumped. It was just her mother. Roxy buzzed the window down and looked at her.

Lorraine smiled stiffly. "I'm very sorry, Roxanne. It's only because I care, you must know that. Anyway, if there's anything Charlie and I can do to help that agent friend of yours, I mean, Oliver, well, just let us know."

"You just rang Charlie, didn't you?"

She looked away. "Yes, he says I'm to be more supportive."

"He's right."

"I know. I know."

Roxy sighed. "Thanks, but there's nothing much you can do, besides, I have to put it aside for a few days. I'm leaving town tomorrow. Got some work to do on the David Lone biography. I'll be up north at Yamba for the next day or so. Perfectly safe."

Lorraine looked relieved. "Lovely! Get away, that's a great idea. Why don't you take a few extra days up there while you're at it? Go all the way to Byron Bay? I hear it's beautiful this time of year."

"I'll just be gone twenty-four hours, Mum, I am very busy."

"Okay, okay. Just a thought. Well, be sure to call me when you get there."

"Mum, I'm thirty-two, not thirteen."

"Writers are being slaughtered in their beds, Roxanne, at least humour me with this one. Please."

"Fine, fine, but it's a long drive so I won't arrive until very late Monday night. I'll call you on Tuesday, let you know I'm okay. I'll definitely be back Tuesday night at the latest. Okay?"

That seemed to make Lorraine happy. She smiled, blew her daughter a kiss and waved as she drove away.

CHAPTER 30

"She's just worried about you, that's all," Max said softly, "and she has reason to be. I'm worried too."

Roxy tried to hide the joy that his concern erupted in her and coughed, swallowing back the smile. She was tucked up on the enormous sofa in his warehouse, Caroline on one side, Max on the other, an opened bottle of wine between them. She couldn't have felt safer, but she knew that Max, Oliver, and yes, even her mother were right. She had better watch her back. It had been over a week since the last murder. Perhaps the killer was getting antsy.

As promised, Roxy had arrived for Sunday night dinner with the Farrell siblings, and was not at all sure what to expect. She knew she had to set the record straight about David Lone. Both Max and Caroline had assumed that she was sleeping with him, and she shouldn't have allowed that. It had been sweet revenge for Max's dalliance with Gilda, but it was time to 'fess up. She glanced around, still expecting the policewoman to appear from the upper bedroom, rosy from an afternoon lovemaking session, one of Max's oversized shirts on, and she had to shake herself a little to remove the disturbing image.

There's no way she could deal with that.

As if reading her mind, Caroline said, "Max has got something to tell you, about Gilda Maltin, don't you, Max?"

She stared hard at her brother who hid momentarily behind his floppy fringe, not meeting anyone's eyes. Caroline coughed and stood up.

"I'm heading out for a ciggie, then I'll see how Max's dinner is going."

"Do you need a hand?" Roxy asked, surprised to learn that Max was actually cooking, and even more surprised by the delicious smells that were now emanating from the kitchen.

"No, you stay here," she instructed Roxy. "And listen to Max. *Max*."

He got another of those stares and smiled slightly. "You're so bloody bossy, Caro. And you promised me you were giving up."

Caroline reached down to the table to grab a packet of cigarettes and a lighter and smirked at him, then smiled at Roxy and padded off. Max took a deep, loud breath and swivelled on the sofa so he was facing Roxy. She went to say something but he held up one hand.

"Please, hear me out." She nodded, relaxed back into the seat and waited. "You seem to have the wrong idea about Gilda and me," he began.

"It's really none of my business, Max, you're a free—"

"Can I finish?"

"Of course, go on."

"That night at the party, I was talking to Gilda."

"Yes, I know, but—"

"Uh!" He held the hand up again. "You're letting me finish this time, remember?"

She smiled, whispered, "Sorry."

"So, yes, we were talking and then it just got so damn noisy, we went up to my room." She shrank back, not sure she really wanted to hear this now. "And then we kept talking. That's all that happened. Lots and lots of ... talking."

She looked at him. Frowned. "Really? Up in the bedroom? Just talking?"

He laughed. "Yes, I know, it's not the usual occupation up there, but that's the truth. Sorry to disappoint you." There was a clouded look in his eyes.

"Disappoint me?"

"Well, you seem intent on thinking that Gilda and I will get together. I don't know why. I don't feel that way about her. Never did."

"But you asked me to bring her to your party."

"So?"

"So I just assumed that ... well ..."

"I asked you to bring her because I thought she'd be fun, and I thought she'd help you lighten up and enjoy yourself. For a change."

"You sound like my mother," she said and he laughed again.

"Sometimes even your crazy mother is right."

Caroline reappeared. "I hear laughter, that's a good thing, surely?" She glanced from Roxy to her brother and back again.

Roxy smiled. "Yes, Max was just setting the record straight. Now it's my turn."

"Not yet, you don't," said Caroline. "Max, your curry is ready to go. We should take this to the dining table, I've set it up and the food awaits us.

"Hang on, Caro. Roxy, what did you want to say?"

"No, no, I'll tell you later, let's eat. I'm starving."

They jumped up and made their way towards a large wooden door that had been turned into a very rustic-looking dining table on one end of the warehouse. Max had a motley selection of chairs around it, some 1950s vinyl and chrome, several wooden ones, a couple of stools. Roxy chose a cushioned chrome one and sat down, placing her wine glass in front of her. Caroline had done a beautiful job of decorating the table with scented candles, matching cutlery and a small vase of fresh flowers.

"I didn't know Max had a cutlery set," Roxy said, and Caroline whistled.

"I struggled, I can tell you, but after rooting around in his kitchen drawers, I managed to find some that look close enough." She pushed a bowl of rice towards Roxy. "Help yourself."

Roxy took a few spoonfuls and then added some Tikka Masala curry over the top. "This smells so good, Max. I didn't know you were such a good cook."

He shrugged. "I can pull it together when I have to."

"Plus he had me as his sous-chef," Caroline said, taking the curry bowl and helping herself.

When they had finished filling their bowls, Max held his glass up. "To better times ahead," he said, glancing from one woman to the other.

"I'll drink to that," said Roxy. Then she added, "And to Oliver, may he get out of this mess, and soon!"

They all cheered and drank.

"I know you're probably sick of talking about it," Max said, "but how's he going? What's the latest news?"

For the next hour, the three friends got so immersed in the Oliver Horowitz case, Roxy didn't get a chance to talk about David Lone, and set the record straight. When the conversation finally lulled, she realised she didn't want to. They were having so much fun and she was finally feeling close to Max again. She feared that bringing up another man, no matter how innocent, was going to ruin everything. So she let it drop for now. She didn't even mention her impending trip to Yamba, to work on David's book. She had a hunch he wouldn't be too thrilled by that either. So she kept it to herself.

Her silence would turn out to be a very dangerous mistake.

Later that evening, after the friends had eaten and cleaned up, Max insisted on walking Roxy back to her car, which was just as well as it was parked well away from his warehouse, the only empty spot she could find.

"You never asked me what we were talking about," said Max as they walked side by side, their arms just brushing, a tingling sensation filling her every time they touched.

"Sorry?"

"Gilda and me, at the party. We went up to my room to talk."

"Oh right. I just assumed you were going through Gilda's life again in minute detail."

He laughed. "No, not that."

"Okay then, what were you talking about you?"

"You, of course. Who else?"

She stopped, turned to face him. "Me? Really?"

"Really." Max stared through his fringe at her, his eyes soft and gooey again and she had to look away. She resumed walking.

"Sounds dull," she said, trying to sound flippant. "So what were you saying? What a pain in the proverbial I can be?"

Max took one of Roxy's arms and stopped her, forcing her to turn around and look at him. "I'll tell you that if you tell me whether you and David Lone are ... together." He said the words as though they cut, and she smiled at him.

"No, Max, we are not together. Never were. Well, I did spend that night, but I was drunk and nothing happened and it doesn't mean anything anyway."

He looked beyond relieved, he looked blissful and he did something that would have irked her once. He pulled her into his arms and he held her tightly for a few glorious minutes. She could feel his strong, sinewy body beneath his shirt and she breathed him in then, the soapy smell of his skin tinged with the scent of fresh coffee and something else, something more masculine, before he was pushing her back out and staring into her eyes.

"Gilda was wondering why I hadn't made a move on you and I was explaining that you didn't like me that way. And she then told me I was a bloody fool, that I was wrong." He hesitated. "Am I wrong, Roxy. Is there a chance ... for us?"

She felt her legs melt as she said what should have been said a long time ago. "Yes, Max. There is a chance." She held one hand up quickly. "But I need to get a few things sorted first. You know what I'm like—hopeless at multitasking. I need to help Oliver and then ..."

He smiled. "Then we'll try again?"

She nodded. "Yes, let's definitely try again."

Max leaned in and kissed her very quickly on the lips, but it was electrifying and she felt all her internal organs dance about, in a good way this time.

"Come on," he said, "let's get you on your way."

Five minutes later, as Roxy waved him good-bye and started her car's engine, her elation turned to anxiety. She had that creepy feeling again. She looked about. The street was dark and, apart from Max who was retreating back to his warehouse, it appeared empty. She scowled, shook her head and strapped herself in. She didn't even bother reaching for her alarm this time. She knew exactly who it was.

That bloody paparazzi guy, she thought impatiently as she began to drive off. *He's certainly tenacious.*

******

From the sidewalk, someone was watching Roxy, had been watching her all night. All week, in fact. He smiled but it wasn't a happy smile. He was bitter, she had betrayed him, and she would pay the ultimate price.

Not long now, Miss Parker, he thought. It will soon be your turn.

Then he began to think of 101 ways to kill a ghostwriter.

CHAPTER 31

Roxy took the first exit onto the Pacific Highway and began the long drive to Yamba, a breezy little holiday town on the NSW north coast. Ordinarily, she liked road trips, but this one felt all wrong, starting with the timing. She didn't need to be heading away from Sydney right now, away from Oliver and his problems. She needed to be back at her desk, Gilda close by, trying to help solve this series of baffling, horrendous crimes.

But a deal was a deal, a book needed to be written and her mortgage still needed to be paid. So she had organized the interview with David Lone's old English teacher for Tuesday morning, and needed the full day to get there. She had a book to write, and she had to get on with it.

Thinking of books, Roxy glanced at the small package resting on the passenger seat beside her. It had arrived by post, just seconds before she'd left, and with no time to spare, she'd simply thrown it into the car, along with an overnight bag, a bottle of water and some fruit snacks, and taken off. She'd open the parcel later, but she already knew what was in it. It had to be the editor's proof of Tina Passion's latest novel. Roxy wished now, as she glanced down at it, and then back up at the road, that it was a talking book. She'd have the whole thing sewn up by the end of the drive. Maybe even be a step closer to solving the crimes.

Roxy clicked her car radio on, hoping a decent tune might distract her instead, but all she could find was news channels, sports channels, and "the best of the '80s, '90s and today!" She grimaced and flicked it off, then concentrated on the road ahead.

Three hours into the trip, she pulled over at a large, neon-lit service station, filled up the petrol tank and purchased a takeaway latté, some dark chocolate and a clump of bananas. She needed all the help she could get to stay alert. Then she quickly checked her mobile phone calls.

There was one from Maria Constantinople at *Glossy* that caught her by surprise and she immediately returned the call.

"Roxy Parker, I've got a bone to pick with you!" Maria boomed on the other end when she'd picked up, and Roxy felt her feet grow suddenly heavier. She did not want Maria picking at any of her anatomy, thank you very much. "And I'm not the only one. Lorenzo Vento is *not* a happy man."

"Really? I thought we got along really well."

"Yeah, so did he, which is why he can't understand why you weren't upfront with him. About Oliver."

Her legs turned to lead. "Oliver?"

"It didn't occur to you to tell him Oliver was your fuckin' agent? He rang this morning, had just heard, somehow, that you were on Oliver's books. He's fuming, Roxy, cranky as all hell. Told me if he'd known that, you never would've got the interview in the first place."

"Hence the reason I didn't tell him, Maria. Look, I didn't want to confuse things; it was irrelevant to this story. I was writing the story for you, not for Oliver. It has nothing to do with him."

"You sure about that? Or are you using us both to get what you want? And by both I mean Lorenzo and me."

She swallowed hard. "No, Maria ... well, okay, maybe I did want to help my agent, but—"

"Ah-ha! I knew you were up to something!"

"But I also wanted to write that article. It's a good story and I needed the work." She glanced at her watch. She needed to get back on the road. "Were you unhappy with it? Was Lorenzo?"

"Well, no, luckily for you it's a bloody good story, but that's not the friggin' point. The point, Roxy, is that you don't muck me around ever again, right?! You want to use *Glossy* for your own personal crusade, you friggin' lay it on the line. You tell me what's going on! No more bullshit. Got it?"

Roxy agreed, apologizing again and hanging up, her heart now heavy. She shouldn't have deceived Lorenzo, she knew that, but she also knew, as Maria had just confirmed, that she never would have got access to him if she hadn't. Then she might never have learned about the strange phone calls before Tina died, and about the missing book.

Still, she couldn't help the feeling of dread that accompanied her on the last leg of the journey. It was never a good idea to get Maria offside, but that's not what was really worrying her. A few free lattés and a bit of flattery and Maria would come around. No, it was not Maria she was worried about at all. It was Lorenzo Vento. He had seemed sweet enough during their interview, but perhaps he had played her all along? From what Maria said, he was clearly quick to anger and now he was angry with her.

Roxy shuddered. She knew what happened to people who pissed Lorenz Vento off.

CHAPTER 32

By midnight, Roxy had managed to push Lorenzo from her thoughts and was focusing on finding the Yamba Holiday Park where she'd pre-booked a small cabin for the night, complete with bedding and blankets. She'd only need a room for a few hours so she wasn't going to waste all her budget on a flashy hotel. When she finally did locate it, she paid the weary looking receptionist at the front office and made her way to the cabin, keen to get some shut-eye. It was extremely basic but it didn't matter. Once she laid her head down, she was asleep within minutes.

A high-pitched scream woke Roxy from her slumber and she sat up, startled. The scream came again, followed by several others and she realized she was listening to white cockatoos just outside her cabin.

Stretching out, she pulled on her glasses and checked the clock on her mobile phone. It was 7:09 a.m., her least favourite time of the day, but she was glad for the early wake-up call. She had no time to waste.

Roxy got up and took the one step required to reach the tiny bathroom. She stripped off, showered, then returned to her bag to find the flowing, animal-print dress she'd brought along. It was crease-proof and perfect for travel. She threw a wide black belt around her waist, some hoop earrings in her ears and short black boots on her feet then returned to the car.

Half an hour later, she was sitting on a park bench, looking down across a startling white Yamba beach, takeaway coffee in one hand, croissant in the other. It was a perfect summer day. Not yet hot, there was a gentle, salty breeze and the caw of seagulls nearby, and she sat for a few moments just drinking it all in, mesmerized by the beauty around her.

For a few minutes she felt a million miles from the horror of the past week in Sydney, from three murders and a good friend out on bail, and she wanted to hold onto that feeling, if only for a little mental reprieve, but she couldn't help herself.

Within minutes she was pulling the brown package out of her handbag and ripping it open. As expected, it was the proof copy of Tina Passion's last novel. Titled *Lover's Delight*, it featured a trademark tacky cover of a buxom redhead standing just in front of a bare-chested man, complete with designer-sized pecs and flowing blonde locks. He was looking down at the woman's neck like he wanted to devour it, and she seemed slightly dazed by it all, her ruby lips parted, her cheeks flushed. Roxy would have sniggered if there wasn't a loud bell clanging away in her head.

She had seen this book before. If only she could remember where.

She flicked through it, noting various marks made on tiny yellow stickies throughout the book, and on the final page the word "proof" had been printed across at an angle. Perhaps she'd seen it at Oliver's office before it went to the editor. She made a mental note to ask him next time they spoke and then dropped it back into her bag. There was no time to give it any more attention; she had to prepare for her interview with Mrs Porter.

Roxy pulled out a notepad and pen, and began to jot

down some questions. More would pop up as the interview progressed but Roxy liked to be organized, so she tried to focus on David Lone and what his favourite English teacher might have to say about him.

He must have shown early promise, but did she really expect him to become quite as successful as he had, to have an international top-selling book and critically acclaimed film to his name?

"Oh, absolutely!" came the giggly reply an hour later as Roxy sat across from the elderly English teacher at her home in an outer Yamba suburb. Mrs Porter looked a little like her name suggested—portly and pink, with fluffy grey hair and a wobbling double chin that was in overdrive now.

She had invited Roxy to her modest brick house for the interview, explaining that she no longer taught English at school, but had moved into university lecturing.

"But I haven't even been at university for the past six months. I'm waiting to take up a fellowship in Literary Classics at a school in London."

"Sounds exciting," Roxy said and the teacher laughed.

"Liar! It sounds dreadfully boring, but I'll just love it. Sadly, most people don't appreciate the classics anymore. They'd prefer quick, vacuous reads, I'm afraid."

Roxy thought then of Tina Passion's novel that was wedged in her bag and smiled. She was probably right. Tina's books sold like wildfire.

"So where would you put David's book?" she asked. "A potential classic or a vacuous read?"

Mrs Porter—who appeared not to have a first name and if she did was not yet telling—gave her a wide, wobbly smile. "Well, my dear, it's a wonderful book! I just knew my little Davey would be a star."

"Why? Was he a natural talent or—"

"It wasn't so much that as his *determination*," she said. "He was always such a charmer, so sweet, but also fiercely determined. When he set his mind to something, he had to have it. I remember we had a writing competition in Year 9, and Davey came second in that. Oh, boy was he disappointed. Angry, even, with himself."

"Angry, why?"

"Because he didn't come first, dear. He had to come first and the next year, he did! He worked so hard at his short story I thought he'd have a breakdown. But it was superb, a truly great piece. That's when I thought to myself, this boy will go far. Nothing will stop him."

"Well you were right," she said and the teacher giggled again.

"But he had to work at, I'll make that clear. He wasn't as natural a writer as some of my other students, but he had the raw determination that sets you apart. Plus, as I say, he was a right charmer. That helped." Her little eyes twinkled and it was clear David's charms still worked on this old teacher. "Of course, not everybody was as enamoured," she added, heaving herself up to fetch more hot water for the teapot.

"Oh?" Roxy said, following her into the kitchen.

"Well, perhaps I'm speaking out of school now—excuse the pun—but, no, I do know at least one of his past teachers who was very surprised to hear of David's success. More tea, dear?"

Roxy held her cup out and Mrs Porter refilled it before waddling back into the living room. They settled onto her old sofa again.

"Yes, if you're going to do this book about him, I guess you need to give a balanced view. You should probably speak to Edward Green, he has a very different take on our Mr Lone." She smiled wickedly. "You'd hardly know we were talking about the same person."

"Edward Green?"

"Yes dear, Professor Edward Green, that was David's Creative Writing teacher at Southern Cross University. We're in the same faculty now. Davey didn't mention him?"

"Not really, no."

"I shouldn't be surprised. Edward was hardly his biggest

fan."

"Really? Why?"

She giggled. "I'm being a bit naughty, aren't I? Being a bit salacious." She said the word with gusto. "Perhaps you'd best chat to him directly, I wouldn't want to be spreading rumours."

Roxy thought about this. David had distinctly asked her not to research his university days and she had accepted that. Yet something Caroline had said, something about his leaving university "mysteriously" had stuck with her, and now Mrs Porter was alluding to something more, something "salacious".

Isn't that what Oliver and the publisher had wanted all along?

"Where is this Professor Green?" she asked and the teacher giggled again.

"I see I have got you hooked! He lives about an hour's drive away. I don't have his number but I'm sure you could locate him easily enough."

An hour later, as Roxy made her way back to her car, she considered what Mrs Porter had said and whether she should call Professor Green. She glanced down at the contact details she had just Googled on her smartphone and frowned. He lived up at a place called Ballina, not far from Lismore where the university was located. It was almost a hundred kilometres away, but then, what was one more hour of driving after such a long journey? Perhaps she should knock this on the head now? Perhaps it was important?

She unlocked her car and slipped in behind the wheel, trying to make a decision. David had been adamant that she keep his university days out of it. *But why?* There was clearly a story here and she would be remiss as a biographer if she did not seek it out. She groaned. It was the last thing she felt like doing, but it was the first thing a good biographer would do. You were supposed to show the whole story, not just one side. You were supposed to be impartial, isn't that what

David had said about his own work? She reached into her handbag and pulled out her mobile phone, then began to make the call.

Back in Sydney, Lorraine Jones was also staring at her phone, willing it to ring. Roxy had promised she would call on Tuesday, but had clearly neglected to, yet again.

"Just leave her be," Charlie said, wandering past as Lorraine reached for the handset. "You promised you'd wait for her to call."

"I know, I know." She dropped her hand back down guiltily. "But why hasn't she?"

"Because she's working, my love. When she finishes, she will give you a tingle then."

Lorraine tried not to frown, it worked havoc on her wrinkles, and returned to reading the latest *Women's Weekly*.

CHAPTER 33

Professor Edward Green was a tall, willowy man, with a bushy beard and gold-rimmed spectacles. He was quite the English professor cliché, right down to the stern attitude and patronizing tone. He was a very busy man, he'd warned Roxy when she'd finally located him over the phone, but if she was willing to make the drive he was willing to find ten minutes to "discuss Mr Lone" as he so eloquently put it.

By the time Roxy got to Ballina, it was close to 2:30 p.m. and she made her way directly to the local library where she was assured he could be found, hovering by the aviation section. A pet hobby, apparently.

It didn't take long to spot him, not only because he personified your cliché professor. He was also one of only two people in the building, the other being the librarian.

"That was quick," he said when she introduced herself. "You must have broken a few road rules on your way here."

She ignored this and indicated a nearby desk. "Do you mind if we sit down and I can record this?"

He'd promised only ten minutes and she wasn't going to waste a minute of it. He nodded and they both sat across from each other, Roxy placing her recorder in between.

Professor Green leaned back in his chair and began stroking his beard, waiting for her to proceed. To start with, she asked if he had read David's book on the Supermodel murders and he sniffed.

"Yes, I have read it."

"And what did you think?"

He stopped stroking his beard. "Well, it's not exactly my style, but that's not to say it's not a very good attempt."

She cringed. It was like red ink all over his manuscript. *Must try harder.* She knew David would not appreciate that review.

"It has been hugely successful," she said, feeling a little defensive on his part.

"Quantitative success is one thing, Ms Parker, quality is quite another."

"He's also had critical acclaim. Not one bad review." He shrugged dismissively. "The book has just been made into a very good movie, and he has two more book deals in the pipeline. That must really surprise you."

"Surprise?" He sat forward. "I'm not at all surprised."

"Really? I got the impression from Mrs Porter that you thought David wouldn't amount to anything."

"Then you got the wrong impression. I would have bet my house that man would become a successful writer. If that's what he wanted." He hesitated then asked, "What sort of book are you writing?"

"I'm doing a biography on behalf of a publisher," she said, adding quickly, "It's not a fanzine. I do want the truth, Professor Green."

"Then I'll give it to you. The David Lone I knew was always a rather tricky character. Arrogant, zealous, a complete charmer. But his charms were wasted on me. I didn't believe he had an ounce of real talent, but I knew that he had drive. And he was driven, really driven to be a writer."

"So why did he leave your writing course then? Mrs Porter tells me it's one of the most acclaimed in the country."

He hesitated again. "Have you asked him that question?"

"Yes. He doesn't want me to pursue it."

"Then perhaps you should respect his wishes."

"I want to get to the truth, Professor Green. I'm not interested in writing a one-sided story. If there's something important to say, I'd like you to say it."

Still the man hesitated. He leaned back in his chair and stroked his beard for some time, clearly giving it considerable thought. Eventually, he said, "I can't see how this can hurt now. I mean, it's a matter of public record after all."

"What is?"

"His departure from the university, of course. He didn't leave, Ms Parker. At least not by choice. He was thrown out."

"Really? What did he do?" Roxy half expected the answer to be something simple and benign. Perhaps he'd played up too much, or missed too many tutorials. Most of her university friends had barely scraped through, their loyalty torn between getting a degree and getting as drunk as possible in the process.

Professor Green cleared his throat then glanced around the room before saying, "You will not quote me on this. You will do your own research and find the facts for yourself. They are easy enough to find. I'm surprised nobody has yet stumbled upon them, to be honest."

"Of course, yes," she said, clicking her digital recorder off, her curiosity now intensified.

He sighed. "David Lone was found guilty of plagiarism." As he said it, his top lip curled upwards, as though he'd just said the word murder, and she winced. It might as well be murder, at least, in a writing degree. It was the ultimate sin.

"Plagiarism," she repeated softly, stunned. She had not been expecting that.

"Yes, I'm afraid so. Not once, but twice, I might add. He handed in two fictional stories that were largely lifted straight from previously published works by a university student in Finland, if I recall correctly. Perhaps it was Sweden. In any case, it was mere chance that we happened upon it—this was pre-Internet age, you understand? And it made me wonder what else he'd stolen and got away with. In any case, we had no choice but to expel him. No choice at all. Of course, Mr Lone was not my first student to be guilty of plagiarism and he certainly wasn't my last. Still, it's a hanging offence at university and he had to pay the price."

She nodded, wondering, like him, why this story had not leaked earlier.

As if reading her mind, he said, "Mr Lone ... asked me to keep it private. I obliged. It was no skin off my nose. But, as I say, it's in the record books. For all to see." Then, sensing her mood, he added, "Ms Parker, I had very little respect for David Lone back then and I'm afraid it does rather tarnish my view of him. You have to remember he was a young man then and if what you say is true, if his work is now critically acclaimed, then he has clearly turned over a new leaf. And that's good to see. Those days are obviously well behind him. Still, it ought to be said. It ought to be said." He pushed his chair back and stood up. "Now, if you don't mind, I have my own research to get on with."

"Of course, yes, of course," she said, glancing down to gather her things and wishing, suddenly, that she hadn't come here after all.

She felt like a traitor, and she knew that once spoken, words could not be forgotten. Or ignored. She could not quote the professor, but she did need to follow this up one day, when she had more time, and it was not a cheerful thought. For now, though, she would try to ignore it, and head back to Sydney. She was keen to get back on the Oliver Horowitz case.

That afternoon, realizing that she had neither the energy nor the time to begin the long drive home, Roxy found a decent looking motel by the side of the road and booked a room for the night. Then, after unloading her bag, she made her way to a nearby Chinese restaurant for an early dinner. The place was packed, mostly with boisterous young families or frowning older couples, but she managed to find a table in one corner and promptly ordered a glass of house red from the flustered young waitress. She had brought Tina's book along to keep herself company and, after ordering from the greasy menu, turned to chapter one and began to read.

As she did so, the bell began clanging again in the back of her mind. There was something about this book. Something important. If only she could work out what. A sudden, loud beep cried out from her phone and several of the oldies turned around to stare at her, their frowns deepening further as she pulled it out. She smiled at them and quickly checked the message. It was from her mother.

Damn it, she'd forgotten to call. But she wasn't about to do it now. They clearly didn't appreciate digital interruptions at this restaurant—although, apparently, screaming kids and flying toys were perfectly acceptable—so she slipped the phone back into her bag and decided to call when she returned to her motel room. Her mum could wait thirty minutes more.

Several spring rolls and a bowl of wonton soup later, Roxy shut the book, paid the bill and made her way back to the nearby motel. The night was now dark, very dark, and there wasn't a soul about. She felt a prickle of apprehension as she walked and she was not sure why. She had that strange sense that someone was watching her again and she tried to shake it off. It was silly. There was no good reason why the paparazzi would follow her all the way up here.

Still the prickle did not go away, so she pulled her handbag closer, placing one hand in to touch her alarm, and picked up her pace. At the motel room door, she grappled for the key and quickly let herself in dropping her bag to the floor with relief before reaching for the light.

But her hand never made it. Instead, a thick wad of cloth was suddenly, violently pressed against her nose and mouth and the overwhelming smell of chloroform blasted her senses. She tried to cry out, tried to push it away, but it was no use, her hands and legs were already turning to jelly and within seconds she had dropped to the floor with one final thought remaining.

She had finally worked out where she had seen Tina's last book, and it struck fear in her heart. But it was no use now. Everything was turning black.

CHAPTER 34

Something hard hit Roxy's head and she opened her eyes, feeling groggy and disoriented. Everything was dark and there was something cold and sharp underneath her right hip and wedged against her cheek. There was an overwhelming smell of grease and rubber, and the ground on which she was lying was rattling and shaking violently.

Where the hell was she?

Roxy went to sit up but her head smacked against something and she cried out in pain, then realized, with horror, that she was in a tiny, contained space, her hands bound together and legs squished up against her chest. She struggled to break free but could barely move an inch. The rattling intensified and it took a few seconds to understand that she was moving fast. Very fast.

Roxy tried to twist around but she couldn't budge so she lay still for several seconds trying to work out where she was and what was going on. That's when she noticed it. The sound.

"Cha-chaa-clunk! Eeeee! Cha-chaa-clunk!"

She had heard that sound before. Roxy's heart lurched. Oh my God, she was in the boot of Oliver's car!

Relief swept through her momentarily before it was quickly consumed by anger and then a sudden, piercing fear. She swallowed hard, felt violently sick, could not believe what was happening.

Oliver Horowitz! Had he done this to her? Had he knocked her out and bound her up and dumped her in the back of his car?

And if so, why? Surely he was not really a killer as the police believed?

No way, she thought, *not her beloved agent.*

The car rattled to a halt and Roxy shrank back, waiting, her eyes wide with terror, every muscle achingly alert, her heart pounding in her chest. A few seconds later the car started up again and continued driving and she felt a rush of relief. She had no idea where she was going or even how long she had been tied up in the car, but she knew one thing: she had to use this time wisely.

Think, Roxy, think.

Back in Sydney, Lorraine was staring at her phone, her own anger quickly turning to worry, and then something that resembled panic. She glanced across at Charlie who was busily cleaning away the remains of dinner, oblivious to it all, then down at her phone again.

Why hadn't Roxanne called!?

She had a thought. She jumped up and fetched her old Filofax, the brown leather-bound diary she rarely looked at these days, and flipped through the pages until she got to the letter M. With one long nail she scrolled through the names, then re-scrolled until she found it—Max's home number scribbled in faded blue ink. Thank goodness Roxy had insisted she add him to her contacts a few years ago. She'd never once called that number, couldn't see the point, and hoped as she did so now, that it still applied. Or did he only use mobile phones like most young people these days?

Max picked up after a few rings, his voice sounding

sleepy, and Lorraine felt her shoulders drop.

"Hello Max, I'm so sorry to call so late," she began. "It's Lorraine Jones here. Roxanne's mother."

There was a pause on the other end as Max tried to compute this fact and then a rushed, "Oh, hi, Mrs Jones. Are you okay? Is everything okay?"

"Yes, yes, dear, please, call me Lorraine. Look, I'm so sorry to bother you but ..." She half laughed. "Silly of me, I know, and Roxy will never forgive me for doing this, but I was just wondering if you'd heard from my daughter? If you know where she might be?"

"Um ... no, I haven't spoken to her since Sunday night. Should I have?"

"Oh no, no, probably not. It's just that I know she went away, up the coast, and she'd promised to call and well ... she hasn't. And she should be back by now, but there's no answer at home, or on her mobile. That's all." She half laughed again. "Silly of me. I know."

"No, you're worried, that's fair enough. Went up the coast, you say?"

"Yes, she had some research to do on another book. She didn't mention it to you?"

"No ... no she didn't. I was wondering why I hadn't heard from her. Um, just a sec." The phone went muffled for a few minutes before he returned. "Listen, I just checked my mobile, there's no messages from her there and my sister hasn't heard a word either. Have you called Oliver, her agent? Maybe she went straight to his place when she got back."

"No, well, I don't have his number, so ..."

"Look, leave it with me. I'll call him and get back to you. I'm sure there's a reasonable explanation. You know what Roxy's like, she hates to be tied down. Just asking her to call makes her want to do the opposite."

Lorraine smiled. He was right. Max clearly knew her daughter better than she'd given him credit for. "Yes, I'm sure she's just teaching me to mind my own business. That's what Charlie thinks I should do, but ... Well, she just never normally waits this long to return my calls, and what with a maniac on the loose ..."

Her voice choked a little and trailed off so Max assured her again that he'd check with Oliver and get back to her. That seemed to placate Lorraine and she gave him her home number and hung up feeling a little more assured.

Max, however, was now starting to panic. He had been on his way to bed when Lorraine called and he sat down on the sofa now, Caroline beside him.

"Everything all right?" she asked.

"Not sure," he replied, grabbing his mobile and looking up Oliver's numbers. His home phone went straight to voice mail, so Max tried the mobile number, which rang and rang before also converting to voice mail. He tried again. On the second ring it picked up and Max sighed with relief.

"Oliver, great, glad I got you. Just wondering if you've seen or heard from Roxy."

"Ro— ... Sorr— ... Max ..." The phone was going in and out of range and Max could hear traffic in the background.

"Where are you?" he asked. "Can you call me back?"

Oliver's phone went dead and Max growled, staring at it angrily. He turned to his sister. "He's out of range. Hopefully he'll get back to me soon."

Caroline nodded. "What's going on with Roxy?"

He shrugged. "I wish I knew. Roxy's mum is worried, reckons she should be back by now from some trip up the coast. I didn't even know she was going away."

A ringing phone caught them both off guard and Max jumped on it, quickly pressing the answer button.

"Sorry, mate," said Oliver, the line still a little crackly. "Friggin' useless mobile coverage out here in the sticks."

"The sticks?"

"Yeah, been staying at my receptionist's place but I'm on my way back to mine now. Can I call you from there or is it urgent?"

"Actually, it could be urgent. We're just wondering if you've heard from Roxy."

"Roxy? Not in the last couple of days, why?"

"Did you know she was heading up the coast?"

"Yeah, doing some research on the David Lone book." There was a pause. "Why? What's going on?"

"Don't know yet, but she's gone AWOL."

"Maybe she got distracted. Caught in traffic?"

"Yeah, maybe ..."

"Listen I'll make some calls. Davo should know."

"Great, thanks. Don't mean to sound melodramatic but her mum's worried and you know what she's like. The sooner we sort this out and get Roxy to call her, the sooner we can all get some sleep. Just call the second you know more. Okay?"

Oliver promised to do that and hung up. Max turned back to his sister, a deep furrow across his brow.

"I'm starting to get really worried, Caro," he said, his voice now a strained whisper.

"Oh, she'll be fine!"

"How do you know that?" he asked. "There's a lunatic out there, in case you've forgotten. Slaughtering writers. Roxy's a writer."

"And she's very, very far away up the coast," said Caroline, giving his shoulders a gentle squeeze. "If anything, she's as safe as houses."

CHAPTER 35

The house was dark and silent when the old Holden pulled up in front of it, and the man stepped out of the front seat and stared at it for a few minutes before reaching in for a balaclava he'd tossed on the passenger seat. He pulled it on, then shut the front door and moved around to the boot. Using the keys, he unlocked it quickly and then stepped back as the boot swung upwards and open. He wasn't taking any chances. Knowing this woman as he did, he was half expecting her to come jumping out, all guns blazing.

Surprisingly, she was still out cold. He checked his watch. He must have used more chloroform than he'd intended. *Oh well, it'll be easier this way.*

He reached down and grabbed the rope around her wrists with one hand and placed the other under her legs, then hauled her up and out like a limp rag doll. He swung her over his right shoulder and began walking towards the house. He staggered up the few stairs and then dropped her gently on the veranda, before stepping over her and towards the front door. It was locked, but he'd expected that.

He crossed to a front window and peered in through the smudge and grime, then pulled his jacket over his elbow and smashed the glass. He reached in and unlocked the latch from the inside, pulled the creaking window up and, brushing the remaining glass away, jumped up and over the ledge into the house. He looked around.

The old place stank of mould and possum piss and decades of dust, and it would do the job very nicely indeed. Barely containing a smile, he moved through the living area back to the front door to open it. As he stepped out and back on to the veranda, he gasped.

Roxy was gone.

"What the hell!" He looked around frantically until he saw her, hobbling slightly in the direction of the main road. "Shit!" he said and began racing after her.

After playing dead in the boot, Roxy had taken the chance to flee while he was inside. But her right hip was aching, and her legs felt heavy, and she knew he was hot on her trail. Far ahead she could see a street light, and beyond that several more lights showing homes, people, safety. She forged ahead and had just reached the end of the driveway when a hand reached out and grabbed her shoulder, whipping her around and down, smashing onto the gravel. She held her bonded hands up to protect her face but it was too late, his fist came crashing down and smacked her hard, knocking her out again.

Some time later, she did not know when, Roxy came to, her right cheek throbbing, her head pounding, her throat bone dry. There was something over her eyes, a dark cloth, so she couldn't see anything but she whipped her head around anyway, frantically trying to get a grasp on where she was, if she was alone. She had been strapped down into what felt like a scratchy old armchair, just like the one in Oliver's office, and her hands and legs were bound more tightly now so they, too, throbbed beneath the rope. It was cold and damp, a stale, musty smell in the air, and a soft scuttling sound at one side.

"Hello?" she croaked, as desperate to hear a voice as not. There was nothing but silence now. "Anyone there?"

Again nothing. She took deep breaths, trying to contain the fear that was racing through her. A small creak startled Roxy and she swung her head around again, a lash of adrenaline whipping down her spine. She craned her neck, trying to hear where the noise was coming from.

There was another creak, then a sudden bang, and she sat upright, trying to steel herself. A door could be heard swinging open somewhere above her head, and then heavy footsteps began to descend what sounded like a wooden staircase. As they got louder they slowed down and then stopped completely. The silence returned, but she wasn't alone anymore. She knew she was being watched, and every hair on her body stood on end.

"I ... I know you're there," she stammered, trying to draw him out. "I know who you are ..."

Her heart was beating a million miles a minute. She was terrified but she was angry, too, and growing angrier by the second. She knew she should harness that, to help stay alive.

She swallowed hard, breathed deeply and said, "I've worked it all out, you know. I ... I know who killed Seymour, and I know who killed William and Tina."

The footsteps started up again and began to move closer, stopping just inches from her shaking knees. Then she could feel someone's breath, hot and heavy against her cheek, and she could smell him, a spicy, sickly aftershave. She did not recoil. She had smelt that aftershave before. That's when she knew for certain what she had suspected for some time.

In a much calmer voice now, she said simply, "Come on, David, I know it's you."

CHAPTER 36

David Lone was impressed. He stepped back and clapped, a slow, muffled clap, then he reached down and ripped Roxy's eye cover off, and stepped away again.

Roxy squinted, looking around anxiously. It was dark in the room, and it took several minutes for her eyes to adjust, but when they did she saw him standing a little way off, leaning against a shadowy wall, a rickety looking staircase behind him, leading up into the darkness. His normally blow-waved hair was messed up around his face, and he was clad completely in black right down to black boots and black leather gloves. There was some kind of bag on the floor beside him.

"Roxanne Parker," he said eventually, the sliver of a smile on his face. "Trust you to work it out."

She swallowed hard, her throat now drier than a country dam and tried to smile back. "Wasn't rock science," she said drolly. Then, looking about, she asked, "Where are we?"

"You're in the basement of my favourite haunted house, of course. Where else would a ghostwriter show up dead?"

She felt her stomach turn. "What are you going to do? Scare me to death?"

"Something like that."

"That's a little cheesy, even for you."

His smile deflated. "Be careful, Roxanne. You're in no position to be a smart arse."

He was right, so she tried a different tack. "Will you at least tell me why? Why you're doing this to me? I thought we were friends."

"Friends?! You were investigating me, Roxy, digging up dirt where you had no right to dig it up."

"I was researching your book. You asked me to do that."

"I asked you to leave my university days out of it, but you couldn't help yourself, could you? You had to go and speak to old fuckwit Green. Is that what gave me away? Did that miserable old bastard slander me?"

"Actually, he was surprisingly restrained, even gave you the benefit of the doubt. It was Mrs Porter, your favourite English teacher, who made me suspicious."

"Oh?" he stepped forward, intrigued. "What did the silly old cow say?"

"She's not so silly, David. She might have found you charming but she also knew what Professor Green knew—that you'd stop at nothing to be a successful writer. They both emphasized your blind ambition, how you'd do anything to be a star, and it got me thinking. How far *would* you go? Your last book on the terror cells was a flop, and there was only so long you could ride on the *Supermodel Diaries* coattails." She took a deep breath and tried to swallow, but her throat was aching. "This new batch of killings seemed too convenient, too contrived. You said it yourself—an investigative writer's wet dream. Then when you got that book deal, my alarm bells began to tinkle. How very convenient for you. I suspected then that you might have had a motive, for all three deaths. But I wasn't sure."

He held a gloved hand up. "Hey, not all three. Don't give me all the credit."

"No, you're right, you had nothing to do with Seymour Silva's death, did you?"

His face lit up, even in the dark, and his smile was eerily sinister. "How opportune was that?! Stupid lunatic must have killed himself to teach his manager a lesson. Or maybe Norm did him in. I don't know, I don't care. It would have made a great story either way, but my bitch-face editor wouldn't hear of it, wanted to kill it off before it had even gained traction, the fool."

"So you decided to take out another writer and keep the story rolling?"

"Come on, you have to admit, it was such a good story—someone popping off famous writers. Besides, William Glad was dying anyway. I just helped him along. That one doesn't count."

"You smashed his head in with gardening shears," she said, a wave of nausea hitting her. She swallowed hard. "You left that poor old man lying in the dirt. I think it does count. To him, to his daughter, Erin."

"Pfft! She's just a gold digger. Was waiting for the old man to croak it so she could profit from his books. I did her a favour. But I had to act quickly. I knew there was a full-time nurse arriving that weekend. You know, I was thinking of planting it all on Erin but then I realized she had five kids so ..."

"How very big of you," she said and, luckily, he ignored this.

"So I decided on that schizo Norm. He had motive for the first murder so it all made sense, I'd have two connected murders and a great story to tell."

"So you placed the gardening shears in Norm's car, but it blew up in your face. The police discovered that Norm had a watertight alibi, didn't they? He couldn't have killed William, so someone else must have planted the shears. That put a spanner in the works."

David shrugged. "Not for long, thanks to Oliver. Yet again he was in the wrong place at the right time. I wasn't going to frame him, you know, not at the beginning, but he made it all so bloody easy." David pushed off from the wall and began pacing around the room, the pitch in his voice rising with excitement, speckles of dust dancing about as he walked. "He was at the funeral so he had access to Norm's car, then, to make it even easier, he'd been studying William's old publishing contract, had even gone to see him the very night he died. Brilliant! You couldn't have planned it any better. He was like a fly straight into my trap."

She thought then of what Gilda had said about David, and realized he wasn't an annoying insect at all. He was far more predatory than that. More like a lone wolf, the name she'd used on his computer file at home. She'd never realised how prophetic that would be.

"Then of course there was the great good fortune of his having absolutely no alibi," David continued. "And not just for William's death but for Seymour's a few days earlier—that'll teach him for walking out on my movie." He stopped in front of her, his eyes flashed. "So I played the disgruntled agent card. It was a great motive. He had been sacked by Seymour just weeks earlier, it all made sense. It was like a gift from the gods!"

"So, you had your story. Two writers were dead. Why kill Tina?"

He shrugged again. "You know how these things work, it's never a strong plot when there's only two. They'll never announce a serial killer until there's a third murder, surely you've seen enough CSI to know that? And again, Oliver made it too easy. When Tina came into his office that day, telling us all about their date that Saturday night, well, it seemed too good an opportunity to pass up. Her fate was sealed. So was his."

She felt a wave of nausea hit her again but she shook it off. She needed to keep him talking. He was right, she'd seen enough murder mysteries in her time to know that the longer she kept him talking the better it would be for her. She didn't know why but that's the way it seemed to work. The truth was, she didn't really believe anyone would find them—*how could they, she didn't even know where she was?*—but she had to buy herself more time, it just seemed like the right thing to do, so she asked, "But ... but how did you know Oliver wouldn't stay the night with Tina? Thwart your plans?"

He sniggered. "As Caroline would say, 'Puh-lease!' She was just a slutty little tease." He paused. "A lot like Caroline, actually. All lovey-dovey but not much putting out. Stupid bitch, pity Caroline wasn't a writer ..." He smiled to himself and Roxy winced. There was such evil in those eyes now, she wondered that she had never noticed it before. Her intuition had been way off on this guy. She had been too blinded by his sparkly success to see the evil lurking underneath.

"Anyway," he was saying, "Oliver was never going to land Tina, been trying for years. It's funny, despite what her dad thought, she was a frigid bitch." Roxy winced again. "So I figured, either way, the world wouldn't miss her much. I waited until she'd kissed Oliver off at the front door, like I knew she would, then showed up soon after, pretending to be Oliver, got access to her townhouse and did what needed to be done."

"Is that why you dragged me back to your place that night? To create your alibi."

"Dragged?' He snorted. "You were begging for it, Roxy. Begging! It all worked out so beautifully. I'd tried to lure you away from Max's party, remember? But you weren't having it, not until that beer kicked in."

"You spiked it?"

"Just a little, enough to fuck you up. I was hoping you'd feel so groggy I'd be able to whisk you away, but when that didn't work, Max stepped in and did the job for me." He sniggered again, brushing a stray lock from his face. "You spotting him kissing up to Gilda was all the encouragement you needed. You insisted on coming back to mine, you made it so easy for me. All of you did. You've only got yourselves to blame."

Roxy's head was now pounding like a jackhammer and her cheek felt like it had swollen to the size of a football, but she ignored the pain and pressed on. "Then you drugged the wine back at your place?" He nodded. "I should have picked it when you said I'd polished off your Pinot Grigio. I would never pick a white wine when there's merlot lying about. Nor would I have got that drunk. Ever."

He stopped walking and sat down on the arm of the old sofa, a puff of dust springing up as he did so, causing her to cough violently for a few seconds. "I didn't have to give you much, you were comatose within minutes, so I pretended to go to sleep with you and then snuck out after an hour or so, when it was clear you were not waking up. By the time I got back you were still out of it. You woke up the next morning and there I was lying beside you ... innocent as a baby, and you ..." He snorted. "You were hilarious, all 'Oh my God, I'm so sorry! I'm so embarrassed!'" He had put on a high-pitched girlie voice and sounded like a psycho, so different from the cool, collected man she had first met just weeks earlier at his film launch. "You were pathetic," he spat, leaning in towards her, "but you did your job perfectly. Now I had my alibi and her name was Roxy Parker, best friend to policewomen everywhere."

Roxy leaned away from him, shuddering at the thought that she had woken up beside a killer; that just hours earlier he had been poisoning poor Tina. As if reading her mind, he leaned in even further and said, "Tina Passion won't be missed, she's a whore, sold herself for her books—just ask her dad. I was doing him a favour, and her. Those Twitter trolls were right, she deserved to die just for her substandard writing alone. She should never have been a success, those books were A-class crap."

"Can't have been too bad. You held onto one of them."

"Ah yes, *Lover's Delight*. The missing proof. Is that what gave me away? I saw it on your car seat, and that's when I knew I had to act fast."

Roxy coughed again. "Actually, it took me a while to work out where I'd seen Tina's book before. At first I thought it must have been at Oliver's office or in Lorenzo's bag, then I remembered. It was at *your* house, the morning after Max's party, when I slept over. You had that copy on your bookshelf. But how could you? There were only two in existence, the one the editor had and the one that was stolen from Tina's house the night before. You must have taken it home with you." She smiled, her lips cracking as she did so. "Get hooked on the A-class crap, did we?"

He smiled back. "Figured I'd keep a memento, didn't realise it was a proof copy. Wouldn't have taken it if I'd known."

"So, you drugged me, slipped away and killed Tina. But how did you know that Oliver wouldn't have an alibi? He might have headed to a bar or to a friend's place after dropping Tina home. You were so lucky he—"

"Bullshit! That wasn't luck; that was foresight. Oliver's always been a total loser. I knew he'd have no alibi, I knew he'd be all alone. Yet again."

She ignored this, her anger growing in leaps and bounds. "And you were also very *lucky* both Tina and William were alone when you killed them. Tina could have had her dad staying. William could have had his daughter over."

He shook his head. "Nope, I checked all that."

"Of course, the elusive mobile phone. What, you rang a few times to check they were home alone? Then you planted the phone at Oliver's office?" He nodded. "That was another giveaway for me. In fact, I have to say, David, I think it was your biggest mistake."

"Oh really?" He stood up this time and leaned into her, menacingly, his two hands at her shoulders, his knees touching hers, his face just inches from her own. "And why is that, pray tell?"

She gulped hard and tried not shrink back this time. "Because it meant it wasn't some random psycho as I was beginning to suspect. It made me realise that it had to be someone close to Oliver. I kept going over it and over it. No one else had access to Oliver's office in that short time frame except you, me and Sharon. I knew I didn't do it and I was pretty sure Sharon didn't have it in her, despite the way she carries on. But why would you do this to Oliver? Why?"

He stepped back and began pacing the room again, and she relaxed a little. "Arrgh, will you get over fucking Oliver already! That's no loss, besides, I hear his lawyer's half decent, he'll probably get off."

"But not before you've destroyed his reputation, his career, the agency he's spent decades building up, that made you the success you are today."

"Hey!" He stopped walking and stormed back towards her. This time she did recoil. "I made *myself* a success. No one can take credit for that, no one!" He took a deep breath, looked at his watch. "This is bullshit, I haven't got time for this."

As he made his way back towards the rickety staircase and the bag he had left there, Roxy could feel her panic rising again.

Did he have a gun in that bag? More poison?

"Yes, but ... but Oliver can't be blamed for this one," she stammered. "He's back in Sydney, he's staying at Sharon's. He has an alibi this time."

He swept around to face her again. "Beeeeep! Wrong again, Roxanne. He's just left me a text message, saying he's on his way back to his place now, via cab. That means he's home alone. Yet again." He did a little bow. "Besides, I've got his car. I'll drive it back to Sydney, leave it a few blocks from his house, your DNA all through the back of it. Then of course there'll be all that CCTV footage of him driving it down the highway." He reached down and pulled an old fedora and a bowling shirt from his bag. "Not hard to look like a tosser these days." He proceeded to put them on.

"But ... but hang on," she said. "You still haven't told me why."

"Why?

"Why you're doing all this? Why you killed William and Tina."

He laughed. "For a smart woman, Roxy, you're incredibly thick."

"It couldn't be the book deal, surely? It couldn't be as pathetic as that?"

He snarled. "Pathetic?! There's nothing pathetic about a top-selling book, Roxanne, but of course you wouldn't know about that. You've never so much as made the top one hundred."

"Hey, my last book reached eighty-seven, I'll have you know." She tried for a smile but he did not smile back.

"You'll get it when you reach number one, one day ... Not that you'll get the chance."

He was going to kill her, that was now obvious and her anger began to edge out the fear. "Oh, who cares about number one—"

"I do!" he boomed, cutting her off. "I was a success, I was Top Dog! Hell, the only reason you looked twice at me was because of that, because I now had a best seller and a shit hot film deal. You don't even remember me when we first met!"

"Yes I do—"

"Don't fucking lie to me. You women are all the same. I had you all eating out of my hand when I hit the big time. Damned if I was going to fade away quietly into the night."

"But you have your other book deal, the one on the elite athletes."

"Wasn't 'exciting enough'," he said, doing the curly finger thing and she wished she could break free of her ropes and strangle him. "You think I'm stupid? People were already starting to call me a one-hit wonder. Damned if I was going to let that happen. No fucking way. Not when there were more gripping stories to be told."

"Gripping stories? There was no story until you fabricated one! Murdered a bunch of people for a bloody book deal. You are pathetic."

He dropped the bag and rushed towards her again, his face contorted with rage. "I don't want to hurt you, Roxanne, so you better shut your fucking mouth."

She wanted to, really she did, but she was almost blind

with rage herself now. She didn't want to die and she wasn't going to go quietly. Besides, he looked comical in the hat and fedora and it emboldened her. "Someone will work it all out, David," she cried. "You *will* get found out, I can promise you that. Take this place, they'll connect it to you, somehow ..."

"You don't even know where you are, do you?" She stared at him, not speaking, and he began to laugh. It was an ugly, cackling kind of sound, and it made her skin crawl. "You won't get found, Roxanne, not for many, many weeks, maybe even months or years! And it only takes a few days without water to die. But that's not the worst of it." He paused and looked around the room. "This house is haunted, Roxanne, there's restless spirits here, you know? It's going to be a very frightening couple of days."

She scoffed, buoyed even further by the realization that he was not intending to kill her himself, that he was aiming to leave her here. "You've got to be kidding me, right? I don't believe in ghosts, David. I'm not four years old. You can't scare me to death."

He sniggered. "*I'm* not going to scare you to death. You're going to scare yourself." He waved around the room. "When I'm gone and the darkness settles in, every little sound will freak you out. Every creak and groan will make you wonder. And if the spirits don't scare you, perhaps the rats will."

A cold wave washed through her. *Rats?* She hadn't thought of that. His grin turned wider. "Ooooh, not looking so brave now, are we? Did you know, vermin don't wait for you to die before they start nibbling at your body? Helping themselves to your doomed flesh?" Roxy's throat constricted, bile filled her mouth. "And it's not just rats, you know. There are lots of creepy crawlies in this house. Snakes, spiders, bats ... Don't worry, Roxanne. It'll be agonizing but it'll be over soon enough. Then you'll be at peace and I'll have my best seller."

She swallowed hard and tried to breathe deeply, tried to

get the thought of nibbling creatures out of her mind. "Can I at least know where I am?" she begged. "Where I'm going to die? This doesn't look like a lounge room."

"It's not. It's a basement. No one will find you down here, not for a long while, plenty of time for you to die a slow and excruciating death. But hopefully in time to finish my book off, complete the final chapter. Perhaps I'll take some evidence to plant on Oliver should I need to speed things up."

He turned back towards the stairs again.

"What will you call this one?!" she cried out.

"Huh?"

"My death? What will you call it? I'm keen to know."

He smiled. "The Haunted House Murder. I'll write that Australia's greatest ghostwriter scared herself to death. Like it?"

She shrugged, feigning nonchalance. "I've heard better."

He stared at her for a few tense seconds than burst into laughter again, shaking his head. "You always were hilarious, Roxanne. It's a pity it has to end this way. We could have been quite a team. I wouldn't have chosen you, you know. For the next murder. It's only that you got too damn nosy. I tried to distract you. I tried to get you onto my book and off Oliver's case. But you wouldn't do it, kept getting diverted. And then when I saw you with Max the other night ..." He paused, his smile now icy. "You're just like Caroline and Tina, you know? You're all fucking bitches, too good for anyone."

"I'm sorry, David—"

"Don't even fucking try!" he boomed back. "You kissed me, Roxanne. You led me on. Then you go running back to that Max dickhead. What's he got that I don't have? He's just a two-bit, half-literate photographer who's never even had a film deal, let alone made one. That's when I figured you deserved to be my third and final victim."

"Final? You're not taking anyone else out?"

"Of course not," he said, a hand to his heart. "What do

you take me for? A monster?"

He smiled sadistically again and began ascending the staircase.

"Please, David," she called out. "Please don't leave me here. I can help you with the book. I can help you write it—"

"Don't do it, Roxanne," he yelled back. "There's no dignity in begging. Don't embarrass yourself."

Then he disappeared into the darkness.

CHAPTER 37

The night wore on and Roxy struggled to break free but it was no use. She rocked and stretched and heaved and screamed but her hands and legs were secured tightly and she realized with renewed panic that she was going nowhere. She was in the middle of a dingy, windowless basement, strapped to an old armchair that was so heavy, no amount of rocking could move it. Apart from the sofa, the room appeared almost empty. Through the darkness she could just make out several boxes in one corner, an old, rusty fan covered in stringy cobwebs, and what looked like a pile of mouldy blankets, and that's where the scuttling sound was coming from. It had started up again soon after David left and seemed to be getting louder by the hour.

What if David was right? What if there was a family of vicious, hungry rats, just waiting for her to fall asleep, just waiting to attack?

Tremors of fear raced through her and Roxy thumped her feet heavily on the floor from time to time, which stopped the scuttling for several blessed minutes before it slowly started up again.

"Go away, go away, go away!" she screamed to no avail. Whatever was lurking under those blankets was not going anywhere.

During the night Roxy heard other noises, too—eerie whistles and piercing cries that sounded far off, above her head, outside of the house perhaps. Yet it didn't seem to matter; each noise sent a shiver down her spine, each cry a stab of adrenaline that made her weary eyes shoot open, her back stiffen, her head pound even harder. She didn't believe in ghosts but that didn't lessen the fear any.

Eventually night turned into day and Roxy struggled to stay awake as she watched a sliver of light come through from the floorboards above. But even with better light, she could see no escape, no shards of glass to cut her ropes, nothing. At least the eerie noises had settled down and the scuttling had subsided.

Silence had finally returned and it was a blessed sound.

At one point Roxy had begun to sob, but very soon she was talking herself around, soothing herself, assuring herself she would be okay. *She was still alive, wasn't she?* He could easily have killed her at any time last night. The fact that he had left her alive was a positive thing. She had to use it, to think, to work her way out.

She had already deduced that this house, long deserted, was a good distance from the main road. If it had been closer she might have got away last night when she'd made her run for it. Still, it didn't stop her from screaming out from time to time, hoping that a stray bush walker or inquisitive kid would wander past. But it was no use. She was completely and utterly alone.

And worse, there was no way anyone back home would know where to find her.

How could they? Max didn't even know she was away, and her mother and Oliver thought she was in Yamba. They had no idea she had driven up to Ballina, a good hour and a half away. And God knows where David had taken her after that. She could be anywhere, anywhere at all.

If only she had called her mum, she might have stood a chance. If only she had done as her mother had asked!

Roxy felt a wet, hot tear trickle down her cheek.

Her poor mother. Lorraine would have worked out by now that Roxy was missing, and she would be distraught. Frantic. But there was no way she could find her. No way.

As the hours wore on and the light slowly turned to darkness again through the floorboards above her head, Roxy felt her desperation return. And she felt an intense thirst, like no thirst she had ever felt before. Panic and fear were working her adrenal glands and every sense was on heightened alert. She wasn't hungry, she realized, just desperate for water. She kept peering around but there was nothing. No hope.

Roxy's head dropped to the side and she finally surrendered to slumber.

A distant screech woke Roxy and she sat up with a start, her neck aching from where she had slept crookedly. She peered out into the darkness, waiting for her eyes to adjust, her ears pricked for more sound. That's when she heard the horrendous scuttling noise closer now, and louder than she remembered it, and her fear peaked. She tried thumping her feet but they were so heavy now, so hard to lift, and eventually fear gave way to exhaustion and she dropped back to asleep again.

"Creak!"

Roxy's eyes flew open, her body went rigid, her ears pricked alert.

"Creeeeaaaaak!"

Was that a door opening above her? Roxy craned her ears. There were more creaks and then what sounded like footsteps on old floorboards above. She felt a wave of relief and was about to scream out when it dawned on her.

It could be David Lone. He could be back to finish her off!

Roxy struggled with her ropes, trying desperately to free herself then she stopped and listened again. The footsteps were now growing softer, they were clearly moving away, and Roxy realized she no longer cared if it was David, she just needed to be heard, she needed to get out of this dingy room and away from those tortuous, scratching claws.

So she took a deep breath and screamed and screamed and screamed until her throat gave way and she could scream no more.

Within minutes the footsteps were growing louder again and someone was rapidly descending the stairs, torch in hand, pointing it frantically around the room. The light found Roxy and rested on her for just a split second. There was a deep gasp, and then someone was hurling himself towards her.

CHAPTER 38

Roxy Parker had never enjoyed a glass of water more and probably never would again. She swallowed the exquisite liquid down quickly then held her glass out for more. The waitress obliged, giving her a puzzled look as she did so. She usually only got this kind of reaction with her coffee.

"Easy, Parker," Max said, smiling. "You'll make yourself sick."

"Sick but alive, Maxy. Alive!" She smiled back at him and then across to Caroline who was seated beside him.

It was two hours later and Roxy was safely ensconced between her two friends in a brightly lit café in the heart of Ballina, a light shawl wrapped around her, the shaking now subsided. The wall clock said 9:13 p.m. and Roxy was waiting for her pasta dish to arrive, but really it was only water that she wanted even though she'd already drunk several litres by this time. In the end the waitress had left the jug at the table, shaking her head as she walked off.

The trio had already been grilled by the local police and were waiting for Gilda to show up. She was en route now, but there was no way Roxy was staying a second longer at that creepy old house. Nor was she about to get carted off to the hospital as the ambulance officers had insisted. It had felt like days and days, but Roxy had only been tied up for twenty-four hours, not long enough to be seriously dehydrated, and she told them as much. Nor was she going anywhere without Max Farrell by her side. Not while David Lone was still out there. Somewhere.

In the end, the ambos had patched up her face and the police had let her depart, insisting she hang around the next day for more questioning, and so the trio had made their way to the nearest, brightest, safest looking café they could find in the heart of Ballina. And Roxy had ordered water, and lots of it.

"So tell me again how you found me?" she said, unable to take it all in the first time.

"Really, Caroline can take all the credit," Max said, giving his sister a smile. "Oh, and your mum."

"Really?"

"Well, it was your panicky mum who first alerted us to your disappearance. If it wasn't for her we might not have thought to start looking. No offence."

"None taken," she said, smiling wearily. "Go on."

"Well, your mum was clearly worried and that got *me* worrying. I mean, I knew she can be a panic merchant at the best of times, but this was not ordinary times. We all knew you were doing some research for David Lone's book, so Oliver figured Lone should know where you were. But he couldn't reach Lone either. And the paper hadn't seen him for hours. To start with we thought you'd *both* come to some danger. I mean, writers were being killed off, you know? Then when Oliver got back to his place and couldn't find his car, he started to wonder if he was being stitched up again. That's when we all began to panic. So we met Oliver at your apartment to have a proper look around."

"Oh, thank God I gave him that key all those years ago," Roxy said.

"To be honest ..." Max paused, his eyes watered up. "God, I was so terrified that's where we'd find you ..."

"Dead, you mean?"

He nodded, glanced at her briefly then away again. Roxy touched his hand, gave it a squeeze. "So what happened next?"

"We started looking through your files, trying to find some evidence of where you might be. Your mum told us you were in Yamba but that's all we had to go on, and bloody hell I wish you'd name your files better. Talk about cryptic!"

She winced. "Sorry."

"Doesn't matter, we eventually found your desk diary and saw that you were meeting with a Mrs Porter, no other details, but Oliver did his Google magic and came up with a number. He rang Mrs Porter and she told us she suspected you'd gone on to see that Professor Green character."

"He was harder to pin down," said Caroline, taking up the story. "We found his number easily enough but he refused to pick up. Slacker!"

"It was pretty late by this stage," Max offered but Caroline waved him off with one bangle-clad hand.

"Big whoop! There were lives at stake, for goodness sake! Anyway, we left him three frantic voice mail messages before the gravity of it finally got through and he rang us back. We thought he might know where you went after your interview, but he had no idea. Completely clueless! He did tell us, though, what he'd told you, about David Lone doing anything to get a good story. That he'd been booted from university for plagiarism, and for threatening Green's life—"

Roxy blinked several times. "What? I didn't know about that."

Caroline sighed. "None of us did. Green told me David had threatened to 'destroy' him if he ever went public with the plagiarism 'rumour' as he called it. Apparently he never admitted to it, even though the evidence was strong. Green's a tough character but David obviously put the fear of God into him because he did keep it quiet, all those years. They agreed David would leave uni and no more would ever be said."

"But why didn't Green tell me all of this when I interviewed him?"

She shrugged. "I reckon he's still a little wary of David. I don't know exactly what David said or did, but it had a major impact. In any case, he said you were on David's side, writing a book for him, so I guess he wasn't taking any chances."

She sighed, too. He was right. She had made the cardinal sin when writing a biography. She had got too close to the subject. Ghostwriting autobiographies was different. You had to get close, you had to take a side—the side of the person paying you to write about them—but biographies were meant to be even-handed. Unbiased. Clearly Professor Green could see she was anything but.

"Okay," she conceded. "So you got the truth out of Green and then?"

"That's when it clicked!" said Caroline. "Up until this point, sweetie, we were trying to find you and David, we didn't suspect *him* of anything. But then we started to think ... if David could threaten an old English professor for a degree, what would he do for his career? I mean, I always knew David was ambitious but I had no idea how much." She shuddered. "I cannot believe I went out with that man—"

"This is not about you, Caro," Max said, interrupting her. "So we started to wonder, what if David did all of this for his articles, for the book deal? We started to imagine, if David was the killer—and we still weren't convinced he was—where would he possibly have taken you? We knew the other writers had died in ways that symbolized their writing style, so we started playing with the idea of a ghostwriter. How would you kill a ghostwriter?"

The waitress appeared with the chicken pasta and Roxy leapt upon it, her hunger now back in all its glory. "So you thought of a haunted house?" she said, twisting the dripping spaghetti onto a fork and thrusting it into her mouth.

"Not at first," said Max. "You see, we all just assumed you had returned to Sydney and David had kidnapped you there. I thought maybe you'd show up at one of your old client's houses, or maybe at that Balmoral bay where that rich socialite had been found dead—one of the places you'd written about in your books. So we rang Gilda and she got onto it, had a search party looking for you down near the rocks."

"Oh God." Roxy thought of the police scrambling across the bay, searching for her body, and shivered. She pulled the shawl tighter around her shoulders. "I didn't realise."

"Yeah, everyone was really worried, and then, well, at some point during the night someone started connecting ghostwriter with ghost train—were you on a spooky ride at some stupid fun park? Then Oliver said 'haunted house'. And it made total sense. That would be the perfect place to kill a ghostwriter, a place full of old ghosts. But we didn't know where to start looking. None of us knew of any old haunted houses in Sydney."

"And that's when it hit me!" said Caroline. "I knew the perfect haunted house! I lived in one back in my university days."

"That's right," said Roxy. "You talked about it at Max's party."

"Mm-hmm, and David was right there with us, remember? He obviously decided that since you were up near Lismore anyway—Ballina's just a quick drive away—well, he'd plant you there. The perfect place for a ghostwriter to die. And no one would ever think to look for you there." She paused. "I just wonder why he didn't put you in the bathroom ... that was the haunted room, after all. We looked there first, hadn't even considered the basement."

"I guess it was too small and there were too many windows," suggested Max. "Anyway, so Caroline reminded us of her old haunted home up near where you were last seen, and we knew that it had to be the spot. It just had to be. So we jumped right on it."

"No you didn't!" she scoffed, slapping him lightly across the chest. "You and Oliver thought it was a crazy idea, until we ran out of options, then you started to see sense."

Max looked sheepish. "It was morning by this time and we were getting pretty frantic. We didn't know what else to do. The police were scouring Sydney but we felt like we needed to do something, and your mother was going nuts. So we decided to come up here and try our luck."

"Except Oliver," added Caroline. "He wanted to come, too, of course, but he would be breaching his bail conditions, so we couldn't let him."

"That's all right," said Roxy, scooping up more pasta. "He's already apologized, about a hundred times over the phone."

"So, anyway, Max and I booked the first flight up here, hired a car and, ta-da!"

Roxy sighed, letting her fork rest for a moment. "And thank God for that."

"Oh thank God!" came a familiar voice across the half-empty café and the three friends looked up to find Gilda striding towards them, a look of relief all over her pretty face. She reached down and grabbed Roxy in a firm hug.

"You are such a bloody worry, young woman! I hope you called your mum. She's been ringing me non-stop for the past twelve hours. She's hysterical."

"Yes, I called her an hour ago. She's so relieved, of course, but I don't think she'll believe I'm alive until she actually sees me for herself."

"I know what she means." Gilda turned to the siblings, hands on her hips. "As for you two! What in the hell did you think you were doing racing up here, acting like the cavalry?"

Max held a hand up. "Sorry, Gilda, but we didn't know what else to do."

"You could have told me what you were up to, or called the local police, let them take care of it! David could still have been in the house."

Caroline spoke up now. "Gilda, to be honest, we thought this was probably a wild goose chase. I honestly didn't think we'd find her here but we had to try. We couldn't sit around in Sydney wondering. Besides, there was no way I could explain it to you or the local police. I couldn't even remember how to get to my old house until we started driving around the suburb. It came back to me then. In fact, we would have arrived earlier if we hadn't taken one or two wrong turns." She glared at her brother.

"Hey, you're the one who couldn't remember the street name let alone the number! You only lived here for a year."

"Six months, and it was like a decade ago! I just knew it was near a bridge, an old mango tree and within walking distance from a pub. Couldn't even recall the name of the pub until we drove past it. That was good luck. That's when we knew we were close." She laughed. "If I'd had a few beers first we might have found it faster."

"Well, scooch along," Gilda said, sitting down beside Roxy. "Wow, that's quite a souvenir you got there."

She took Roxy's chin gently in one hand and inspected the damage. The skin below her right eye and cheekbone were a lurid shade of purple now, and there was considerable swelling, but the throbbing had subsided thanks, in part, to painkillers and thanks to the sheer, overwhelming joy of freedom. Once Roxy had caught sight of Max dashing towards her in that dank, old basement, the pain and fear almost dissipated on the spot.

"Yep, he's all gentleman, that David Lone," Roxy replied.

Gilda growled. "The bastard. He's lucky I haven't got my hands on him yet." She paused. "Look, I know you've got a giant story to tell but I won't make you go over it all again now."

"Thank you, my voice is hoarse enough as it is. At least tell me you've got the bastard in custody now, please."

"Done and dusted. Or fingerprinted to be more precise. He reappeared at his office late this arvo, acting all nonchalant, apparently. Wish I'd seen his face this evening when they told him you'd been found, alive and well. I was already on my way to Yamba. I wanted to question that English teacher who'd seen you last. I thought she held the key. Little did I know the Mopsy Twins here were two steps ahead of me." She glowered at Max and Caroline, then paused to order an herbal tea from the hovering waitress who knew something big was up but didn't have the heart to ask what. As she shuffled off, Gilda said, "I just can't believe Lone didn't kill you. Like he did the others."

Roxy felt a shiver down her back. "Well, his plan was for me to die of fear, and as ridiculous as it sounds, I have to tell you, it was beginning to work. It was terrifying in that old house."

Max curled an arm around Roxy's shoulders and gave her a hug. "You're okay now," he said.

"Okay? I feel like the luckiest woman alive!" She sank down into his warm body.

"Luck had a *little* to do with it," Gilda admitted. "But Lone was getting sloppier with each murder and he just assumed there was no way anyone was going to find you. And when we eventually did, he figured we'd automatically pin it on Oliver. Or maybe even Caroline here. It was her old house."

As Caroline's jaw dropped at the thought, Roxy sat up and said, "Well you coppers were all pointing the finger firmly at poor Oliver."

"Not me," Gilda replied firmly. "I told you that. I didn't think he did it for one second, but I just couldn't work out who else did. You were considering suspects like Lorenzo and Erin but they just didn't stack up, and Frankie, the detective in charge, well, he had to follow the evidence trail and, unfortunately, it kept leading back to Oliver."

"All thanks to Mr Lone. So when did you start suspecting David? I mean, he had such a good alibi for Seymour's death. I thought it put him out of the running."

"Not in my book, it didn't. My colleagues always knew that Seymour had killed himself. That had been so obvious, despite what David was trying to whip up in the press. It was as clear as day. The sleeping pills Seymour had overdosed on were in his name, he'd secured three separate prescriptions a week earlier from three GPs who identified him from photographs, and the wounds to his wrists were clearly self-inflicted. The coroner said it was open and shut. It was only when William Glad showed up dead and then Tina Passion that things started to look shaky. That's when we decided to look at that case again."

"So why did Seymour do it?" asked Roxy. "Why kill himself?"

"That's where Lone was almost correct. Silva's manager, Norman Hicks, was getting fed up of playing second fiddle to his fake writer and had only just told Silva he was going to come out. His new agent had been badgering him to do it for the past month, apparently. Sales for their last book were pretty dismal and she thought this new scandal would reinvigorate the *Alien Deliveries* series. You know what they say, any publicity is good publicity."

"But Seymour wasn't keen?"

"'Course not! His whole *raison d'être* would vanish. Everyone would know he was a fraud and Hicks would start to get the credit for the books, the credit that Silva had been happily living off for years. He knew he couldn't stop Hicks from revealing the truth, so he decided to teach him a lesson, to at least put his death on his manager's conscience. If he has one. You have to remember, Silva was a few sheep short of a paddock."

"But it played so beautifully into David Lone's scheme," said Max, and Gilda shook her head.

"I don't think there was a scheme, not at the beginning. Lone just truly believed that Silva's death was suspicious, would make a great idea for a series of articles, maybe another top-selling book. But when the story died in the water and the coroner declared it a suicide, it must have infuriated him. He had his sights set on another book and he wasn't going to let anything get in his way. I think that's when he hatched the plan to kill Mr Glad."

"To keep the story rolling," Roxy said softly, sadly.

"Yep, supposed murder number two. And as you say, it got him off the suspect list because there was no way he could have done the first 'murder'. Hundreds of people saw him sitting watching the *Supermodel* movie at the exact time Silva was dying. Couldn't have been the illustrious author. All he had to do then was link that death with the next two and he was off the hook. If he couldn't have killed Seymour Silva, well, he mustn't be guilty of William's and Tina's deaths either."

"Plus I gave him that alibi for Tina's murder," said Roxy, unable to meet Max's eyes.

"He drugged you," Max said, forcing her to look at him. "If that hadn't happened, would you have stayed the night?"

She shook her head vehemently. "No, of course not."

He looked relieved. "There you go then."

"What I don't get," said, Roxy, "what I keep coming back to is the fact that I was up drinking with David until 2:00 a.m. before I passed out. Tina was killed at midnight."

"No, David said you were up drinking until two and then freaked out when you saw the time and headed to bed. Even if that was true—and your memory was hardly very reliable—he could easily have changed the clock, put it forward a few hours to deceive you."

Roxy groaned. "I was such a fool."

"Ahh, don't beat up on yourself. That alibi never counted anyway," said Gilda, waving it off. "You being passed out in his apartment counts for nothing. David could have slipped away at any time. Plus, when you told me you'd drunk a bottle of white wine back at his place even though he had plenty of merlot on hand, well, it's not what you'd call incriminating evidence, wouldn't stand up in a court of law, but it certainly got me thinking. You asked me when I started suspecting David? That was the moment."

"But why did you even consider David in the first place?" asked Max. "When all the evidence was pointing at Oliver? I mean, I thought he was a tosser but that doesn't make him a killer."

Gilda laughed. "I don't know, it was more than that. He'd just always been a slippery character, you know? I knew he'd sell his mother for a headline."

Caroline was nodding her head furiously. "I sensed that side of him when we were going out all those years ago. I tried to warn you about him, Roxy, that day I came to your apartment, but I didn't know how to say it. I mean, I liked the guy—God help me—but he had a dark side ... I just had no idea how dark."

Roxy sighed. "He fooled us all, Caroline."

"Not me," Gilda repeated. "And I kept wondering how the hell he was always one step ahead of us. He had all the information on the crimes, even before we did. I thought maybe he was sleeping with one of the team, but I couldn't pin that down. Finding the gardening shears in Norm's car also had me stumped, and we were all looking at someone at the funeral at first until it dawned on me. Duh! David could easily have slipped into the car park while everyone was inside the Crematorium. So that left his alibi open." She took a sip of her tea. "My biggest stumbling block, to be honest, was the strychnine."

"Oh, yes, the poison that killed Tina," said Roxy, sitting forward. "How did he get hold of that?"

"One of the new detectives worked it out, actually. Young Milton, he's going places, that bloke. Milton works out a bit at the Police Boys Club, lifting weights and stuff, well, he reminded me that strychnine is still used in very low doses in performance enhancing drugs. It's one of the ingredients they look for when testing drug cheats."

Roxy sat back with a thud. "Of course, and David had been working on a book about doping and elite athletes."

"Got it in one. Milton was in the process of questioning a supplier down at a dodgy gym where David had been doing some of his investigations, when we got the call about you going missing. I don't know what he found but I'm sure it'll come in handy for the prosecution." She glanced at Max. "Jesus, you sent a shiver down my spine when you phoned me and told me Roxy had vanished. Freaked me right out."

"Really? I got the impression you thought I was overreacting."

She laughed. "Sorry, I was just trying to calm you down and get you to stay right out of it. It clearly didn't work." She shook her blonde locks at him. "To be honest we might have got to David days earlier if I could have persuaded Frankie that Oliver was a red herring, but we all kept stumbling on the question of motive. Oliver had motive in spades." She held a hand up to Roxy's raised eyebrows. "Sorry, but that's how Frankie saw it—so I had real trouble persuading him to release some of his team and divert them to David Lone. Eventually he let me have Milton, but in the meantime that's why I was snooping around. I felt like someone had to consider other options. It was just pinning down a motive that had me second-guessing myself. I just couldn't get my head around why Lone would do it. I still can't. Honestly, slaughtering a bunch of people so you can write a bloody book? It's beyond me."

They all looked at Roxy then, as though expecting her to explain it and she shrank back. "Hey, don't look at me. I clearly don't have that kind of fierce ambition. I couldn't kill a fly for a best seller, let alone two innocent human beings."

"Nearly three," said Max softly.

"I blame Professor Green, in the library," said Caroline, her eyes defiant and they all turned to stare at her.

"How you figure?" asked Gilda.

"Well, he should have spoken up years ago about what a monster David Lone was. I had a teeny weeny inkling of it, but nothing concrete. You just have to wonder if the truth had got out earlier, about how he'd been booted from university and threatened a teacher, I wonder whether he mightn't have got away with so much."

Gilda thought about this. "People forgive a lot of bad behaviour in youth, Caroline. I don't think that would have counted for much." She drained her cup dry. "Okay, we should call it a night, you all look bushed, especially you, Ms Parker."

Roxy stretched out like a cat, letting the shawl fall away and giving herself a shake. "Yes, well, being tied to an armchair and stalked by killer rats for twenty-four hours will do that to you."

"Oh, you'll survive. You've survived worse."

Roxy thought about this. Gilda was right. This was the second time in less than two years that her life had been threatened; it was becoming way too familiar for her liking.

"I'll accompany you to the Ballina station in the morning," Gilda was saying, taking care of the bill, "but for now you need a decent night's sleep. You booked in somewhere yet?"

Roxy looked from her to Max and smiled. "I'm staying where my knight in shining armour is staying. Just in case my bad track record continues."

"Hey, Parker, no one is going to threaten you tonight," he said, his floppy fringe dropping across one eye, a worried frown settling on his brow. "I won't be letting you out of my sight. Not for one second, so prepare yourself."

"Promises, promises," she said, feeling ridiculously happy despite it being one of the worst nights of her life.

Watching the two of them flirt with each other openly across a neon-lit café, Caroline glanced at Gilda and the two women shared a conspiratorial smile.

EPILOGUE

David Lone still looked dapper, even in his prison greens. He had slicked his hair back and was freshly shaven, a sliver of a smile on his lips as Roxy was led towards the cubicle where he was sitting, prison guards loitering close by. As she sat down across from him and peered through the separating glass, she was heartened to see scratches down one side of his face, and the remains of what looked like a fat lip. Good, she decided. He deserved that, and more.

Her own bruises had long vanished but she was sure her fear of scuttling critters and dark, dank corners would take a lifetime of therapy to overcome.

"Hey, Roxanne, delightful you could drop in," he said through thin slits in the glass, his tone light and breezy, as though they were chatting over lattés at Lockie's.

She nodded, unable to speak for a few minutes. She could barely meet his eyes. Roxy was still so furious with him, and with herself for falling for his charms so easily just a few months ago. The truth was, she *had* been seduced by Lone's success and, more so, by his fascination for death. Roxy had thought, once, that it made him sexier and more compatible, but she realised now that he wasn't just fascinated with death as she was, he was *fixated* with it. He didn't just live for true crime, he killed for it, too, and there was nothing sexy about that.

Once upon a time she had criticized Max for his disinterest in crime but she knew that he was exactly what she needed—her counterbalance, the one who could snap her out of her morbid moments and bring her back to the land of the living.

Thank God for Max, she thought. *Perhaps if David had had a counterbalance of his own ...*

She shrugged the thought away—it was too late now for what ifs—and looked up into those icy blue eyes. "What do you want, David? You've been hassling me for a meeting for months, so here it is. I'll give you ten minutes, then I'm out of here."

He stared at her. "No need for the attitude, Roxanne."

"There was no need to kill two innocent people and leave me to rot in an old house either, but that didn't stop you." She sighed. "Why have you asked me here? What's so life and death?"

"I'm just wondering about the book, that's all."

"The book?"

"You were writing my 'tell-all', remember? I've been waiting for it to hit the stands. I mean, there is so much to tell now! But I wait in vain. There is still no book."

Her jaw dropped and she shook her head at him. "Arrogant as always, I see. You're right. There is no book, David. There never will be."

He mock gasped. "No book?! But it's such a terrific story. You could make millions! Surely Oliver has told you that?" He paused, glanced down at his nails, held them out as if inspecting them. "How is Mr Horowitz, anyway? Get over his bad press, did he?"

"He's great, David. Fantastic, in fact. Has a stack of new clients. Your little stitch up has made him quite the celebrity. He said to thank you, by the way."

That last bit was not true but she couldn't help herself.

This horrendous man had tried to destroy a perfectly innocent, big-hearted human being and she needed him to know that he had not succeeded, in that, at least.

Her mind went to Tina now, and then to William, the tragic victims of his unchecked ambition and insatiable appetite for a good horror story. Both writers had finally been laid to rest properly, and Oliver was able to attend their funerals with his head held high. Tina's father, Lorenzo, had sought them both out after the burial, thanking Roxy for her help, and even managing to shake Oliver's hand, and that was enough for him.

Oliver and Erin had not published William's old gardening books, as per his final wishes, but Erin had set up a special, public memorial garden in her father's name, not far from his house, and his grandchildren helped tend it every weekend. William would have loved that. It was the only legacy he needed.

David Lone, however, was after so much more.

"Have you at least done a rough draft?" he was asking and she stared at him aghast. Did his ego know no bounds?

"I'm not writing your bloody book, David. It's the last thing I would ever do."

"I'm just saying, Roxanne, it would be a best seller for you. People are *intrigued* by me! I get fan mail, would you believe? Dozens of letters every week, telling me what a genius I am. Had a few offers of marriage even. You could put them in your book. Out there, they think I'm great!"

"Well, I'm out there, and I don't think you're great. I think you're the opposite of great. You're not worth a sentence, let alone a book, certainly not one from me. I won't be wasting any of my energy on you."

She sighed and looked away. David was right, of course. His biography would have been a huge success for Roxy. She had the inside scoop, after all. She had almost been one of his victims; she had known him intimately. It was sure to be a best seller for both her and her agent, probably the most lucrative book she would ever write. But she didn't care about that. Never had, and neither did Oliver. They both understood that writing a book about David Lone somehow justified the murders of his two victims, and they weren't about to give him the satisfaction. He could tell his own story, but she was not going to be a party to it. She was not going to profit from Tina's and William's deaths. She did, however, have the whole story contained in her Crime Catalogue at home. She couldn't help herself. She felt that pasting it in was putting it to rest, or at least containing it a little. But she wasn't about to tell him any of that.

David's smile had turned into a snarl and he stared at her for a few stony minutes before speaking. "You need to get off your moral high horse, woman," he said eventually, "because I've handed you a gift. A gift! Without my story, you'd have nothing. What, you think a few books about crusty old socialites will ever help you crack the big time?"

"I don't need to crack the big time. I've told you before, I'm not interested in that."

"You're a fucking fool then!" he spat and a guard stepped forward, placing a warning hand on David's shoulder. He glanced around at him and then at Roxy, his smile back in place but this time it was glacial. "You've never had any real success so I'm going to forgive you your stupidity, Roxanne, just this once. But let me tell you what having a best seller is like since you'll clearly never know. There's nothing better, Roxanne. Nothing! Nothing better than watching your book go from ... what did you get to? That's right, eighty-seven." He sniggered. "Well, imagine watching your book go from a lowly eighty-seven to Number One in a matter of weeks, right around the globe. Knowing your words are in the hands of millions and millions of people, from here to Hong Kong, Berlin, Paris. Knowing that reviewers at the *New Yorker*, the *Guardian*, are all reading *your* words, gushing over them, falling over themselves to interview *you*. To get *you* on the phone. No more waiting for celebrities to call you. You are the fucking celebrity! You're the one everyone wants to talk to, hanging on your every word. They live for you."

His once dazzling blue eyes flashed a viciousness she wished she had seen a lot earlier, and several strands of hair had dislodged and were flying about as he spoke, making him look more like the lunatic that he was. "You could get out of that crappy little dive you call a home. Make millions! But you know what, it's not even about the money, not really. Having a best seller is better than all the money in the world, Roxanne. Hell, it's better than the best sex you'll ever have. It's orgasmic."

Roxy shook her head and smiled. "You've been locked away too long," she said. "You're just horny."

He stared at her for a quiet second then laughed his cackling, ugly laugh, which made the prison guard look up. "I always loved your sense of humour, Roxanne," he said, calming down. "We could've been dynamic, you and I. We could have made waves."

"I don't need to make waves, David. I like my life the way it is, nice and calm."

He scoffed. "Like I say, you're a fucking fool." He whispered the words but again the guard looked up and this time he gave a warning cough. David glanced around and then held his hands up. "Doesn't matter anyway. I don't need your pathetic, boring drivel. I'm writing my own book. You wait until my memoir is out. It'll be the biggest book to hit the stands since ... since ..." He sniggered again. "Since *The Supermodel Diaries*." He paused, his eyebrows arched. "I wonder who will play me in the movie this time? Maybe your old favourite Brad Pitt might be available?"

"I would think he has better things to do," she said. "In any case, I don't give a shit. I won't be watching it. I won't be reading it. And you, you'll be stuck in here, unable to enjoy any of the fame and fortune you so desperately seek." She stood up. "You've wasted enough of my life, David. I'm done with you. Don't hassle me again, I won't be coming back."

She turned to the guard who nodded and began to lead her away.

"Oh, and by the way," she said, turning back. "There are plenty of things that are better than a best selling book. Or even a movie starring Brad Pitt. I'll say hi to Max for you, shall I?"

With that she walked out of the prison and away from the biggest story of her life and towards her brooding photographer guy who was waiting patiently in the car park, a worried look of love across his soft, brown eyes.

And she smiled widely because she knew that he was the only happy ending she needed.

ABOUT THE AUTHOR

Christina Larmer is a journalist, editor, blogger and the author of nine books including six in the popular *Ghostwriter Mystery* series as well as *An Island Lost*, *The Agatha Christie Book Club*, and the non-fiction book *A Measure of Papua New Guinea Story* (Focus; 2008). She was born and raised in Papua New Guinea, spent several years working in London, Los Angeles and New York, and now lives with her musician husband and their two sons in the Byron hinterland of Northern NSW, Australia.

Connect with C.A. Larmer online:
www.calarmerspits.blogspot.com/
christina.larmer@gmail.com
Facebook
@CALarmer